SOLI BULA

SOLI means to give or offer.

BULA means life or soul.

SOLI BULA is the Fijian phrase meaning to submit life to some valuable cause or worthy belief. In a literal sense, it means to give life or sacrifice life.

SOLI BULA

Stephanie Hoffman

SALT & SAND
PUBLISHING
LA JOLLA, CA, USA

Published by Salt & Sand Publishing,
La Jolla, CA, USA

Stephaniehoffmanbooks.com

Artwork by Brett Hoffman
Edited by Neva Sullaway
Graphic Design and Layout by Karl Hunt

Printed in the United States of America

Library of Congress Cataloguing-in-Publication Data has been applied for.

p. cm

ISBN 978-1-7347681-1-4

Women—Fiji—Fiction
Woman—Doctor—Fiction
Leprosy—Islanders—Fiction
Pacific Islands—Fiction
Australia—Medical—Fiction
U.S—Medical—Fiction
Alzheimer's—Dementia

Inspired by my patients, relatives, friends, neighbors, ocean friends, and others along the way, your need has become my purpose. I am grateful and privileged to be on your path.

Acknowledgements

THANK YOU to the Tribe, once again, who help shape my life with adventure and gusto, as well as joy and reverence. And to my mentors along the way who remind me "nobody cares how much you know until they know how much you care."

Courtney Hoffman—My beautiful daughter, who is one of my greatest teachers. Your wisdom and compassion are beyond your years. Your view on one of the characters in this story helped shape the arc of his journey.

Brett Hoffman—My talented and thoughtful son, helps keep my personal navigational chart on track. Your ability to capture emotion and tell a story from behind the lens is astounding.

John Hoffman—My husband, who gives me eternal clearance to be me, and tell stories the way I see them.

Vanessa Vosberg—My sister, whose view on nursing includes always treating others with dignity, has helped shape some scenes in the story.

Neva Sullaway—My relentless shaper of words, scenes, and dialogues, with the ability to stretch my story-telling; I am forever grateful for your views, proofreads and edits.

Finally, to all the lost souls and hearts this year from a variety of ailments: You all gave me wise words, gracious thanks, and final smiles. You taught me the concept of "good enough" and I listened, carefully, to what that really means.

Part 1

1

THE newborn was deep asleep, snuggled into Reagan's breast. The swaddled baby rose and settled, matching Reagan's inhale and exhale. She nuzzled the baby's scalp, intoxicated by the alluring aroma—a cross between sweet and sour, maybe an over-ripe mango, or peach, or even a ten-day-old tuberose. Reagan breathed in the scent that enveloped her two-day-old daughter. There was nothing like it, not even at her home back in Fiji. Sure, the tropical flowers were great competition, so was the smell of salt-crusted skin from hours of surfing, or fresh-cooked yellowtail with ginger. But this was different—this was her daughter.

Her miraculous, beautiful baby was unscathed by the ravages of Reagan's dual diseases. She avoided thinking about what may have happened over a year ago. She looked over at Jeremy, passed out in the hospital chair that couldn't contain his 6'2" frame. One arm hung down to the floor with periodic twitches in his finger. His head was too far bent for comfort if he had been awake, creating an irregular snore. Sleep had finally conquered Jeremy after he had been awake for the thirty-six hours of Reagan's labor, followed by the elation of their baby's birth. Distant memories crept back in—what might have happened if he hadn't come back for her, or worse; if he had agreed to help end her life.

Looking back at her daughter, Reagan let go of the nagging past. She smiled, thinking of her baby's name Laura, named after her dear friend Roger's infant, who had passed away too early in life. Reagan couldn't wait to get out of Sydney General Hospital and back to her home in Fiji to celebrate the arrival of their baby with Roger and the islanders. Her smile broadened, cracking the edges of her parched lips. Reagan emptied a gulp's worth of water from the yellow plastic pitcher. The sink was only six feet away, but the thought of disturbing the unusual calm in the hospital room didn't seem worth it. She licked her raw lips, tasting remnants of orange juice, then glanced at the emptied juice glass on the morning breakfast tray. She sighed.

Reagan tied her auburn blond hair into a half-knot and dropped her head deep into the pillow. She stared at her arm—a faded island tan with fresh postpartum splotches that had appeared overnight. She switched her focus back to her home in Fiji—the waves, her ocean friends, Maura and the girls, the islanders she took care of, and all the tranquility of nature that surrounded her there. Reagan imagined the salty blue ocean that bathed her skin and soul. She closed her eyes. The tropical sensations of her past soothed her.

Somewhere in her hazy reverie, she heard two knocks on the heavy metal door. Reagan rolled her eyes—more vital signs. The interruptions were endless, but maybe they could fetch the water or help her get to the bathroom. Both seemed to be such monumental chores at the moment. She resisted leaving her dream-like state and images of teal surf with dancing dolphins, but the strident sound of the creak in the metal hinges woke everyone in the room. Baby Laura whimpered.

Now, with the door fully ajar, Reagan froze. She stared at the last person she had ever expected to see in Australia. "Mom! What . . . how . . . what are you doing here? How did you find me?"

The woman stood motionless in the doorway. Reagan winced at her familiar strained smile—an act that was used to demonstrate to others that she was capable of simple pleasantries such as a social smile. Silver strands of hair hung loosely around her face, in a way that might appear unkempt to some, yet was fitting for the woman who stood in the threshold. Her piercing gray eyes were dark and unsettling as they inspected the monitors above Reagan's bed. She appeared much smaller than Reagan remembered. When had she last seen her? Maybe five years, or was it more?

Jeremy stumbled out of the chair and tripped over his shoes, "What, who now—"

A baby's soft cry turned into a full wail. The calm was gone—the storm broke loose, shifting everyone's attention to the insistent call-to-arms. Jeremy picked up their six-pound, four-ounce daughter, supporting her ragdoll head, and hummed lightly into her ear. A momentary reprieve.

"I'm Jeremy," he raised his head.

"Dr. Rozalynn Caldwell, head of . . . oh, never mind."

"Oh, isn't this a surprise? How do you do, Mrs. Caldwell—"

"Dr. Caldwell." Roz corrected, leaving Jeremy's hand in midair.

Jeremy had heard about Reagan's strained relationship with her mother and the lengths she went to avoid her mother's medical prestige. He glanced at Reagan before saying, "This is your granddaughter, Laura Rose."

Reagan's mother looked beyond her and Jeremy to the vital statistics on display overhead. Reagan had a hunch the numeric values of the heart rate, pulse, and oxygen levels registered more important to this woman than the person they were linked to. Were they norm values or not? Were they adjusted correctly for the insufficiencies? What about the compensation values versus how the patient felt? Reagan knew this woman too well.

"How did you know I was here? What are you doing in Sydney? I don't understand . . . it's been . . . a while . . . and well—"

"I was at a Genomics conference in Tokyo, so practically in the neighborhood." Roz kept her eyes on the medical apparatus above Reagan's bed. "A colleague mentioned you were in the hospital."

Reagan hesitated, "Of course."

Dr. Rozalynn Caldwell had disapproved of her daughter's academic path since the day Reagan announced she was going to medical school. The potential complications were too much for Roz; the twice-awarded medical laureate, whose achievements in gene therapy were world-renowned. What if her daughter didn't rise to the level of competency her mother would insist on? Roz had dissuaded her for years.

Reagan noticed her mother's tight red lips and disapproving glare at the inadequacies of the Australian hospital. Roz would usually be more poised and confident—more in charge, but there was something out of place, something impalpable. Reagan swallowed, desperate for water.

What would have been a clipboard propped against Roz's torso was now a small book with a bow on top. She took slow steps toward Reagan—her usual overconfidence was lost in this scene of her daughter and newfound family. She extended the book to Reagan.

"It was your favorite book," Roz steadied her voice. She tucked her hands in the pockets of her button-down blazer and stepped back.

Jeremy took the book from Reagan, opened it and flipped through the pages. "Oh, *The Giving Tree*. I remember this when I was little."

Reagan looked at her mother. "But as I remember, you said the author got it all wrong. You told me life doesn't go that way—that if you give it all away, you end up with nothing."

"I . . . I am sorry . . . I shouldn't have come, so soon." Roz turned to leave.

Reagan bit her lip. There was so much she could have said regarding her mother choosing her profession over her family or her mother not approving of Reagan's decision to leave Western Medicine, or a host of other things. Instead, she relaxed; "Wait, please stay. You are here now . . . and I am grateful, Mom."

The words hung in midair. Silence penetrated the room.

"We would like you to stay." A softness tempered Reagan's words and she smiled at Jeremy. She had learned so much from Maura and the islanders—the only certainty was today—the moment. She could hear Maura's silent message in her head; *Grudges are like rust on an anchor, makes things sticky and too much work to clean it up.*

Roz stared blankly.

"Mom, what's up? What's going on?" Reagan looked into the dark circular chasm of her mother's eyes; the answer was too deeply hidden.

Jeremy finished changing the baby and placed her back in Reagan's arm, handed her a glass of water, and kissed her forehead.

Reagan brought her daughter close to her chest and touched the silky skin along her cheek. The baby's eyelashes curled upward perfectly, as if someone had crimped them. Reagan figured they were from Jeremy's gene pool, since her own lashes were stubby. Baby Laura even had Jeremy's eye color—a hazel center with strands of seagrass green. Reagan had been drawn to Jeremy's eyes when they first met. Now she reveled in their similarity. The infant's eyes blinked several times before she dropped them shut and collapsed back asleep.

Roz stared at the scene, without words. Mothering was never easy for her with the child-rearing years handled by a variety of nannies. There was no time for breast-feeding or cooing moments. Her career took precedence over her family duties. Who else could solve such important medical issues? Her husband was much better at those parenting tasks anyway—when he was around.

Reagan's dad, Earl, was a surfer and musician. Similar to Roz, he traveled all over, but his passion was the ocean and finding a beautiful, unspoiled island in the middle of nowhere, with a perfect wave. He crossed numerous oceans several weeks at a time, in search of teal waters, no crowds, and a pointbreak that faced the perfect direction to receive all swell angles. He surfed hollow waves most mornings and played his koa-wood guitar in the afternoons, composing melodic riffs. Similar to Roz, Earl was known for helping others, in his own way. He brought water filters to Bali, set up farmed fisheries in the Mentawai Islands, and taught music to schoolchildren in developing countries. His passport stamps were impressive—documenting travel to exotic places all over the South Pacific. He didn't appear to miss the limelight that his wife lived in—seated with heads of state for yet another award that Roz Caldwell would receive.

As a child, Reagan imagined what it would be like to travel the world. Earl sent her spices from Portugal, puka shells from Tahiti, and rib bones from the narwhale that washed up on the beach at Normandy. Reagan begged to join him but her mother simply wouldn't allow her to go, stating Reagan was too young, there would be a host of immunizations required and she couldn't miss school. When Earl did come home from his extended travel, he would steal Reagan away for off-the-grid surf trips to Baja California where no immunizations were required and communication with Roz impossible.

"How's Dad?" Reagan asked, watching her mother's eyes shift back to the hospital monitors.

"Oh, about the same. Dementia is tricky. Lucid moments come and quickly flee." Roz flipped her hand up in the air.

Reagan had given Jeremy snippets of information about her parents—they were somehow still married yet lived apart until a few years ago when her dad was found wandering the streets of West L.A., looking to pick up his young daughter from a local elementary school, which his daughter hadn't attended for thirty years. Earl was diagnosed with Alzheimer's, and Roz had allowed him to move back in with a full staff of caretakers. Reagan told Jeremy it was her mom's penance and, besides, it was similar to raising her—very hands off.

Roz walked closer to Reagan's hospital monitors and adjusted a knob. "I told your father I was going to a conference in Venice. But every few hours he will ask the caregivers if I am still at the clinic or was I at yoga. So, it doesn't matter where I am."

"You've taken up yoga?" Reagan was suspect of why her mom would ever practice self-care ahead of her sacred work.

"I try, sometimes. I still don't get it." She smirked. "Why would anyone want to sweat in a room of bacteria-laced petri dishes, waiting to cluster and explode?"

"Why are you here?" Reagan tilted her head.

"Like I said, a colleague at Cedar's Research said you were sick. But now I see he didn't have all the facts."

"Well, it was a hard pregnancy," Reagan lied. It was the most pleasant eight and a half months of her life—all the doting from Jeremy, Maura and the kids. The islanders had numerous celebrations, in anticipation of the new baby. Reagan had never felt more pampered, but her mother didn't need to know how easy it was. Roz spent her last trimester, when pregnant with Reagan, in bed due to complications.

"Why would a doctor at Cedar's—" Reagan started to ask.

Jeremy chimed in. "Why don't you tell her about the special testing?"

Reagan read the body language from her actor boyfriend—his forward lean, with veins in his forearms distended, and his drawn lips. She loved this man. All they'd been through over the last year and a half, and now they were a family. The questions she had about him and his Hollywood lifestyle the previous year had all vanished. She turned to her mother, "What do you know about Hansen's disease?"

2

REAGAN had agreed to deliver their baby in Australia since it was close to Dr. Yiung, the doctor who had guided the care of her two previous illnesses. She knew that immediate blood work on the baby was essential to test in case any residual toxins had found their way into Reagan's system during her pregnancy.

"You will be my guests for a few months during your last trimester," Dr. Yiung had told them. "Otherwise they might not let you on the plane much later than that. Plus, the clinic could really use you. Lots of pregnant women these days and they all admire you."

Sydney Annex was Dr. Yiung's community clinic with a holistic approach to illness and treatment. Reagan's paradigm shift occurred the previous year when she had first met Dr. Yiung at the 'no fee for service' facility—one of Reagan's core beliefs. He introduced her to a new way of seeing disease and illness, including the patient in the plan of care.

"But I have patients in Fiji to look after. Maura is deteriorating quickly and Joni tips the chart with febrile seizures every time she spikes a fever." Reagan tried to justify staying close to her island family, ocean and waves. She had left it once before, and the Pandora's box of side effects had erupted.

"I won't take 'no' for an answer. You know we have to test the baby soon after he or she is born, and the guest room in my home is already set up for both of you." Dr. Yiung had a way of convincing his patients what was best for them.

Reagan was perplexed by her mother's unannounced hospital visit. There would be an answer soon—her mother always had an agenda, none of which included social visits. Reagan wished she would have stayed in Fiji, where access would have been more difficult for her mother.

"Of course, I know about Hansen's, and I've heard that you are working with some afflicted cases on that island." Roz had a forbidding tone to match her penetrating eyes. She stepped forward and tapped the top of the IV bag with her red-polished nail. "Such a tough bacteria to control . . . one day it's rampant, the next it's dormant. Genetic susceptibility against those acid-fast germs. Stigma is far worse than the disease itself."

"Have you treated anyone with Hansen's?" Reagan straightened.

"You mean for the stigma? Not really, what's the point?"

Shocked, Reagan jumped back, "How could you—"

"Relax, honey. You don't understand me. The point is, the disease isn't that devastating; it takes its own course. Better not to get in the way."

Reagan countered: "That makes no sense, have you ever seen—"

"Of course, I've seen the devastation. Have you seen how society treats someone with leprosy? Even in L.A., where some new cases just popped up. Better off avoiding it all."

Jeremy stood and began to speak, "Uh, do you—"

Reagan raised her index finger toward him—there was no reason to fill her mom in on her own diagnosis. She wondered how much her mother knew about her work with the islanders. Reagan had always sensed a deeper reason why she helped end the lives of those suffering with leprosy. She hadn't considered saving them from society.

Roz looked out the window for an instant, "It's not *how* you end the suffering. It's when. Do you spend your life locked up and hidden just to avoid the cold harsh world? I'd rather be dead." She turned back to the machines. "You haven't seen hardship as I have. Disease doesn't always make sense, and none of it is fair. All I know is, it makes no sense to be miserable all the time."

Reagan dropped her shoulders back against the hospital bed. She looked over at Jeremy and noticed his intense stare. She could tell how irritated he was by the woman with the upper-crust accent. But Reagan didn't feel the need to pave the way for a relationship between them—her mother would be gone soon and out of her life just like before.

Roz adjusted the knobs on the cardiac telemetry unit and just as Reagan was going to ask what she was doing, three knocks on the door caught everyone's attention.

"What an honor." Dr. Yiung's voice was expressive and uplifting. He looked up at Roz, "Dr. Caldwell, I am Jay Yiung, Reagan's physician." He smiled at his patient, "and friend." The doctor walked over to Jeremy and patted him on the shoulder. "You do good work, buddy. She's an early bird but very healthy."

"What about her blood panel?" Roz interjected, "Her sed rate should be lower, don't you think, doctor . . . what was it? Jung?" Roz perused the casual floral button-down shirt that Dr. Yiung wore. She ended her glaring stare on his slip-on shoes with Hawaiian print on the sides.

"Mom, you're not the doctor here, Dr. Yiung is." Reagan emphasized the correct pronunciation of his name while she gripped the side rails on her bed. "Dr. Yiung's the one who saved me last year from . . . well, never mind. It was a holistic approach, no pharmaceuticals."

Roz huffed, "Western medicine's not good enough for you?" She pointed to the screen. "Those values are too high. How about you up her potassium. And get new blood work. Could be human error, God only knows—in this upside-down part of the world."

Reagan's heart rate escalated. The alarms on the monitors beeped annoyingly. She reached for the shut-off switch, but Jeremy stopped her hand and stroked it.

"Actually, those values are within—" Dr. Yiung countered.

"They're only within normal limits if you don't care." Roz turned to leave.

"On the contrary, Doctor. Because I care, we leave them be, because they are within normal limits." Dr. Yiung beamed toward Reagan.

The empty silence was palpable, and Reagan didn't interfere. The sleeping baby on her chest reminded her of the priorities in life. For the moment, she let the tension of her mother go.

Jeremy watched Roz walk out of the room and across the hallway to the nurse's station. He followed her to the edge of the door, fearful of what she might say or do. He saw her pick up a pen and tap the counter repetitively, creating an annoying resonance in the small nurse's hub.

One of the nurses asked, "Can we get you anything, Dr. Caldwell?"

"Yes, I understand Dr. Tom Dover is chief of staff here. I need to speak with him."

"Dr. Dover is in a—"

"STAT!" Roz ordered.

3

MAURA pulled back the traditional sarongs, acting as window covers, earlier than usual. It wasn't even nine a.m. and the bure was already hot. The Fijian trade winds were sluggish at best, leaving a heavy stench of dry-salted fish in the air. Springtime on the island slowed everything down, creating doldrums and fatigue, even for those not afflicted with leprosy. Maura's eight-year-old daughter, Joni, was drenched in sweat, and even the slightest breeze helped with her fever.

"Mama, when will Auntie Reagan be home?" Joni peered up at Maura with one eye open.

Maura released her strained smile as she blotted Joni's damp forehead with her deformed hand. The washcloth slipped several times until she finally secured it with both fists. "Should be home any time now, sweetie. Jus' a few more sunsets. Auntie Reagan misses you more dan' all da' coconuts on da' island and can't wait for you to meet baby Laura."

"Is baby Laura my cousin?" Join attempted to prop herself upright with her twig-like arms before sinking back onto the pillow. A heavy sigh followed.

"Of course she is." Maura's daughters had always called Reagan "Auntie" so they figured her baby was their cousin.

"I will tell her the bird stories." Joni forged a smile as she pointed across the bure. The traditional Fijian hut was a simple dwelling with thatches of palms stacked together for the roof and open windows to encourage the ocean breeze to waft in and out. Maura's bure showcased a modest collection of local handcrafted décor, but the outstanding item in the room that Joni was pointing toward was a hanging bookshelf made of koa wood and nautical rope, attached with carabiners to the ceiling. Reagan made sure it was full of books from afar, to expand the girls' dreamscape.

Joni's older sister, Lelei, walked in and handed her mother a bunch of assorted leaves. Her strong stature with shapely defined arm and leg muscles was a sharp contrast to both her mother and little sister. "I made da' tea, and now I will wrap her arms in Musa leaves."

Maura beamed, "You are beautiful Kōkua, jus' like your Auntie Reagan."

"Only I'm not getting no 'island sick', no way. I'm doing my skin checks." Lelei rolled her arm back and forth, flicking at her usual freckles.

Maura dropped her head and shielded the look on her face, tucking her gnarled hands into her side pockets.

Lelei walked over to her little sister and made a silly grimace, scrunching her nose and mouth. "Who wants to be a swamp monster today?"

Joni giggled and contorted her lips to match the monster-like face her sister made. "Me, me . . . make me into Nessi, from the far away swamp."

Lifting her sister's limp and skinny arm with the finesse of a heart surgeon, Lelei wrapped the wet Musa leaves around her upper arm and tucked them into her armpit. She split the stem with her teeth and rubbed the inner sap on Joni's forehead. The scent was musky with strong wisps of black cohosh and meadowsweet, the herbs she soaked the leaves in. The tincture would allow the body to cleanse out the toxins and lower the fever. Auntie Reagan had taught her well.

"Come, help move your sistah over there, so I can clean da' sheets." Maura's eyes indicated which direction. There were no designated beds for the girls and with only two mattresses in the room they slept where there was space—usually three to a mattress. But on special occasions, Maura would sleep with Joni, to keep an eye on her symptoms and remind her of the most treasured job. Joni was in remission from Hansen's disease and currently recovering from a staph infection that surfaced intermittently. Although recurrence of Hansen's was common, the sulfone drugs that Reagan prescribed for Joni kept the disease at bay. But the mysterious infection that chronically haunted the small girl persisted—a never-ending fever being chased. Maura caught it at the earliest detection and started the holistic regime that Reagan had taught them.

Lelei placed Joni's freshly wrapped arms in her lap and carried her across the room. "You're in charge of keeping those hands still."

"Cava?" Joni asked.

"Why? Because leaves fall out if you move. Nessi needs to stay hidden." Lelei had learned from both Reagan and Phaeole—the healer on the hill, to include the patient in their care. *The patient always needs a job in their own healing*. Reagan's message stayed in Lelei's subconscious. She was an ambitious student, already practicing herbal medicine. Only sixteen years old, and she could distinguish which plants lowered a fever and what soil, when mixed with sand, could act as a healing salve. She frequently had sprigs of cago, the natural antiseptic, in one pocket, and ground turmeric wrapped in fabric in another.

Lelei was also her mother's physical support since Maura's hands had shriveled, claw-like, over the last year. Her leprosy was so severe that even the sulfone drugs weren't enough to erase the crippling effects, before she had started treatment—before she had met Reagan. Maura had lost sight in one of her eyes, and her previous stagger would have been welcomed compared to the newest inward collapse of her hip when she walked. Lelei appeared just at the right moment, so her mother wouldn't fret too long or even notice what she couldn't do.

"Will you read to me?" Joni yawned, with her arms at her side, mummified in leaves.

"Of course, you want big story or small today?" Lelei walked to the hanging bookshelf.

Joni raised her head as she heard the familiar creak from the wooden steps outside the door. She managed to straighten her body upright on the mattress without using her leaf-bound arms for help. Her smile widened, her legs wiggled back and forth and her big round eyes looked at her mother.

"Is my girl awake yet?" the husky voice made Joni squeal.

Maura's smile matched Joni's as she opened the bamboo door for Roger. "Ah, you come early, my friend. We all excited."

He nodded—they all missed Reagan. Roger assumed a fatherly role for Maura's girls after Reagan had left for Sydney. He brought fresh lettuce and asparagus, bags of rice, and paper goods weekly. But it was Joni he perked up to each time he visited.

"Rogi," Joni sat up with renewed vigor. "Read to me, kerekere, kerekere, please, please."

"That's why I'm here." Roger held out two new books for Joni. "Are you a tree today?" Roger poked at the leaves around her arms. "What are you hiding in your branches?"

Joni giggled as he tickled her underneath the wet healing Musa leaves.

Maura's husband—the chief of their tribe, had passed away with Reagan's assistance two years previous. His suffering was endless, to the point there was no other option than to get medical support from Reagan to end his life. It was one of Reagan's roles with the islanders—end the suffering when the time had come—respect their right to die with dignity. She was the person, their Kōkua, who had the passion and strength to help with *life goes*.

Now in Reagan's absence, and with no husband for support, Maura looked forward to Roger's visits. The island community took care of each other. Maura was instrumental in making Roger part of the Islander's circle, even though he lived across the waterway at the resort where Reagan lived.

"How long 'til the leaves need turning?" Roger asked.

"'Bout an hour." Lelei adjusted the few stems that tried to escape.

"I can do it. Things are pretty quiet at the resort." Roger sat next to Joni and opened the first page of *The Girl and the Seabird*. The heat penetrated through the leaves and Roger pulled his hand away, "Youch! You're cookin' today."

"Vinaka, Roger." Maura got up gingerly from the wooden chair. "Lelei and I do some cleanin' outside. Big winds las' night leave big mess. Be back before lunch. Cold water is in da' coconut shell, and fresh poi on the cooker."

Joni stuck her tongue out as she heard the word *poi*. "Eki."

"You eat like da' gecko, lil' one. You need to grow, eat the poi," Maura said.

Joni smiled at Roger—a knowing secret that there would be no consumption of poi.

"You take all day if you need to. My girl and I are staying put. I mean the tree and me." Roger placed a few extra leaves on his head.

Joni giggled and rubbed her feet together, "We both trees now."

Maura gazed at the two nuzzled up together. Small beads of sweat gathered on Roger's forehead. Maura admired the connection between them, the close fatherly love. She knew Roger understood Joni's need to feel like a normal kid, not one with a potentially debilitating future.

"We be quick." The warmth in Maura's smile clearly said; *Vinaka, thank you for being here . . . you are her person . . . I couldn't do this without you.* "Come Lelei, the baskets, we go now. . . ." Maura's attention was on her daughter as she turned to leave. She felt the blunt force pain immediately. The large beam, in the middle of the bure, had always been there, but suddenly she slammed into it, nearly missing her eye. Blood gushed from the corner of her eye, streaming in a narrow red river down her neck, eventually soaking her sarong.

"Mama!" Joni yelled.

Maura started to spin toward the floor.

"Maura!" Roger rushed to her side.

Maura pressed on her upper cheekbone and squeezed her eyes shut. Crimson red swelling erupted, distorting her face. "Didn't see—"

"Oh, my dear, sit down, come let me look at this." Roger kept his voice low.

"No, I go. I get Aloe." She wrapped her sarong around the side of her face, into a fashionable scarf-turned tourniquet, pulling on the ends. "I go with Lelei, stay with Joni. I be back."

"Are you sure? That looks bad, maybe you should lay. . . ."

"No worry." She tried to open her eye but decided to keep it shut. She searched for Lelei with her one good eye.

Joni sat upright, with her eyes welling. Her arms broke loose from the Musa leaves. "Mama—"

"Listen to Mama, I help her, you stay with Rogi," Lelei guided her mother's arm up, and held pressure on her swollen eye while leading her out the door.

Maura hobbled out of the bure with a trail of blood left behind.

Roger winced at the stray wisps of black curly hair stuck to the beam. He snatched them with one hand and wiped the bloodstain off the wood with the sleeve of his shirt. Gathering his emotions, he picked up the book.

Joni pouted until Roger was back at her side with the first page opened. "There once was a small girl, who lived in a tropical Chimichimi tree. . . ." Roger pulled her into his side, adjusting the half-soaked leaves around Joni's arm as they tried to unravel.

4

REAGAN was flustered from the commotion her mother had created. It felt as if a swarm of hornets blew in her hospital room and back out, but they were ready to return at any moment. She tried to calm Laura, who squirmed—lifting and lowering her head with no control, squeaking small sounds of need. It wasn't feeding time yet.

"Why is she here?" Reagan handed her daughter to Jeremy.

Jeremy shrugged his shoulders and cuddled the baby.

"She wants something. I just know it." Reagan looked first to Jeremy and then toward Dr. Yiung, who flipped through the clipboard at the foot of her bed.

"Well, currently she is going to visit Dr. Dover, head of the hospital," Jeremy casually mentioned as he rocked Laura.

Reagan noticed the alarm on Dr. Yiung's face. She'd never seen him angry or fearful—she sensed this was a combination of both.

The excessive beeping of the hospital machines attached to Reagan escalated again, adding to the anxiety from her mother's intrusion. The siren-like noise reverberated against the window, creating a steady upheaval in the room—its cataclysmic effect vibrated down Reagan's spine and throughout her entire being. She threw the sheets off violently and got out of the bed, holding the water pitcher in one hand and the IV pole in the other. Stabbed with a sharp pain in her stomach, Reagan's hand slipped off the aluminum rod and she fell to the floor.

Jeremy was at Reagan's side mid-fall, catching her with one arm before she hit the floor. He balanced baby Laura in his other arm and stooped to the floor to support Reagan. "Hold on there, Champ. Not quite ready for the races . . . or getting upset by your mother. Come on, back to bed you go."

Dr. Yiung was at her side just as fast, holding her other arm. "Slowly, Reagan. Your body ran a few marathons two days ago, yah know."

Jeremy lifted Reagan's legs onto the bed and covered her with the hospital blankets. Then he placed baby Laura on her chest, stroked Reagan's head and hummed an island tune.

The baby's eyes followed Jeremy's voice. The crying stopped and the cooing began. He continued the lullaby while Laura's eyes fluttered closed.

"Why do you think she's here?" Reagan whispered to Dr. Yiung.

"No telling," Dr. Yiung shrugged. "Guess she wanted to meet her granddaughter."

Jeremy kissed Reagan on the forehead, then her cheek, and finally her lips. "I love our daughter, and I love you. Let's not worry about Granny being here. . . ."

Reagan's heart rate monitor abated its alarm and quiet in the room returned. Her eyebrows furrowed into deep creases as she whispered, "I don't trust her for a minute."

"Relax, my love." Jeremy stroked the baby's head with one hand and placed his other hand on Reagan. "My family . . . so beautiful, so precious."

Dr. Yiung headed for the door. "I'll be back in the morning to check on you girls, but we do need another bilirubin profile this afternoon. Stay cozy and I'll get it ordered." He left the room and went straight to the nurses' station. "Ladies, anyone happen to see where Dr. Caldwell went?"

A nurse pointed down the hall, "Dr. Dover's office."

"Any idea why?" He pushed his glasses up the bridge of his nose.

"Not sure. She said something about needing someone in charge." The nurse peered from her eyeglasses and stared at Dr. Yiung.

"Of course, she would." Dr. Yiung turned from the nurse and picked up his pace. Taking the back stairs down to the administrative level, he made one detour by the digital exam room. There she was, standing with the chief of staff at Sydney General, looking at a large computer screen. Dr. Yiung walked to the next door, which was a colleague's office, and head of radiology.

"Hey, Ted, how's the new knee?" Dr. Yiung held his arms open.

"G'day, mate, where yah been?" The two embraced.

"Just keeping things interesting at the free clinic. You should really come moonlight sometime. The classroom is alive with new ways."

"Yeah, if I had half your luck. Gotta keep services reimbursable around here."

Their smiles widened.

"How can I help yah, Jay?"

"My patient, Reagan Caldwell, is here and I'm hoping to look at her latest bilirubin and liver enzymes." Dr. Yiung looked over his shoulder twice for anyone within earshot.

"Well, labs aren't my department, but let's take a look at her order." The radiologist leaned against a tall stool and made several clicks with the computer mouse, before leaning closer to the screen.

Dr. Yiung was always welcome in other facilities—he had hospital privileges all around Sydney. His reputation preceded him. With expertise in nontraditional healing methods, other medical professionals held him in high regard. He was also the kind of doctor who asked about a practitioner's family and remembered small details of stories once shared. Jay Yiung had an incalculable quality—humility permeated his brilliance, rendering a unique personality, friendly and approachable.

"Huh, the bilirubin might have to wait. There's a push order for her genotype profile and placenta tissue biopsy. Could take a while."

"Placenta biopsy? What the—"

"Yeah, that tissue is all the rage. You know, all those mesenchymal cells. Helps with inflammation and the immune system. Practically a black market for the organ."

"Any consent on that order? Did the parents sign off?" Dr. Yiung asked.

Ted rolled his eyes before shaking his head, "Mate, you think someone like Roz Caldwell can't get around a scribble mark?"

"Come on, Ted, you know that mother of hers is just throwing her academic weight around."

"Maybe, but it says right here: STAT, MD orders—priority."

"It's not right, mate, is it?" Dr. Yiung stared at his colleague.

"Not for me to judge what other docs do."

"Even if it's unethical?"

"Even if it's illegal," Ted whispered with a cocky smile.

5

JEREMY answered his cell phone quietly as he covered baby Laura's pink ears. "Hey there, Jean, how's the script coming along?"

"Jeremy? I thought you'd be back in L.A. by now. Where are you? Why are you whispering?" Jean Michael's voice was much louder than Jeremy's.

"I have to stay quiet or I'll wake the baby . . . our baby. She came early. Jean, you should see her, oh my god, she is so amazing . . . her eyes, her smile." Jeremy's voice sped up.

"Sounds like a proud Papa." Jean softened.

Jean Michael Raava was more than a producer and director to Jeremy—he had become a good friend and confidant, unveiling the source of Reagan's radiation exposure. Jean was now Jeremy's partner in exposing the fraud and blackmail of the energy company—Hollywood-style.

"How's Reagan?"

"She's beautiful, never better. And our baby, Laura . . . well, you will just have to meet her, and soon. I promise." Jeremy beamed.

A few moments of silence changed the tone of Jeremy's voice. "Hey Jean, do you remember . . . uh . . . back in Fiji, on the dock the night before we left, what we talked about?"

"Something about how you found yourself, after being lost," Jean answered.

"Yeah, I was just thinking about that feeling . . . it was pretty heavy, almost too big to handle." Jeremy cleared his throat.

"Life gets that way, at times . . ." Jean paused, ". . . Jeremy, are you okay?"

There was a flash of static on the line followed by a muffled cough.

"Jeremy?"

"I'm here . . . I'm fine, really. It's just—"

"Just what?"

"There's this massive wall pushing at me. More like a concrete bulldozer. I can't let it in, it's too much. But I should be the happiest guy alive. Makes no sense."

"Jeremy, you listen to me. You're overwhelmed, that's all. You probably haven't slept in what . . . two or three days . . . go easy on yourself. You just became a father, and in my eyes, you won—you're with Reagan. She's amazing and that scares you. That's a normal fear."

"It's more than fear, I just can't identify it." Jeremy's voice cracked. "I mean what if something . . . happens to her?"

"Nothin's gonna happen to Reagan, she's—"

"Not just Reagan. I'm talking about our baby, our daughter. She's so tiny, so . . . vulnerable." Jeremy stroked his daughter's cheek. There was a soft innocence of her deep sleep—no strain, no struggle, just peace. Things would be different for her. He would make sure no one could harm her, the way his father hurt his mother.

Jean Michael said a few more things that Jeremy didn't fully hear. He kept stroking Laura's cheek, silently overwhelmed. *No one will ever hurt you, I promise.*

"Did you hear me, buddy?" Jean's voice broke through.

"What's that, Jean?" Jeremy half-whispered.

"I said, when are you coming to L.A.?"

"Probably a few weeks. She's a little premature, and Dr. Yiung wants us to stay put for a month or so."

"Okay, I can keep working the sideline shots. But man, are you gonna freak when you see the new info that your nurse Lydia keeps feeding me. It's fantastic, almost unbelievable. Lucky we didn't go documentary . . . they'd come after us for sure."

Jeremy could sense the distraction from Jean. The long-distance static broke up the call. "Wait, say that again, Jean. You're breaking up."

". . . such a . . . strange . . . bystander on the. . . ."

"Jean, Jean, I didn't get any of that. Say it again."

"No way to tell . . . such a coincidence. . . ."

The line went dead. Jeremy returned to stroking his daughter's pink cheek. He wondered what Jean meant by *strange coincidence*. The hospital room suddenly felt cold and too white. It bounced a glare of light toward him. A dagger of dark threat poked at him. It prodded, but Jeremy wouldn't let it in.

Jeremy looked at Reagan fast asleep in bed, while his daughter's breath flowed over his chest. Love and fear held him motionless. In the last year he'd gone from spoiled indulgent actor to meeting and falling in love with Reagan, who barely survived her debilitating disease of leprosy and radiation poisoning. All leading to this powerful moment of watching these two sleep—the two females he couldn't live without. The dark thing rushed toward him again; he had to work hard to avoid the terror of it—the memory of it. Careful not to let his fear steamroll him, Jeremy pulled Laura closer to his face and whispered, "I love you, little one. I will always be here for you." He buried his face into hers and dozed off.

The creak in the hospital door woke Jeremy. A nurse peeked in and cleared her voice.

"Yes?" Jeremy looked up, startled.

"Oh, excuse me . . . uh, sir. I mean, Mr. Black. The doctor is waiting, I mean he asked to see you, uh, somewhere, I mean . . . in his office."

The nurse tripped over her words. Everyone knew Jeremy Black—his stardom was international.

"Oh, Dr. Yiung just left, said he'd be back tomorrow," Jeremy whispered, while covering baby Laura's ears.

The nurse looked at Reagan, asleep in the bed, and lowered her voice, "Dr. Dover wants to see you. He's head of the hospital. I'll show you to his office."

6

REAGAN had longed for the crystalline teal water of her favorite surf spot in Fiji—the one accessible only by boat and unknown to most surfers. Pumping her legs to stay ahead of the raging water, she outran the tumbling peaks of white water at the crest of the wave. The glassy interface between calm and turmoil breached as she made a hard bottom turn into the next section. Then quiet—for several seconds, which seemed an eternity in surf-tube time. Ducking her head and keeping one eye open, Reagan revelled in the distant light at the end of the barreling waterfall. She stretched her arm toward the expansive sunlight and the energy pulled her out of the jaws of the wave. Her skin glowed, revealing shiny scales in a multitude of colors. Reagan felt fish-like. Then both eyes opened, with full clarity, more light saturated her body, and then the full panorama unfolded—colonies of purple coral heads, extravagant colored fish, her island, her life. Panting, chest heaving, she turned her board up and over the end of the wave with precision.

Reagan lived for the exhilaration, even though it had been a distant sensation over the last year of her life. The joy of surfing compressed her lifeline into segments of over-the-top happiness. It was very reliable. But her illness and pregnancy had kept her out of the surf too long. Fortunately, her vivid dreams kept her in the waves, and in the ocean. Now, as her eyes popped open in response to someone shaking her, the fluorescent light in the hospital room brought her back to reality. She embraced the rapid rise and fall of her chest, desperate to hold on to the fading surf scene.

"Miss Caldwell, you have a phone call." A nurse nudged her arm.

"Where? What?" Reagan jumped as the nurse pointed to the bedside hospital phone.

"Says she's a nurse from L.A. and it's urgent we wake you."

Sitting upright, Reagan reoriented. A small grin grew larger as she picked up the bedside phone. "This better be the nurse I think it is."

A lighthearted squeal preceded a race of words, "Hey girl, I heard you had your baby, but evidently you have no cell cuz there be no messages here on my phone . . . which I'm sure you would have called. Do I have to hear everything through the Hollywood grapevine?"

"Lydia!" Reagan lifted herself high in the bed and gripped the phone with two hands, hearing the voice of her rescuer.

Now alert, with Laura sleeping next to her, Reagan softened her voice. "Yes, she is right here and beautiful—perfect APGAR score, but impatient. She came a bit early and I've been a little preoccupied. My mother's here, unexpectedly, and—"

"Damn."

"What . . . Lydia?"

Reagan heard the tepid cough on the other end of the line. "Lydia. Did you know my mother was coming?"

"Well, not for certain." Lydia's voice choked again. "I hoped this call was ahead of her. I was jus' fixin' to tell yah when yah woke up. Sorry friend. I was hoping to prep you. That's why I told them the call was urgent. Your doctor Mama be askin' all kinds of questions and you know I don't be doin' the talkin' 'round here. Not to no one who doesn't need to know."

"And?" Reagan's tone surged, stirring the sleeping baby next to her. She softened, "And what?"

"Well, your Mama knows how to throw her name around, is all I'm tellin' you. She's one bossy lady doctor—got her way all right. Them doctors 'round here practically kneel down to her."

Reagan snuggled into her baby, inhaling and absorbing the scent. There was a hint of plumeria in Laura's hair, or was it her skin? She closed her eyes and held back tears.

"They be sayin' she's got some confidential therapeutic or vaccine of some sort. It's all hush-hush roun' here. Even the big guns at Cedar's told us to keep our mouths shut."

There was stark silence for several moments before Lydia broke, "Reagan, you still there?"

Keeping her eyes fastened shut, Reagan swallowed, "Vaccine for what?"

"The intel is still out on that one. Don't think she's got any civil liberties in mind, so not gonna help my people. That mama of yours hangs with big Pharma and big money, so could be just stackin' the patents."

Reagan wiped her eyes with her gown sleeve. "Well, I'm sure there's some award waiting for her, right?"

Lydia laughed, "Oh, girl, I can't wait to hug you and that baby of yours."

An eerie silence once again extended the long distance between them.

"Lydia, why would she travel all this way? What does she . . . want?"

"Not sure, my friend, not sure." Lydia's voice matched Reagan's tone.

Retreating farther into the bed, Reagan wrapped her arms around her daughter and let the tears bathe her.

"I'll do my best to find out, hopefully before she start blowin' up a storm. You jus' pay attention to that baby girl and don't mind that doctor Mama of yours. I'll make tracks on this. Don't you worry. You hear me, girl?"

"Thank you, Lydia. Talk soon." Reagan slowly replaced the receiver and dropped her head on the pillow in exhaustion.

With a heavy heart, Reagan's dad entered her mind—she suddenly missed him and worried if he was okay—would he get to meet his granddaughter, or worse, what if Reagan never saw him again. Guilt-ridden threats attempted to take over her emotions, but then she thought of her mother. *Why is she here?*

7

JEREMY listened as Dr. Dover threw out a variety of medical terminology, to somehow justify the need to further test baby Laura. He sat stiff, perched at the edge of the oversized leather chair in the doctor's personal office. Jeremy heard words such as 'displacement' and 'recovery tracking', then something about 'cell reabsorption' and 'stem cell' something or other. He couldn't help but notice the word 'gene' was cautiously planted in most of the phrases. Reagan needed to be here. He couldn't comprehend any of it.

"You are the father. You can sign off on all of this." The doctor looked away from Jeremy as he tapped the end of his pen on a stack of papers.

"What about Reagan? She needs to know about this." Jeremy's voice got louder. His heart pumped erratically; he feared an impending panic attack. Placing his hand over his chest, he temporarily stopped the excessive movement. He got out of the chair and started to pace but found himself taking only a few steps, then turned to repeat the same number of steps in the other direction. The office was small to start with, and the four adults in the room occupied much of the needed floor space that Jeremy needed to work out his anxiety. The vinyl slats echoed his concern, as the rubber sole of his shoe squeaked with each turn. *I can't breathe. I need to . . . need to get out of here . . . need air.*

"Actually, we can go with *your* consent. Reagan is exhausted and likely not thinking clearly with all the meds she's on." The doctor looked down at his desk. "We just need a few tests."

"But I don't understand any of this. Why—" Jeremy threw his hands in the air.

"We don't expect you to understand." A commanding voice interrupted him.

Jeremy turned around at the sound of the familiar tone. "Roz, I didn't know . . . didn't see you there."

Roz Caldwell had been sitting in the corner of the office all along. "This is why I'm here, to be your advocate, rather, Reagan's advocate. I do understand. I'm a doctor and I can help you with what you need to know."

"This is starting to feel like an ambush." Jeremy inventoried the room. "What else is going on here?"

The heavy hospital door flung open with a thud, hitting the back wall. An apologetic nurse followed Dr. Yiung.

"What the hell is this?" Dr Yiung's anger brought everyone to attention. Several pieces of paper were clenched between his white-knuckled hand.

Dr. Dover stood up. Roz followed.

"What happened to patient rights? These orders are a sham." A small distended vein erupted on the side of Dr. Yiung's eyebrow.

Jeremy stood ready to defend Reagan's doctor—their doctor, their buddy. "What's going on here?" Jeremy squeezed the back of the chair.

"I'll tell you what's going on here. Your daughter's prize-seeking Grandmum thinks she rules the roost and can use her blood relatives as guinea pigs. Easy way to bypass human subjects review." Dr. Yiung turned and faced Roz. "I can practically smell that Nobel Laureate. Can't you, Dr. Caldwell?"

"I'm really confused." The blood had left Jeremy's face.

"Now, now, both of you," Dr. Dover attempted to mediate. He held both arms out toward Roz and Dr. Yiung, his fingers outstretched with his palms outward.

"I'll spell it out for you, Jeremy. Granny here is on the brink of a new gene-blasting phenomena—"

"Splitting." Roz interrupted.

"You call it whatever palatable word you like. It's still playing 'God' and you don't even come close. Abducting embryos left and right, exploiting newborns for their placenta and stem cells . . . didn't exactly get permission from them, did yah now?" Dr. Yiung stood a few feet from Roz's face. His upward stare held her hostage for a split second. "It's all about the notoriety. Am I right, Doctor?"

Roz picked up her Hermes purse, snapped the latch shut and walked toward the door. "Your perception is way out of line, similar to your wacky practice, Dr. Yiung. It's a wonder you're not banned from this upside-down part of the world. Your reckless abandon of Western medicine will leave plenty of innocent patients with unnecessary suffering. What happened to your oath, Doctor?" She whisked out of the office leaving everyone in stunned silence.

Dr. Yiung bent to the malice like a palm tree in a cyclone. He stooped over making him appear even shorter than his five-foot-six frame. Pushing his glasses farther up the bridge of his nose, he conceded, "Jeremy, my friend, she is bad news for you and Reagan—bad news for your daughter. I'm sorry to say, I don't really have the power to stop her. Roz Caldwell will probably get her way here. She could drain the hospital's funding in one phone call." He shook his head without looking at Dr. Dover.

As Dr. Yiung headed for the door, Dr. Dover finally spoke. "We are finished here. I will have our chief resident reassigned to your patient. If you lost us a dime . . . I swear. . . ."

The heavy door shut with a solid thud, shaking Jeremy further. The twisting knot in his stomach strangled his gut—holding his body hostage.

Dr. Dover continued his diatribe, but Jeremy had gone numb. A strange mute-like sensation took over. Jeremy willed his feet to take one small move, then another. His breathing was erratic and he had to remember to exhale so he wouldn't pass out.

Jeremy edged his way down the hall to the exit stairway, then up a flight of narrow concrete stairs toward Reagan's room. He sensed for a moment that the walls moved in on him and that the ceiling dropped several feet. His breaths shortened and strained. When he reached the top step, he pushed the door open with more force than needed, creating a loud slam on the back wall. This would not be easy. He rehearsed the untenable script in his head. He knew the doctor had purposely thrown a bunch of medical terminology at him. "This is what I heard," he rehearsed. "The doctor thinks Laura needs . . . what did he say . . . some sort of genoprofile, something or other." He couldn't remember the exact words. "And Dr. Yiung feels. . . ."

As he turned a corner, he bumped into a nurse who was holding a tray of food, almost knocking her over. "Oh, so sorry, I didn't see—"

"No worries, mate, just watch your step. Oh, so sorry, Mr. Black, sir. Are you okay?" The nurse straightened up and steadied her tray.

Jeremy saw Reagan's door opening and he ran toward it. His heart rate shot up as he darted in. "Dr. Yiung, you're still here? I thought you were . . . I mean, I thought you left." He looked to Reagan.

Jeremy always searched Reagan's eyes for the truth. They stood out as her most prominent feature, not for any specific hue, but for the expression they took. He had learned to read her eyes over the last year. He studied them now, searching for what she already knew.

"You're welcome." Dr. Yiung took Jeremy's hand and laid his other one over both of his. "I filled her in. I'll work on your discharge." He walked out the door.

Jeremy looked back at Reagan and noticed the gentle forgiving slant to her eyelids, relaxing her mild crow's feet. He was confused.

"Reagan, I'm so sorry. This is all so confusing . . . I don't even know what she wants. I swear, your mother is—"

"Stop." Reagan took his hand and brought it to her cheek. "Just stop. It will be okay. She won't harm Laura. Dr. Yiung has arranged a transfer."

"To where?" Jeremy knew the nearest hospital was over fifty miles away.

"What about Laura? Is she ready to leave?" His hands were shaking.

"She'll be fine. Our daughter's a fighter. Look at these arms." Reagan stretched out her baby's arm, stroking the long, yet petite limb. "These arms will do so much in life and we will make sure no one pokes at them, without good reason."

Jeremy picked up his baby and smelled her familiar fragrance—it was part Reagan. He had never smelled a newborn before until she arrived. Holding her calmed him. His hands settled and he pulled Laura tight to his chest. "I love you, my little girl."

8

SHADOWS of the morning sunlight stretched and contoured Reagan's body as she extended her arms toward the sky. The small lanai off the guest room at Dr. Yiung's home was a perfect way to greet the day. After several minutes of quiet, she was drawn to the smell of a rich smoky sweetness melded with the aroma of French roasted coffee.

The kitchen was spaciously arranged so a gathering of people could easily contribute to what dish was being prepared. One by one, members of Dr. Yiung's extended family entered the grand room and inevitably picked up a long wooden spoon and stirred a pot on the stovetop. The smells were alluring for anyone within several rooms of the kitchen.

Reagan and Jeremy stayed at Dr. Yiung's home, as their interim hospital while Laura gained her would-be birth weight. The new baby thrived with her milestones and showed off new antics daily—flirtatious smiles and cooing at different pitches, lifting her head on her own to inspect her surroundings, or an outburst of giggle in her sleep. The couple fell more in love with their daughter with each new blossoming milestone.

Reagan and Jeremy felt safe at Dr. Yiung's home, well away from the hospital, beeping machines, the constant interruptions, and the threat of Roz Caldwell at their door.

"What's this?" Reagan inhaled into the glass double-boiler on the stovetop. She let the rich and complex flavor surround her. A subtle trickle of smoke lifted high toward the kitchen fan then evaporated, leaving a hue of orange in the air. She picked up the bamboo spoon at the edge of the pot and stirred the dark syrupy liquid. A kaleidoscope of brown and burgundy colors swirled in a hypnotic circle.

"Cacao. Theobroma, that is. See these pods . . . it's the food of the spirits." Dr. Yiung responded as he poured the last few drops of herbal ginger tea into a cup and handed it to Reagan.

"Sounds like something Phaeole would make." Reagan missed the wise Shaman elder on her island, the person who had shown her how not to get in the way of her own healing.

"I'm sure Phaeole is making his own healing brew right now. These are just some nibs for the day." Dr. Yiung wiped his finger along the inner edge of the bowl. "Almost there. Needs a bit more chili."

"Working on your heart health, I see." Jeremy walked into the kitchen and picked up the spoon and stirred the dark chocolate.

"Wow, someone's upping their game on medicinal intel," Dr. Yiung chuckled.

"Gotta stay up with this crowd, for sure." Jeremy looked toward Reagan, who was silent and stood on one leg with the other foot perched at her ankle.

"What's up, my love?" He moved toward her and took her hand.

Methodically peeling a mango, Reagan's eyes stayed on the task as she answered, "Time to go home." She took a bite of mango then looked up at him.

"But I thought . . . I mean . . . I hoped you might stay here a while longer with Laura and Dr. Yiung while I go to L.A." Jeremy peeled another mango, dissecting the pit perfectly. Years ago he would have never known what to do with this fruit. He took the paring knife and finely sliced the pieces of fruit. He placed them on a plate with a small orchid flower in the center and rotated it so the petals reached toward Reagan. "Jean Michael said only three weeks to film. I can be back here to fly home with both of you."

Reagan moved in closer and softly kissed him on the lips, lingering for a moment. "It's time for us to go home, to Fiji. You can meet us there when you're done." She fed him a bite of mango.

Jeremy flung his hands in the air with the paring knife still between his fingers. He looked over at Dr. Yiung, who was busy with the melted chocolate concoction. "How about a little help here, Doc?"

"I got to go check emails, you're on your own. And put that weapon down." Dr. Yiung left the kitchen.

"You know, I taught you how to use that knife." Reagan spoke softly, reminiscing about how she had introduced him to a new way of living in Fiji. It was a far cry from the pampered actor he had been when they first met, where every aspect of his life was managed so he would be spared the slightest scratch. Peeling and arranging a mango would have been a long shot back then.

Reagan remembered how distraught Jeremy had been when she had asked him to help end her life—he couldn't. She wondered now, if his inabilities then, spared her life. The memory haunted her; their eyes met.

"Do you remember . . . last year, when I left—" Jeremy began.

She put her index finger on his lips.

"I will never leave you again."

"Except L.A. this week." She raised an eyebrow.

"You know what I mean."

Reagan put her cup of tea down on the counter. She did know what he meant and wasn't surprised by the comment since he recited it on a regular basis. This was the first time he'd said it since Laura was born. "Maura and the kids can't wait to meet our daughter. They want to meet her *as a baby*." She emphasized the last few words.

Dry winds wafted into the lanai entry. The Aussie sun crested the mountain scape and Reagan raised her head to greet it. She closed her eyes and envisioned her ocean across the way. The dolphins and rays called to her. Maura, the kids and her many patients on the small island of Ravanuu, needed her as she needed them.

"And Roger, he is desperate to meet Laura. You know how much he helped me last year and well . . . I will need to explain the namesake in person." Reagan bit the edge of her lip and wondered how that would go—Roger's infant, Laura, had died from SIDS only a few days old.

Turning back to Jeremy, she caught his stare and was drawn to his blended eye color. She was attracted to his new look of ruggedness—once-groomed hair now out of place, a prickly golden beard and his sun-parched skin.

She pulled her fingers through his beard with a gentle tug. "It's time, my love. It's simply time."

Jeremy raised Reagan's hand to his lips and kissed it. He lingered with her scent and acknowledged his defeat. "Well, it's settled then. I'll book our flights and make plans to join you."

"No, I can do this on my own, really." Reagan stretched upward as she spoke.

"But it's no problem. I can take you back, the film can wait."

"My decision is mine. I want to do this on my own. Like you said, you will be back in a few weeks. Go to L.A. and get the film done." Her smile grew. She longed for the moment of not needing anyone else to help lift her, care for her, or dote over her. It was her turn to take charge.

Dr. Yiung appeared again, suggesting the chocolate needed tending to—he smelled the rich liquid.

"What do you think, Doc? You can't possibly agree with her going back to Fiji on her own." Jeremy turned to him.

"Oh, you mean I get to keep the little one?" Dr. Yiung beamed.

Reagan walked over to the pot of simmering chocolate, picked up the spoon and drizzled the medicinal liquid over her plate of mangoes. She grinned at Dr. Yiung.

"I agree. Your people need you." Dr. Yiung looked straight at Reagan.

"Thanks, Doc. Big help." Jeremy dropped his head.

"My friend, what you need to understand about Reagan is that her hunger is fulfilled by helping others. She's played the role of patient long enough. Now it is her turn to nourish herself."

Reagan absorbed his words. She too, knew what her soul needed.

"But before you leave, you owe me a day at the clinic, right?"

"Of course. How about today?" Reagan begged. Excitement ran through her.

"Sounds perfect. There are some baby admirers who want to meet Laura, so let's give it a go." Dr. Yiung turned off the stove, covered the chocolate, and smiled triumphantly.

Jay Yiung was raised on the island of Yakushima in the East China Sea. As a young man he had fished with hand-sewn nets and fed his community daily. While handing out fresh tuna, he took time to interact with his neighbors. Some of them presented with different types of ailments—an irritated rash, fever, or a lopsided hobble. Jay would offer Ayurvedic treatment advice, using ocean kelp and other naturopathic remedies he had collected from the sea. He understood, at a young age, the delicate balance between the mind and spirit, with the body acting as a barometer. He had attended medical school in Syndey, Australia, but kept in touch with his community in Japan, traveling home monthly to stay connected with the family traditions. As he aged, many of his relatives joined him in Australia to escape the economic hardships in Japan.

He had always envisioned a society that took care of each other like the people in his fishing community did. When he finished medical school, he built a free clinic with that concept in mind. Dr. Yiung created a medical facility where holistic treatment and teaching patients self-care was the cornerstone of his practice. He established a work-trade program for those who couldn't afford to pay. Pharmaceutical companies were not welcome, insurance reimbursement did not exist and managed care was incomprehensible. Patients naturally transitioned to become volunteers, the facility ran flawlessly, and the community was well taken care of. *Sydney Free Clinic* was a place where medical inequities did not exist.

When Reagan had first met Dr. Yiung at his clinic, she couldn't comprehend the concept. She figured the most destitute medical cases were simply sent there as a last resort. At the end of that first day at the free clinic, she had shifted her view of medicine and resurrected her belief in helping others and not just putting money in the pockets of shareholders.

The entry to the free clinic had its usual long line of patients. Some stood on their own accord. Others rested on nearby benches. Several people were in wheelchairs; some with missing limbs. Most of the patients displayed various physical ailments. Reagan acknowledged them all, touching several patients on their shoulders as she headed to the entrance. Baby Laura was wrapped in a sarong on her chest, while Jeremy followed, stopping to make silly faces to the children in line.

As Reagan approached the steps that lead to the front door, a young girl ran toward her, half-tripping amid the crowd. She held a big towel close to her stomach. "Miss Rea . . . Miss, Miss Reagan!" The girl was out of breath, "Please . . . help me . . . I mean, me pup. Me dad is gonna kill 'im . . . says he won't make it . . . with only three legs."

The young girl appeared to be nine or ten years old. Her dark brown hair was partially pulled back in a ponytail, with strands of dust-ridden hair stuck to the tears on her face. Her trembling arms held a small puppy under the towel. "I cried all night, then heard you're coming today, so I ran here as fast as I could. Mum and Dad don't even know I'm gone. I knew you would help 'im. You saved me grandmum last year on Boxing Day. Please help 'im, please—" She used the wet sleeve on her bleached T-shirt to wipe away more tears. Her drained eyes stared at Reagan as she held the small dog up and waited for Reagan's response.

Reagan touched the stumped front leg on the blue heeler. The dog seemed to be a few weeks old and not moving much. She pressed her ear to his heart and heard a good steady rhythm. The pup opened his eyes and blinked several times.

"I call 'im Atta Boy, since he walks just fine. But me dad says no one will want this bluey. Please Miss Reagan, can you help? Can you do your magic?"

Tears flooded the girl's face, drenching the pup's ear.

Jeremy walked up, smiling at Reagan, "Well, what do we have here?"

Reagan picked up the pup and kissed it on the nose. "Would it be okay with you if he lived with us in Fiji?" She asked the girl. "My baby Laura will love him just like you do. He will run around all day long and play in the surf with us."

"Ye . . . yes . . . that would make me so, so . . . happy. I packed some brekkie for 'im." The small girl kissed the puppy on its head and handed Reagan bites of sausage in a napkin. "He really loves singing. I sing to 'im at the nighttime." The girl kept one hand on the puppy's head while the other hand stroked his stumped leg. The tears had ceased. "And you can give 'im a proper name too, if you don't like—"

"I think Atta Boy is a perfect name." Reagan stroked the girl's head. She took the pup and tucked him in her sarong, next to baby Laura. The baby curled into the puppy and they were both asleep in minutes.

"Our family's growing fast." Jeremy kissed Reagan affectionately.

Reagan headed into the clinic to say goodbye to some of the patients she had known and treated over time. A long procession had formed near the exit, and one by one the well-wishers gave their best recommendations for how Reagan and Jeremy should raise their child—no solid foods 'til six months, no peanuts 'til one year, let a sleeping baby lie, wake your baby to feed on a regular schedule, don't let the baby sleep in your bed, always let your baby sleep with you—the suggestions were endless. Reagan soaked up the attention from everyone around her.

After numerous kisses and hugs, thank yous and goodbyes, Reagan and Jeremy fastened their seat belts and waved out the car window. As they turned out of the clinic driveway, baby Laura started to cry in the infant seat. Reagan turned to soothe her but stopped when she saw the puppy crawling into the baby's lap in the car seat, nuzzling and calming Laura.

"Atta Boy."

9

JEAN Michael scrolled through the working screenplay marked up with symbols and highlights, comments and question marks. He had a black ink pen behind his ear and a red ink pen in his hand. He hovered over the stacks of paper and periodically shook his head and switched out the pen color and jotted notes. He longed for a dinner break but couldn't pull away from the edits that needed to be addressed. The studio cafeteria had closed hours ago and there may have been a greasy taco truck in the lot, but instead Jean opened his third energy bar and took a big bite.

Jeremy and Jean had compiled plenty of convincing information, enough to indict the power plant for corporate negligence as well as the coverup that followed. This was Jean Michael's passion for working in film—telling the truth and exposing the perpetrator.

"Mr. Raava, sorry to interrupt, there's a Mike Peters on line four . . . says he's a friend of Jeremy Black." The receptionist held the phone up.

"I'll take it." Jean Michael was quick to respond. Mike was a new friend of Jeremy's and one of his closest liaisons. He had become an integral member of Jeremy's house staff, not on the payroll, but rather he worked for his keep. There were plenty of odds and ends to handle around the property and Mike, who had completed three tours of duty, the last one in Iraq, knew how to get things done. And he was deeply loyal to Jeremy. The veteran had watched many of his men die, some in his arms, and upon his return stateside he had struggled with all the trauma and death he'd seen. He had ended up homeless on the streets of L.A. before Jeremy had rescued him.

"Mike Peters, what a surprise. How's the homestead doing?" Jean leaned back in his chair and propped his feet on the desk.

"The home on the hill is in good order, sir."

"I'm hanging up this phone if you don't call me Jean."

"Sorry, sir . . . I mean, Jean."

"What's up, my friend? Are you picking up Jeremy tomorrow?"

"Yes, sir . . . Jean, sir. I will be there on time, don't worry, sir . . . Jean."

"Relax Mike, something up?"

"Uh, yes, something came up today. Well, not that I need to tell you how to do your business, sir, but I'm familiar with your plot, shall we say."

"Out with it, Mike."

"Well, I've been working with Lydia and she's been looking for more info on Charlie Grant, your whistleblower guy from the plant. She even tried to call the guy, several times, about his doctor follow-up."

"Yeah, I know the guy. What about him?" Jean sat upright with his feet back on the floor.

"Seems like he may have turned up at the hospital morgue today. They're still matching prints." Mike stopped, then sighed, "And a strange item was left at Jeremy's house midmorning, sir."

Jean Michael froze as he heard the words. "Wow, the guy was pretty sick, but I never imagined this would happen so soon." Jean remembered how Jeremy described Charlie Grant and his restless leg as he revealed what he knew about the malfunctioning equipment at the power plant, creating a deadly radiation leak. "What's the strange item?"

Mike cleared his throat, "Someone dropped off a notebook at Jeremy's entry gate. First page says: *Here's the whole story. The truth.* I'd say there's about a hundred pages here with dates and everything, and a bunch of names."

Jean Michael kept quiet. Charlie did know the truth and did need to tell it.

Mike continued, "There's a scribbled signature at the end followed by: *Sorry, I can't live in hiding anymore.* A sort of goodbye letter, like I'm leaving town. But the real kicker is that Lydia said his body showed up at the hospital morgue this morning at five a.m.—dead on arrival, and this notebook was dropped off today around noon. Seems to be someone else blowing a whistle here."

Jean Michael leaned forward, holding his cell phone on his chest for a second.

"Are you there, Jean? Sir?"

"Yeah, yeah, I'm still here. He was a good guy trying to do the right thing."

"I know where that gets you," Mike blurted. "Usually face down in the trenches, defending what you thought was right."

"I really appreciate this, Mike. How can I get that notebook?"

"I'll get it to yah. Hey, another thing," Mike added. "Thanks for what you do . . . you know . . . the movie thing. I saw your documentary *War at Home*. You got it right."

Jean Michael lifted his head and listened.

"In Iraq, I was drawn to anything that could make you feel somethin', you know . . . engage your heart, not just feed you the bad news. But these days it's hard to feel anything. I mean we're all suffering. Most of you guys in film get it right from time to time, get people like us to sign up, make a change. I'm grateful for that."

Silence echoed on both sides of the phone.

"Now I've said too much, sorry man . . . I mean, sir."

"No, Mike, you've said just enough. I know what to do."

10

PREVAILING winds out of the south blew Reagan's scarf off her neck as she de-boarded the plane in Fiji. Hands full of baby and puppy, wrapped together in the sarong around her body, she let the scarf fly. The latent heat sat heavy in Reagan's lungs, with a smattering of small thunderheads far off in the distance. No rain in sight today; she would have welcomed a break from the stagnant air. Little Laura and Atta Boy were sound asleep against Reagan's chest. The past twenty-four hours together fostered a strong connection between the two. Where a newborn puppy would normally be overly energetic, this little blue heeler was calm and protective. Reagan loved watching them sleep together, paw over baby's hand.

"Auntie Reagan, Auntie Reagan," the first few voices bellowed down the gangplank and across the airport walkway.

Reagan first noticed Joni running toward her, followed by Lelei and Massina; all three of Maura's daughters had matured while Reagan had been gone. Maura hobbled behind them with a large walking stick. The hand-carved wooden staff was a new accessory, one that Reagan had fully approved of even though Maura didn't feel it was necessary. Reagan forced a smile as she watched Maura's deteriorating limp.

Joni hugged Reagan's leg, "You came back, you came back!"

Reagan welcomed the distraction from witnessing Maura's worsening physical state. "Of course I came back. I really missed you guys." She wrapped her elbow around Joni's head.

Joni rose up on her tiptoes to see her new baby cousin. When Atta Boy nuzzled out of the sarong, Joni jumped back and screeched. "Oh, oh, what is that? Na koli, na koli." Joni jumped up and down. "Mama, Mama, come quick, it's a puppy too."

Lelei put her hand on Joni, holding her back. "Calm down, little one. You'll wake the baby."

Reagan hugged Lelei. "Good job, my beautiful Kōkua."

Lelei smiled back. "How can I help?"

"How about holding Laura?" Reagan offered the easier of the two babies at the moment.

Lelei blushed as she opened her arms. She enveloped the baby and nestled her into her chest, just like Auntie Reagan.

Reagan bent down to Joni's level. "And you, my little plumeria petal, can hold Atta Boy."

"What kinda name is that?" Joni scrunched up her nose as she extended her arms to hold him. "Oh! No leg? What hap—"

"Now, now, lil' one, na koli doesn't need four legs to be loved, does he?" Maura smiled as Atta Boy squirmed in Joni's arms. Her gentle lesson camouflaged the heavy exhaustion of the illness she struggled against.

"No, they don't." Reagan wrapped her arms around Maura and held her close. She thought of the chief and his passing—the impact it had on Maura. It wouldn't be much longer for her as the disabling effects of Hansen's disease were winning. Reagan remembered the chief's words; *my family is now your family*.

"He would have been so proud of you." Maura responded to Reagan's unspoken words. She hobbled to baby Laura and stroked her cheek, "Akeakamai."

Reagan tilted her head, questioning.

"It means desire for wisdom," Maura said.

"Sounds Hawaiian."

Maura smiled. "Yes, but us Fijians blend with all our Pacific Island ohana, the Hawaiians don't mind."

"We'll add it to her birth certificate." Reagan said.

Reagan watched as Maura recited words in Fijian while making the sign of the cross on Laura's forehead. She didn't have to ask for the translation. It felt like a loving blanket being spread over all of them, tucking them in as a family.

Reagan felt the gentle tugging of her sarong. "Massina!" A new wave of emotion hit Reagan, as she hugged Maura's middle child, already a young woman at age thirteen. "There you are . . . my special girl." Reagan pulled her into the hug with her mother.

"I've missed you all so much. I wanted to come sooner, but—"

"Hey, what about this ol' man?"

Roger's voice had deepened since Reagan had last seen him. It had only been a few months, yet he'd aged. Thickened crevices surrounded the edges of his lips. Yet when he smiled, his cheekbones lifted, erasing the months of grief he must have gone through. Reagan suddenly realized how the last year of her illness had affected him.

"My friend." Reagan opened her arms. "You have done such a great job with Maura and the girls. Thank you."

"Where's our new addition to the family?" Roger's voice shook slightly.

Reagan nodded toward Lelei and Maura, and prepared for Roger's response.

Roger approached the baby and stopped a few feet away. He shifted from side to side. "So you named her Laura, eh?" He gazed back at Reagan.

When Reagan and Jeremy had discussed naming their baby after Roger's deceased daughter, she knew an explanation would be needed. There were many nights spent practicing what she would say, about her admiration for Roger and what he'd endured. She held her breath for a moment and watched him move closer.

Lelei turned baby Laura to face him, allowing Roger a full view of her little face. Baby Laura stared at him.

"Do you want to hold her?" Reagan asked as she joined them.

"No, not just yet." Roger's voice was barely audible. There was a mild, yet noticeable tremor in his left hand. He placed his finger in the baby's outstretched palm.

Reagan covered her mouth as Laura wrapped her tiny hand around Roger's index finger, grasping it tightly. His tremor settled.

Roger softened. "It's a good name. She's beautiful, just like my—" He cleared his throat and lowered his sunglasses over his eyes.

"I think she has Jeremy's nose." Reagan rested her arm on Roger's shoulder.

"I think she has your . . . beauty." Roger's voice cracked.

Reagan's cheeks turned pale pink. She wiped the beads of moisture from her brow. "I forgot what the tropical heat does to me. Let's get inside."

"Better yet, let's get everyone to the boat. We have a quiet sea today, lucky girls." Roger linked arms with Maura and Reagan.

"I've missed it so much," Reagan smiled at each of them.

11

JEREMY paced the LAX airport terminal, as he waited for Mike to arrive. Exhaustion weighed on him as the crowds brushed by. He was irritated with the oversized jacket, low-brim hat and dark glasses. He glanced at his watch for the fourth time. "Where are you, Mike? And what the hell is that smell?"

A woman, dragging a roller bag with a smaller bag tethered on top, walked past him with a baby squirming in her arms. She dropped a small toy, looked at it, shook her head and kept moving.

Jeremy ran behind her and picked up the toy. "Excuse me, Ma'am, you dropped this." The woman turned and Jeremy could see layers of swelling under her eyes. The baby was crying, her other arm shook and the oversized diaper bag slid down her arm, bursting the top open. Diapers, wipes, rattles and a variety of baby toys descended, landing all over the sidewalk.

"Let me help." Jeremy lifted the remaining bag off her arm and guided her over to the edge of the wall. "Relax here for just a moment." After taking off his hat and glasses, he gathered the items on the ground, rearranged and packed the bag and zipped it shut.

"Aren't you that actor, Jeremy Black?"

"Just call me Jeremy. Do you need help to your car? Is there someone coming to pick you up?"

"No, no, it's just us. We're getting on the bus. Not so easy doing the travel thing by yourself."

Jeremy felt a pang of regret.

"How nice that you would stop and help, or even notice us, you being so famous and all," the woman said.

The words stabbed at him. "You just seemed to need a hand."

The baby had settled, and there was a cart nearby. Jeremy situated her three bags on the cart, took the infant blanket and made a makeshift sarong around her body to wrap the infant inside, freeing the woman's arms.

"Now that's impressive. I don't think anyone has ever been so kind. You will make a great father someday when you settle down." The woman stared at the newly secured infant wrap.

Her words stabbed him again.

"We'll be on our way now. Thank you again, Jeremy." The woman looked back at him twice after she had walked away.

Jeremy froze. The dark emotions walled up again—the fear, the unrelenting panic, the pressure in his head. He dialed Reagan's number. No answer. *Breathe, just breathe. What's wrong with me, she's not gonna have her cell tucked in her sarong, this is stupid . . . I'm stupid, what have I done? I've left her again.* He fumbled for his dark glasses and took quick steps over to the pickup area.

Jeremy had told Mike to drive the old pickup truck used by his gardeners and meet him just beyond the international terminal. The less attention drawn to him the better. As the cars sped by, Jeremy couldn't remember what kind of truck he had—he'd never driven it. He put his hand up at several trucks as they went by before dropping his arm, seeing there was no Mike in any of them. A sense of disorientation snuck in and Jeremy tried to call Reagan again. Still no answer.

"Hey J, is that you?" The voice echoed across the median.

"Mike, buddy," Jeremy tore off the hat and glasses. "What a relief."

Mike jumped out of the truck and ran across the street. They bear-hugged then slapped backs affectionately. "Nice coverup. You okay?"

"Yeah, yeah, I'm good. Let's get out of here." Jeremy wiped the sweat from his face.

Mike grabbed Jeremy's bag. "Follow me. I'll clear a path. Put those stylish glasses back on."

They walked in line, Jeremy two steps behind Mike, with his head downward. The last thing he needed was a frenzy of fans recognizing him.

"How's that baby girl of yours?"

"Mike, she's amazing. Her eyes—the way she stares at me. Like I was her whole world. When she wakes up, she scrunches her nose and looks around for our voices. . . ."

Jeremy beamed as he described his daughter, but there was a gnawing twist in his stomach—the undeniable ache of separation anxiety.

"Why, just the other day Laura rolled—"

An overweight man walking next to them on the sidewalk bumped into his shoulder, knocking him off balance.

"Hey, watch where you're goin', bud," Jeremy said with a glare.

The man had a wide face with an overgrown beard and a swath of colored lines, shaped like a bolt, tattooed on the side of his face. He stared back at Jeremy then leaned in toward his ear, "Stop the film, now."

Jeremy stopped walking, "What are you talking about?" He ripped off his glasses and matched the guy's stance.

"You heard me, *Big Shot*. Stop it now. No second chances." The man with the facial tattoo gripped Jeremy's arm as he spoke into his ear.

Mike turned to look for Jeremy and darted back toward the man, pulling him off of Jeremy and throwing a punch at the side of the man's face.

"Mike! Stop." Jeremy was too late.

The man fell to the ground with a loud thud, attracting much attention, including three airport security guards.

The guards pinned Mike to the ground before Jeremy could defend his friend. "Get back!" One of them yelled as he pulled out a taser gun.

The Panama hat flew off Jeremy's head as he lurched toward Mike. "He's my bodyguard. He's with me."

Swarms of people stopped in their tracks, hearing that familiar voice and now seeing the famous actor.

"It's Jeremy Black," yelled one woman.

"Is he hurt?" Another person got her phone out.

Cameras were out and the action began. Police and airport security swarmed the crowd yelling: "Get back, clear the area. . . ."

Jeremy hovered over Mike, protecting him from the chaos of the fast-growing crowd. As he looked up, he saw the man with the tattoo on his blood-soaked face weave through the crowd and away from the police.

12

LYDIA parked her car at the end of the studio parking lot—the one with extra space and a slight decline, in case she needed to roll her car to get it started. She knew how to plan for her own rescue. The '78 Volvo was showing its ninth life and she needed to help it last a few more months.

"Excuse me, Ma'am. No visitor parking here. This area's for studio staff only." The parking attendant seemed older than he probably was, with a side-to-side hobble as he walked toward Lydia. He wiped the sweat from his face with a well-worn bandana, then tucked it in his back pocket.

"Hi there. I'm Lydia and I'm here to see Jean Michael Raava."

"Yeah. Who isn't here to see him? Don't matter what yo' name is. Still can't park here." The African American man smiled wide, exposing his gleaming white teeth.

Lydia smiled back. She felt akin to him in skin color and his need to stick to the rules. He reminded her of one of her old uncles.

"Where you from?" She exaggerated her slang.

"Louisiana, Ma'am. West side, near Carroll Parish."

"Oh, you mean Province."

The man let out a hearty chuckle, "Yes, Ma'am. You know da area?"

"Oh sweetie, not only do I know it, I spent my summers swimmin' in that lake across from the State Cotton Museum. Nasty water color." Her smile grew as she glanced up at Jean Michael's window. Lydia needed to get up there. She was already ten minutes late, but the visitor lot was a mile away with a shuttle to bring her back to the studio.

"How 'bout I bring you a cup of coffee when I come out and we talk a little story then?" Lydia glanced at her watch. "I'll be lickety split."

The attendant looked over his shoulder, then back at her car, "Well, okay Ma'am. Seein' as you're gonna be quick an' all. How 'bout two packs o' suga and one of them curly donuts in the lounge, the ones with the maple."

"Here's my keys, in case you have to move the car for someone else." Lydia handed the man her keys and winked at him as she made her way up the stairs to the entry.

"Two packs o' suga, don't forget." He wiggled her keys in the air.

As Lydia opened the grand entry door, Jean Michael almost ran into her.

"Hey, where you goin' in such a hurry?" Lydia touched his arm. "I know I'm late and all. . . ."

"Let's go. Jeremy's downtown at the police station. Something about a brawl he was in at the airport." Jean grabbed her elbow and led her down the stairs.

"Now, that don't sound right. That boy is way too pretty for a brawl."

"Come on, ride with me." He directed her to the convertible BMW parked right outside the entrance in the "reserved" section.

Lydia got in his car and waved to the parking lot attendant as they exited, mouthing: "Sorry, gotta go."

As Jean Michael sped out of the lot, he further explained, "Mike Peters went to LAX to pick up Jeremy, and now the cops have him in custody and they need a bail out."

"Well then, there's jus' never a dull moment 'round here, is there? You know who came up pulse-less today at my hospital?"

"Let me guess . . . Charlie Grant?"

"Man, you movie boys are *good*." She drew out the word 'good'.

"I already talked to Mike, before he left for the airport." Jean glanced at her, raising one eyebrow.

"What? Are you two buddies now?"

"Just using all my informants, you know, for the film."

"Well, do you also know the cause of death?" Lydia turned toward him, looking for a response.

Jean shrugged, "I could take a guess, but no, not really."

"Yeah, I didn't think so." She settled back in her seat, facing forward. "You guys only know so much, and then the assumin' starts takin' over, and you know what that word spells . . . it jus' makes an ass out of you and—"

"Yeah, yeah I got it." Jean grinned.

"The problem is no one listens to us nurses. It's only them docs who get your ear. They gone and sold out a long time ago. They don't even know what's killin' their patients. God only knows they don't take notice of that kinda trivia. But us nurses, we notice everything. We close every door and latch every window, if yah know what I mean."

"Well, no, I don't know what you mean." He chuckled a little. "But I'm guessing you're into more detail than the docs?"

"Not just detail, child," Lydia turned in her seat again, to face him directly. "We be into treatin' humans like humans, not just another patient number. Us nurses know you inside and out—even your loved ones. We get the whole picture, not just the part."

"I appreciate your honesty, Lydia. Wish there were more like you."

Lydia blushed, then cleared her voice, "Charlie Grant died from the biggest burden in life—keeping a big fat secret. It was too much for his soul to handle. They buried him alive with their greed and threats. He died a long time ago, but just today he stopped breathing."

After they parked in the drop-off area of the police station, Lydia led the way to the entrance. The media had already gathered and were being corralled by an officer in the parking lot. Lydia lowered her head and moved toward the entrance. She opened the door for Jean Michael.

"You really shouldn't spoil me that way. I don't think it's *all* nurses. I think you're one of the special ones." He took the door from her and waved her in.

Jeremy stood up first as they came into view. "Lydia!"

"Oh, you poor little actor boy, what kinda trouble you in now?"

Jeremy hugged Lydia, "I miss you too."

"And how's that little baby girl of ours? I can't wait to meet her."

Jean Michael was at the desk speaking to the chief of police, shaking hands with several of the office staff and smiling.

"Good sign over there," Lydia smiled. "You boys be smooth as honey."

Mike Peters came out of a small room and shook hands with Jean Michael. A thickened swath of dried blood on his knuckles was in full view as he held an ice pack on the side of his face. "Appreciate it, sir."

"Sir? Really?" Jean glared at him.

Mike grinned as he re-adjusted the ice over the red contusion on his face.

"Well, I'll be damned, if it isn't you guys again." The man was dressed in casual clothes; his wrinkled cotton shirt barely supported the detective's badge.

Jeremy turned to him, momentarily confused.

"You're that fancy actor . . . and your buddy got clobbered over the head last year." The detective looked at Jean Michael. "It's been awhile. He survived and you're back in town, back at my police station. Huh."

"How could I forget . . . Detective Burns." Jeremy let out a stilted laugh.

Jean chuckled nervously, “You haven’t stalked us recently.”

Detective Burns looked around the hallway. “Strange coincidence, I thought of you recently. Last year . . . that CDC van thing. They didn’t really want Reagan. It was a wild goose chase for sure.”

“What did they want?” Jean leaned in.

“Oddest thing ever. Thought I’d seen it all—” Detective Burns stopped talking as two officers passed them.

Jeremy whispered, “Let me guess, not really CDC?”

“How’d yah know? I’m thinkin’ thugs, related to the power plant company. We got some leads . . . this one weirdo old guy, but nothin’ turned up, so we put the case to bed.”

Mike looked over at Jean and both remained silent.

“Anyway, I meant to call yah . . . and . . . well, tell yah—” Detective Burns looked away. “Clear the air so to speak.”

Jeremy started to respond and Jean interrupted. “Well, we all make mistakes, from time to time. Thank you, sir. We need to get going now.”

“What about the power plant?” Lydia blurted.

Jean took Lydia’s arm, “Like I said, we need to get going.”

Lydia glared at Jean, but kept quiet.

“Why don’t you guys take the back door to avoid the media frenzy out front and I’ll send an officer out with a statement.” Detective Burns pointed down a hallway to a nondescript door.

Walking out to the car, Lydia shook her arm from Jean’s grip. “Hey, what’s with the hush-hush in there?”

Mike shook his head back and forth, knowing the truth.

“What do y’all have?” Lydia stopped walking and stared at Mike.

No one answered her for several moments.

“Come on now, you boys know I can get it out of yah. Give it up and save us all the inside tradin’ crap.”

Mike spoke first. “It was in Charlie’s notes. The ones dropped off today.”

"Go on." Lydia perched her hands on her hips.

"The energy company was up for sale but there were some unsettled claims on wrongful deaths."

"If those incident reports leaked, and if proven accurate, those corporate guys would be off to prison for a long time and no sale." Jean sighed, "They paid big bucks to shut people up and get rid of anyone who knew anything."

"So, they heard 'bout Reagan's case and figured—"

"You got the picture." Jean opened the door for Lydia.

Mike whispered something to Jean Michael as they got in his car and drove away.

13

BRITTLE sounds of twigs being dropped into a sparrow's nest woke Reagan. She felt a great sense of calm; she was finally home in Fiji, back in her bure, with boundless island fragrances and tropical flowers growing outside her door. Laura had been asleep for close to seven hours and Reagan didn't dare wake the sleeping baby. She respected the advice of the well-wishers at Sydney Annex. Reagan caught a floating scent of jasmine in bloom. Beaming, she walked out onto the lanai to welcome the burst of light projecting at her feet. Her room was one of the only bures that spanned east to west, enjoying the welcome of the day as well as the sunset. Translucent rays dropped down from the rising ball all the way across the adjacent horizon, reaching toward the direction of Malibu, California. It created a sense of longing, missing Jeremy.

Reagan picked a plumeria bloom from the branch hanging near her lounge chair. The delicate orange and yellow petal tickled her nose and she drew another expanding inhale, deeper than the first one. She placed it behind her left ear, thinking of Jeremy. Closing her eyes, she listened to the musk parrots chirping their morning tune. The yellow-breasted birds squawked and sang in a distinct conversation as they dipped between the cassava patches to feed. Reagan opened her eyes and caught a glimpse of several fruit bats diving and foraging for breakfast. *Home. At last.*

Turning toward the harbor, Reagan saw swaths of teal ocean swirled between darker shades of blue. She envisioned her reef just a boat ride away—the pitching peaks that brought her so much pleasure. It was only a matter of time until she would submerge in the serene beauty of it all. Her surfboard was propped against the edge of the bure, where she last left it. Wads of wax held tiny webs, new homes for some local critters while she was gone.

As she walked back into the bure, she laughed at the sight of Baby Laura and Atta Boy, both on their backs with all limbs extended, still asleep in the middle of her bed. "We're gonna need to improve on this sleeping arrangement, but for now it'll do."

Hanging over the bamboo divider, the exam light was perched, unplugged, in the corner. She hadn't used it for over a year. The incandescent light was used to detect any blemish or outward sign of leprosy, but it hadn't found the three small brown spots on her back, the first sign of Hansen's disease. That was thanks to Jeremy's strange and lovely handwritten letter . . . a love letter in an era of email and texts, no less, which prompted her to search for the "faint row of freckles" he had found so endearing. His description had saved her life. She looked away from the light, wondering if the inspection was even needed anymore . . . at least not today.

Hunger pangs interrupted her memories of it all, as she foraged the counter for a quick snack. The handwoven fruit baskets were empty, so she opened the small refrigerator, only to find empty shelves.

A whimper caught her ear. "Oh, my sweet little girl. Is it time for breakfast for you too?" Reagan was famished. She had been traveling the previous day and the excitement of seeing everyone had distracted her from eating enough. She attempted to nurse Laura but realized she wasn't producing much milk. She tried to fill a glass of water with one hand, when the puppy awoke and whimpered.

"What do *you* need?" Reagan searched for a bowl to fill with water for the pup, while nursing Laura. Then Laura started crying—the milk was not flowing. Reagan tried to console her while she rummaged with one hand, through her travel backpack for any remnant of nutrients. A half-eaten granola bar had stuck to the inside lining of her bag, but specks of sand and dirt were now woven in the nuts and raisins. Her heart rate escalated as baby and puppy whined in unison.

"Okay, you two, give me a minute to get it together." Reagan raised her voice as she opened cupboards in the kitchen. Boxes of rice, quinoa and pasta, cans of pinto beans, cornmeal, oats—nothing quick.

"Crap, nothing here. We need to go get some fruit for me, baby girl."

"Well, how about this fresh omelet from the kitchen?" Roger was at her bamboo-slatted door holding a plate of food. "And why don't you hand me my sweet little girl while you get yourself fed first."

"Oh, Roger. Such timing, I wasn't quite prepared." Relieved, she handed Laura to him and took the plate in one swoop. The food tasted decadent. She chewed feverishly and savored the fresh spinach wrapped in home-hatched eggs. She made herself slow down just enough so she wouldn't choke.

"How about some of this too?" Roger handed her fresh coconut water in its husk, with a bamboo straw.

"This is amazing. It's so fresh! Nothing even close to what I've been drinking out of a carton." Reagan handed a few bites of omelet to Atta Boy, who inhaled the food even quicker than Reagan. The short-term chaos abated.

"Looks like compliments to the chef from everyone around here. Thank you so much, Roger. I was feeling a bit desperate."

Roger held Laura securely on his lap, cuddling her. His hands shook sporadically so he extended his fingers and hovered over the small baby. He held still for moments before he silently kissed her forehead.

Reagan stopped chewing as she watched Roger's gentle love flow over her daughter. She put the plate down on the table and walked over to them. "She will be okay, Roger. Trust me. We will all be okay. We're home."

"I thought you might not come home." Roger looked up at her.

"But I did."

"And last year, when we first saw those spots on your back, I was afraid you—"

"Sorry, I was so frantic. I didn't mean to scare you."

Swallowing several times, Roger finally responded. "You always think of others before yourself. I've never met anyone . . . who truly does that."

"You do the same, Roger. Look at all you've done for Maura and the girls, and how about the boatmen you hire. I know what their circumstances are, below poverty level and no education. You've provided gainful employment and purpose for those boys. And you've given me a home. I could go on and on—"

"And I worried you might not make it." Roger looked away from her.

"But I did." She spoke softly. "The Hansen's is all cleared up and the radiation poisoning is gone—completely gone."

"Reagan, you are my family, the one person I really care deeply about. If something were to happen to you, and little Laura, well—"

"I'm here. Roger. I'm here." She kept her hand on his shoulder for some time.

14

THE first few weeks back at the resort took some adjusting to baby Laura's needs, the puppy's needs, and her own adjustment to nursing and sleep schedules; all of which was a pleasure, since she was home. But Reagan had yet to return to any doctoring, until Roger mentioned a young man who had traveled from the U.S. to seek her medical advice.

"He has just arrived and booked a bure for two weeks with the hopes of meeting you," Roger explained.

"What does he need? I wasn't really planning on seeing any patients yet, let alone anyone who's not an Islander." Reagan handed Laura to Roger to be burped.

"Well, not exactly sure . . . something about his sick mother." Roger took Laura with natural ease, positioned her on his chest, and began the ritual. He rocked side to side and made circles with his hand on her small back.

"Kinda hard to treat someone via someone else, yah know."

"Well, maybe I don't have it right, which I've been accused of before." Roger walked around Reagan's bure and shifted back and forth. He swayed little Laura in his arms—a slow dance, dipping her from time to time and placing kisses on her fleshy pink cheeks.

"She's the best little girl ever." His own little Laura had never made it to this age. "Look how strong she is, and her eyes are so intent." The proud parental bragging was endless.

"You are such a good grandpa, Roger. I'm lucky to have you in our lives. Jeremy will be happy to see you both when he gets back. You know he comes in just a few more days." Reagan beamed as she prepped a bowl of fresh fruit, handing a piece of papaya to Atta Boy.

"So, will you meet with the patient? Or I guess the patient's son, or whatever the case is."

"Of course, Roger, anything for you. But how'd he find me?"

"Not sure about that either . . . seems to me people know about you."

"Oh, please don't remind me, my mother suddenly showing up in Sydney, it's just all a bit weird."

Roger took Baby Laura to the changing station—a smooth wooden board with bamboo fronds weaved together by Maura and the girls, covered in a handmade blanket. He changed the baby's diaper, dressed her into a fresh onesy, and cleaned up the area without a glitch.

"You are getting really good at that, you know."

"How about noon today?" he asked.

"Noon today, what?"

"See the new patient." Roger returned to slow dancing with Laura.

"Let me check my schedule, huh . . . nurse, sleep, eat . . . yeah, I see an opening at noon. Book it. I presume you'll watch Laura?"

Roger extended his smile, "any day."

The gaunt young man stood before Reagan, off-balanced and awkward. Reagan focused on his eyes, and the dark circles magnified by his thick glasses. She wondered how old he was. Beyond his facial features, his long arms and fingers stood out giving the appearance of a sickly aged albatross. She considered that he could very well be the patient.

"My name is Windsor Rhoades." He pushed the wide rim glasses farther up the bridge of his nose. "You may have heard of my grandfather, Dr. Giles Rhoades. He's kinda famous."

Reagan couldn't recall any Dr. Giles Rhoades, famous or not.

"I live in Dayton, Ohio. But I'm hoping to go to medical school at Northwestern, someday."

"That sounds great, so you're interested in medicine?" Reagan asked. His mannerisms were perplexing—the twitching of one eye, the restlessness of his body as he stood, like he was ready to run at an instant's notice, his inability to look directly at Reagan for more than a few words.

"Have a seat." She pointed across the table.

Windsor looked around the empty restaurant before sitting across from Reagan. He dropped his worn backpack on the floor and grabbed a napkin out of the holder to clean his glasses. "It's really hot here."

Reagan sipped her ginger tea and stayed relaxed in her chair.

Windsor flattened the napkin on the table and turned it around and around, corner to corner, staring at the glass of water. "Is this water . . . is it clean water? Where does it come from? I don't usually drink out of glasses."

Reagan leaned toward him and placed her hand on his arm.

He pulled back abruptly like his arm had touched a searing flame.

"It's okay, I won't touch you. Yeah, yeah, it's good water, fresh from a waterfall." Reagan reassured.

Windsor picked up the glass with both hands and gulped the water until the glass was empty.

"You've come a long way—several planes, I'm sure, a few boat rides and a bus probably. What can I help you with, Windsor?"

"Can I get some more water, please?" he looked over at the bartender several yards away from them.

Reagan noticed the carafe of water completely full next to the glass he had just finished. She looked at the bartender and shrugged her shoulders. Drawing a deep breath, she steadied her patience. Her breasts were full, telling her she needed to get back to baby Laura soon.

After the bartender walked over to their table to pour more water, Windsor emptied the second glass, gulping at a frantic pace. He knocked the glass over as he placed it back on the table, "Oh, sorry, sorry. I didn't mean that . . . I didn't mean to knock over the glass. It didn't break . . . the glass . . . it's okay."

"Yes, It's okay," Reagan lowered her voice. "The glass is just fine. Why don't you tell me why you're here."

Windsor resumed his napkin spinning and looked around the restaurant, which was still empty. "Um . . . well . . . I want to hire you . . . I mean I need your help, or advice, on something."

"Okay, on what?" Reagan shifted in her seat, attempting to release the pressure on her bladder. She hadn't planned on the necessary preparations of a new mom going back to work. She wasn't planning on seeing patients so soon, except for the islanders' needs, or maybe Dr. Yiung's free clinic. But right now she wanted to get on with the patient in front of her, so she could get back to nursing and peeing and not being sidetracked with—

"On how to kill someone."

Reagan stopped moving in her chair, her basic needs were suddenly overridden. She sat up attentively, hearing the chilling words from the young man.

Windsor held eye contact with no problem. He sat motionless—no more nervous body language, just stillness.

"Did you say kill someone?"

He nodded, still watching her eyes.

"And did you say hire me?"

Now it was Reagan who reached for the water glass and gulped it down.

"I'm sorry, you came to the wrong person. What made you—"

"I was told you were the best." He interrupted.

"The best at what?" she raised her voice, as she pushed her chair back.

"Please, please, stay . . . stay, Dr. Caldwell." His hand was on hers, digging his fingers into her forearm, anchoring her to the table.

Reagan looked at the bartender, who was headed her direction.

She nodded to him, indicating she was fine and looked back at Windsor. Reagan lifted his hand off her arm. *No problem with me touching you now.*

Leaning toward her, Windsor whispered, "Let me say it differently. My grandfather says I need to work on my words. I need help ending someone's suffering."

Reagan let out a deep repressed exhale. She was confused how this young man got to her; the work she did was sacred here. Yet here was this odd young man begging for her help to end someone's life.

"Your grandfather seems to be a smart guy. Who is suffering?"

Windsor straightened his glasses. The rims were bent at such an angle that they sat crooked on his face, needing regular adjusting. He fumbled to pull another napkin out of the holder and they all fell onto the table. He used several to clean his glasses and left the rest scattered about.

Reagan held back her desire to roll her eyes and clean them up.

"It's my mom. She's dying . . . I think. She doesn't say much and grandfather won't help. He wrote us off when Dad left us. He says Mom had it coming."

The tension in Reagan's upper back extended to her fingertips. This young man, a boy really, had the gall to ask for her help. It wasn't the way she worked. "It sounds complicated. I can't help. Sounds like you may need a psychologist."

"No, no, really she's dying . . . I mean suffering . . . or whatever the right word is. I never know what to say, everyone's always correcting me, but I do know she is suffering . . . and dying." He pushed the glasses back on straight, and this time wiped the edge of his eye.

Reagan looked around the restaurant. Her body was heavy with fatigue. It seemed easier to stay put than move. Her patience was waning. She hadn't experienced this at Dr. Yiung's clinic. It was just so easy there—the holistic and natural approach to medicine. Reagan didn't know how to help the young man biting at his hangnail. She wasn't sure she even cared enough. There wasn't a connection with the patient, rather a desperate and somewhat irrational person asking how to kill someone. And the thought of being hired. . . .

"I sit with her every morning . . . the days that she wakes up anyway. I open all the windows that have the sun coming through them. She loves to be warm. Then I bring her chamomile tea, just the right temperature, not too sweet either. I hold the cup for her." He stopped talking for a moment and looked at his water glass. "I don't understand why the teacup can be so slippery, but for some reason it slips out of her hands, so I hold it the whole time, sometimes for an hour, until she finishes."

Reagan pictured the scene—the boy's love for his dying mother, it helped soften her, to connect with him. "What is she sick with?"

"Don't know, they won't tell me. They think I'm too young. 'He's just a boy,' they mock me. They think I can't do anything, but look at me now. I'm across the planet, talking to Dr. Reagan Caldwell, taking care of my mother."

"You're both lucky to have each other. Is there anyone else who lives with you two?"

"Oh, she doesn't live with me. She's at the nursing home. I live at the dorms. But I go there every day. She worries if I don't."

"Does your mother want to end her life?"

"No idea, she doesn't talk anymore. She just does her needlepoint and feeds the birds outside her window."

"Sounds lovely." Reagan relaxed a bit.

"No, she can't even talk, some days she doesn't know who I am. My grandfather always says if he gets that old and can't remember anyone, just shoot him."

Reagan stood up. She knew how to help.

"Where are you going?" His mouth dropped open.

"I need to go feed my baby. Meet me back here tomorrow and I will let you shadow my patients on the island."

"But what about my mom? I came all this way . . . I don't want to see any patients."

"Just meet me here tomorrow." Reagan started to walk away, but then turned back to face him. "By the way, what kind of medicine was your grandfather practicing?"

Windsor lowered his eyes and softened his voice; he had nothing to lose. "He started the Hemlock Society."

Reagan stood still with her eyes fixed on his. "Well then, you have a lot to learn. Meet me here in the morning, at nine."

"And you'll teach me how to um . . . help . . . um . . . end her suffering?"

Her mouth opened slowly then shut. She walked away. *Hardly.*

15

WALKING back to her room, Reagan recalled the group from Santa Monica in the early '80s that championed 'right to die' issues. She had taken courses on palliative medicine before medical school—it had always interested her. As Reagan learned more about the Hemlock Society, she really wished the advocacy organization would refer to it as 'Right to Choose' and rally with the 'Pro Choice' group. Both issues were one and the same to Reagan—so much in common—choice, dignity, control. She considered their motto: good life, good death, compassion and choices. She wondered if they had considered what she had discovered about losing oneself through illness, only to discover a new beginning—a second chance at redefining the illness. Her own experience with Hansen's disease and radiation poisoning was a death sentence, one that she had begged Jeremy to help end on her terms. Luckily her extended family—Phaeole, Dr. Yiung, Maura and Roger, had helped her see the rays of light shining through and not just the shadows on the wall.

She contemplated what it all meant—assisting others to end their life, their suffering, if they could no longer go on, doing no harm. The weight of it seemed—

"Reagan!" Someone called out from the dock.

She had to get to her room to nurse Laura; her breasts were starting to leak. Whoever it was could wait.

Sounds of fast-moving steps chased her down.

"Jeremy!" she jumped into his arms. "I thought you weren't coming back 'til—"

His lips on hers silenced them. The magnetic suction of their bodies melded into one. When he finally let her breathe, he pulled her into a strong embrace. "I missed you both so much. I had no idea. There was this woman at the airport and she was with her baby . . . and, well, the whole scene made me think of you and Laura, and how could I let you travel by yourself. What was I thinking?"

"But I told you we'd be okay. And we are fine," Reagan said.

"I should have insisted. I came back early because . . . because, well, I need you both."

Reagan stroked his face, "And we need you, but at least we made the first run okay. We—"

"Where's our daughter?"

The words were a perfect symphony to Reagan—every chord matched, resonating a strong response.

"And what's going on here? Did you fall off the dock . . . you're soaked." He pointed to her wet shirt, drenched in breast milk.

"That's how it's been going these days . . . a bunch of wet T-shirts telling me what time it is." She kissed him again, softly.

Roger met them on the path, holding baby Laura. "Here you go, my friend. Great to see you, Jeremy."

Jeremy scooped up his daughter in his arms. He kissed her gently all over her face. "I missed you so much, my little girl."

Reagan was touched by the scene; Jeremy's towering protection over their daughter, his wide smile, and the loving look in his eyes.

"She's grown so much. Look at her hold her head up." Jeremy beamed.

"That's what happens when all you do is eat and sleep."

Baby Laura started to fuss, which added to Reagan's wet shirt. "Okay, enough of all this, time for her to eat, for my sake."

Roger patted Jeremy on the back. "Welcome home, Papa, go be with your family."

As they walked down the path to Reagan's bure, a voice yelled, "Thank you again, Dr. Caldwell. See you at nine." The young man at the restaurant waved at her.

"Do I even need to know?" Jeremy asked.

"You stop it, he's my intern or rather a patient of sorts. His name's Windsor Rhoades, grandson to the *great* Dr. Rhoades." Reagan accentuated the word *great*.

"Yeah? Why's he so great?"

"Not sure yet. Maybe he published a bunch of great research. That's what makes you great, you know."

"Yeah, right." Jeremy stopped to pick a twig of jasmine and handed it to Reagan.

She sniffed the white flower and let the fragrance dance before she responded. "Dr. Rhoades was an advocate for 'right to die' patients. He introduced palliative care into the mainstream."

"What does that mean?" Jeremy asked.

"Well, it means an entire branch of medicine is dedicated to mitigating suffering and optimizing quality of life with a person who has a serious illness, with the time they have left."

Jeremy stopped and looked back at Reagan, "Is that why the guy's here?"

"Not sure. We just met. He needs my help somehow."

"Did you tell him you're on maternity leave?"

Reagan laughed, "Doesn't exactly apply here. Illness and suffering don't take a break, so why should I?"

He pointed to her drenched shirt, "because you need the break. You just had a kid and, well, I just don't want you to feel overwhelmed like the woman in the airport. She could barely manage."

“But she did. She managed to get you to help her.”

“I’m just saying, I don’t want you to feel stranded or without help, ever.”

“Have you noticed how much Laura is in demand? I have boundless help here. Between Maura and the kids, Roger and the staff; I’d be lucky if I ever had a day with just Laura and me.”

A brisk tropical wind swept through them creating a small whirlwind of leaves on their path.

Jeremy stopped walking and faced Reagan. He moved blown strands of hair out of her eyes and placed his hand on her cheek. “There will never be a day with just you and Laura, without me.”

16

REAGAN met up with Windsor the next morning. She watched him trip down the boat ramp, dropping a brown paper bag. She rolled her eyes as he picked up the spilled items.

"I'm ready." Windsor landed upright next to the boat.

"Hop in, my friend. We got a little ride across the pond first."

"What pond?" He looked around. "You said ocean and—"

"Never mind, Windsor. Just hop in."

Before Reagan's arrival ten years earlier, the islanders who were afflicted by leprosy died young, presumably by "natural causes," but as Reagan began to treat those who were trying to survive with the disease, it was clear that quality of life was the hardship. Handling even the most basic daily activity was more than a chore, so often the task would simply be neglected. Basic hygiene was even aborted—the fourth time the toothbrush dropped out of a clubbed fist was enough to put off the task for later. It was just too much effort.

Windsor was as clumsy getting off the whaler as when he got on. The islanders' dock creaked and moaned as he swayed like a sailor who'd been at sea for months instead of the short passage from the resort. Reagan walked in front of him, introducing the gawky character that traipsed behind her. "Adi, this is my friend, Windsor. He's come a long way to see your work. Can we watch?"

Adi was one of the strongest of the young men, but his hands were already crippled from leprosy. He had high cheekbones, alluring sky-blue eyes that would make him extra handsome if not for the scarring of his disease. "Sure, we jus' dig new hole, fix pipe dat' broke."

Windsor froze, staring at the adaptive tool at the end of the shovel. "How does he hold on? What happened to his fingers?"

"It's a claw-like transition. The scarring of the peripheral nerves tightens all their connective tissue, shrinking the muscle and scarring it down. Mobility is hard to come by with Hansen's."

Windsor adjusted his glasses. "So how—"

"We adapt their equipment and tools to help them get the job done."

"Why don't they just get help from someone who's not deformed?"

Reagan softened, "Is that what you would do if your hands didn't work?"

Kicking the dirt under his Nike tennis shoe, Windsor looked away from the islander. "Why did this happen to them?"

"Different reasons for each of them. It was a bit out of their control. The disease originated in Eastern Africa in the eighteen hundreds. Throughout time there were waves of migration and with them came various diseases."

"Yeah, but can't they just take some medicine or something?"

"Yes, we are treating them with sulfone meds, as well as other plant-based remedies, but doing the job themselves is also their medicine." Reagan recalled that finding her own purpose, once again, after she was ill, was the primary medicine she needed.

Windsor watched as Adi's shovel slipped from his hands several times. He kept adjusting and readjusting it and returned to digging.

"Someone should make some gloves with Velcro so the handle won't keep falling out of his hand."

"Now, that's a great idea, Windsor."

Over the years, Reagan had adapted many tools for the islanders who couldn't use their hands for gripping. She used foam from shipping cartons to widen handles of tools and utensils to ease the strain on their scarred fingers. She also built up the sole of a shoe to help balance a severely shortened leg— Maura's right leg was two inches shorter than her left one. An endless list of occupational and functional adaptations was needed to ease tasks of those afflicted by the crippling effects of leprosy.

Windsor watched the islanders reach, grasp, twist, and tighten items using various adaptive tools. He looked at his own hands from time to time, bending and straightening his fingers. Then he shook them out and gripped the side of his pants. "I don't get it. How are they doing this so easily?"

"Gotta get the job done. Those holes can't dig themselves and the old pipes need to be repaired," Reagan answered.

"Yeah, but look at their hands, their bodies . . . I mean . . . I just don't get it."

"Miss Reagan . . . need boy to help . . . turn the wrench." One of the men, with blotchy red skin and a patch over his eye, looked desperate; his claw-like hands could barely hold the thick metal tubing about to burst. "Please, Mu'm."

Reagan elbowed Windsor to get over there.

"What's a goddamn wrench? I don't know how to use a wrench." Windsor looked to Reagan for a clue. He began to hyperventilate. It was all too much. He opened the brown paper bag and took out his inhaler.

"Windsor, calm down. He's offering to teach you."

After looking back and forth from Reagan to the men, Windsor put the inhaler back in the bag. He shuffled toward the men who attempted to fix a pipe under the outdoor community sink. There was a steady stream of water escaping the rusty pipe, creating a pool of mud cascading down the trail. He hesitated, as he got closer, staring at the man's deformed hands.

"Don't be 'fraid, I show you how. I Dakota, call me Dak." The man smiled, exposing several missing teeth.

Windsor looked to Reagan, but she had turned away. He faced Dakota, who held the wrench in the air. The whites of his eyes were glassy and expansive, drawing attention to the distinct outline of his pupil. Windsor reached slowly for the tool, then moved in toward the leaking pipe. His hands trembled.

"See this . . . place da' wrench where metal comes together . . . hold tight, don't let it move." Dak had a gentle voice.

As Windsor brushed up against the islander's dark mottled skin, he froze—subconsciously paralyzed, while the two men continued to twist, pull and turn the large pipe attached to the sink. The wrench that Windsor held moved in a staccato fashion. More water escaped, spewing all over the men.

"Hold it still." Dak turned his face away to avoid a mouthful of high-pressure brackish water.

Windsor gasped at the older men, now drenched. He tightened his grip, using both hands and clenched forearms. He dug his legs into the muddy earth and let out a bloodcurdling scream. "Aaggghhhhhh." The water pressure diminished.

"That's da' way." Dak wiped his face.

"More, more. Almos' got it." The other man added.

Windsor's smile grew, with a red glow to his cheeks. The water stopped.

"I hear da' scream, almos' tribal." Maura limped along the path and stood next to Reagan. "New hire?"

"Maura, meet Windsor. He's my intern for the day."

The sweat on Windsor's face attracted the dusty residue of clay soil, creating an orangish-brown appearance on his skin. The dirt-stained glasses had slid too far down his nose while his hands stayed fixed on the wrench.

"Somethin' different 'bout him, no?" Maura whispered.

Reagan nodded.

Windsor sat in a low squat, knees stuck together with his feet angled outward. His shoes had uneven wear at the heels and the holes in his socks drooped over his bony ankles. He attempted to scratch his nose with his shoulder, which torqued his neck in a contortionist pose.

"Where you from?" Maura asked.

"Ohio. It's far away, in the United States of America, which is North America." He answered loud and slow.

Maura smiled first at Reagan, then back at the young man. "Sounds like a good place. First time in Fiji?"

"Yes, Ma'am." He answered loud enough to be heard by everyone.

"You learn good from Reagan. Stay nex' to her."

Reagan smiled at Maura, putting both hands up in the air.

Maura kept her voice low. "You go up mountain to Phaeole?"

Reagan nodded.

Windsor stood up from the sink and handed the wrench back to the man. "Uh, thank you, sir . . . I mean . . . well, it was nice to meet you."

The man patted Windsor on his back with his deformed fist. "You good boy."

Reagan and Windsor left Maura and the two men to finish cleaning up. Windsor brushed himself off and was overly focused on readjusting his glasses. No position on his nose seemed to suit him. Reagan turned to him as he continued to twist and bend the wire frames to the ridge of his nose. "So, what do you think so far?"

"Hell, I think that's why you're here to help kill . . . I mean . . . end their suffering. Did I say it right this time? I get that they're all messed up. Isn't that why you're here?" He wiped the sweat off his brow with the back of his sleeve.

"Why do you assume they want to end their lives?" Reagan asked sharply. "Do they seem unhappy?"

"Well, no, not at all, they seem . . . well . . . to be busy and doing . . . some sort of job."

"And do they appear to need *my* help? To end their suffering?" She glared at him.

Windsor scratched his head and looked down at the ground, "No, not really."

"Okay then, stop judging and assuming." Reagan turned away and headed up the trail to Phaeole's house.

"Wait, where are we going now?" He trotted up to stay with her extended stride.

"Going to see our first patient." She kept her pace.

"Isn't that what we've been doing so far?"

"No, none of those people are patients." Reagan smiled.

It had been awhile since Reagan ventured to Phaeole's. The broken trail to his place was overgrown with thorny bushes, half-split tree branches, and dried-out fronds, long departed from their palm tree. The dense tropical rainforest preceded the mountainous terrain, and as the trail steepened Reagan heard endless groans behind her. The fresh rain made it a challenge to keep a shoe on, since the mud suctioned with every contact.

Windsor slipped several times. He grabbed at branches and yelled with every missed step. "Why the hell would someone live up here so far away? Don't they have roads to drive on? Why would. . . ."

The endless complaints, disguised as questions wore on Reagan. The scene reminded her of a first-year medical student who was clearly not cut out for the job. "Maybe you should turn back," *all the way to Ohio*. "This is surely more than you had bargained for when you asked for my advice."

Windsor grabbed the bristled branch that had just left a bloody scratch on his right cheek. He broke it in two. "This sucks!"

Reagan stopped short and turned to face him. "You wanted to know how to kill a person?" Reagan spoke fast. "Well, here it is . . . run up a rigorous trail with deadly snakes, dart frogs and other poisonous creatures, lead 'em to quicksand, and let them bleed to death." She hadn't even seen his bloody cheek, but she was running low on patience.

"But, I didn't mean me . . . I mean it was really . . . about . . . you know, my mother. Not me, I swear. Not me."

The heaviness of the silence that followed hit Reagan like a twenty-foot wave crashing in front of her. She stopped, clearly hearing the unspoken surrender—the silent beckon for help. Reagan's full attention was now on him. Taking the small daypack off of her shoulder, she laid it on a large boulder. She opened her water bottle and offered it to Windsor.

He took it hesitantly, smelling the water.

"The water is fine." She stayed calm.

"But you touched—"

Reagan held her hand out to take the canteen back.

Windsor kept it and sniffed at the opening. He held the spout several inches away from his mouth and poured the water down his throat, leaving a stream of wetness down his neck. He caught her stare, and handed the water back to her.

Reagan noticed the shades of green and brown foliage surrounding them. A crackle of sunlight entered the fronds' folds, casting shadows on the trail. She inhaled and recognized the scent of wild lilac and thyme growing on the hillside. It was a good time of year for the herbs, plenty of fresh rain daily. Then she took a small sip of the water and replaced the cap. She let the offshore breeze run through her. The silence was like a welcome mat before opening the door.

"How long have you been thinking about taking your life?" She stayed focused on the greenery and beauty around her, not allowing her eyes to meet his gaze.

"What do you . . . mean? I'm not going . . . to . . . what I meant is I need to know for . . . my mom, you know," his voice cracked several times.

Reagan remained silent. Many valuable lessons had been learned from the islanders—be patient with your questions, and in time, with trust, people tell you what they need to. There was plenty of information in the silence: his locked arms, flared nostrils, and the way he swayed unevenly.

The distant sound of the cascading waterfall was a good reason to stay quiet and wait. She loved how the sound had layers of decibels with the falling intensity. She pictured the water's long flight down the mountain, streaming midair, to land in a still pool of water.

"It started about a year ago." Windsor looked out at the smattering of remote islands. "One day my mom asked if I was her new nurse. I looked around the room for someone else, but it was only me."

Reagan picked a branch of cranberry bristle. She split the leaves from the stem and smelled the root. Hints of licorice and honey wafted upward, so sweet in fragrance, yet poisonous to eat. She continued to wait and listen.

"Then I made the mistake of going to Grandfather to ask him how to do it. I wanted to end it all. He got so mad at me . . . said I was a spoiled brat . . . that my only worry should be about my mom, not me. That was the last time I saw him."

Reagan let out an audible sigh, not intentionally at first, but she welcomed the sound of pent-up resistance. She looked at him and thought of her daughter. Then she remembered asking Jeremy to help end her life—the unfortunate resemblance to this young man.

"It's time for you to meet Phaeole." Reagan picked up her pack, put it on her shoulders, then made a motion with her head for him to follow.

17

WAFTS of jasmine and tuberose floated through the entry path to Phaeole's bure. The rickety wooden steps usually announced visitors, but today Reagan stepped heavier than normal to cover up Windsor's grunts as he followed her up the stairs.

"Who goes there?" the gravelly voice demanded.

Windsor pulled back, grabbing the edge of Reagan's backpack.

"Who is this guy . . . this patient of yours. What's wrong with him?"

"Actually, nothing." Phaeole had been doing great compared to a year and a half ago. He had found his purpose—the holistic sage had returned. His life had been resurrected by his need to help others, including Reagan.

"But you said something about your first patient."

"*You* are my first patient." Reagan laid her hand on his.

Windsor looked at her hand and then to her eyes. "But . . . I thought—"

"Save that thinking for medical school, Windsor. Come on, there's someone I want you to meet."

They walked across the extended porch to enter the plantation-style bure. The room was simple in design with homemade bamboo furniture. There were no unnecessary accessories—only a few wooden chairs, a low table, handwoven pots supporting herbs and some dilapidated shelves. Most noticeable were stacks of artwork—sketches and paintings, some finished, some still in progress. Fresh glasses of water, with brushes recently placed in them for soaking, accented the room next to their canvas paintings.

"Hello, Phaeole, it's Reagan. And I brought a friend from the U.S."

Windsor froze at the sight of Phaeole. The old man's facial features were worn with the engrained etchings of leprosy—bulbous ridges diving into cavernous descents throughout most of his exposed skin. His clawed hand was in full sight, and his muffled breathing left a roughness around his words.

"Ah, my beautiful new mama." Phaeole embraced Reagan, kissing her on each cheek. He had softened since their first meeting, now welcoming her as family.

Windsor backed up against the wall, pressing both hands into his thighs.

"How is our new totoka? I hear a girl? A surfer girl, of course. When did you get home?"

"Just a week ago, but still trying to get settled in. Sorry, this is the first time I've come for a visit."

"Who is your friend?" Phaeole turned toward the wall where Windsor was plastered.

"He is a young man visiting me . . . to discuss end-of-life issues for his mother." Reagan watched for Windsor's reaction.

"Oh, she must be grateful for you." Phaeole, although completely blind, looked in his direction. "I make tea. Sit, sit . . . I be back."

As Phaeole disappeared into the kitchen, Windsor whispered: "What the hell, he is hideous. Is he contagious? I can't believe the guy . . . I want to go."

"Sit down, Windsor. Come off the wall and just sit down and pay attention."

Creeping away from the wall, Windsor walked to the most distant chair and half-sat on the edge of the seat with his knees buckled inward. His left cheek twitched. "Why did you bring me—"

"You drink kava tea?" Phaeole was back, holding a tray with his crippled hands. He extended a wooden bowl to Windsor. "Made sure to add suga' so you don't spit it out."

"What's kava?" Windsor's hands shook as he accepted the wooden bowl of tea. He held it at the rim of the bowl, with the tips of his fingers, avoiding where Phaeole had touched the cup.

"Kava tea different from ceremony kava. Any way you drink it, make you feel good, help quiet fear. Is your mother ill?"

Windsor put the bowl of tea down on the hand-carved table. He crossed his legs and pulled his feet away from Phaeole. Sitting on his hands, Windsor faced him. "Yes, sir, my mom is . . . she is real sick. No one . . . well, probably someone . . . no, no, we don't really know . . . but she is for sure sick, real sick. She lost her memory. Doesn't even know what day it is. All she does is hum to the birds and do her needlepoint."

"Ah, a perfect day." Phaeole glanced toward the window sill, as the yellow-breasted sparrow chirped.

Reagan breathed in the earthy kava tea and sipped it slowly. The numbing agent sat heavy on her tongue, expanding and thickening it. She had missed Phaeole. He had helped her heal, and, along with Dr. Yiung, was instrumental in how she viewed her own illness.

Phaeole was educated in shamanistic practices, through generations of ancient healers and dukuns from Indonesia. At one time, the islanders believed Phaeole was a sorcerer, practicing black magic with his mystery herbs. Unable to convince them otherwise, he left the village and made his home up on the Koro, a type of Fijian fortress, high in the mountains. The chief of the village finally absolved the rumor and befriended Phaeole. After the chief's death, Reagan and Maura continued to look after him.

Reagan sat back into the worn wooden couch and waited for the lesson to begin.

"Birds sing for different reasons," Phaeole lifted his head. "Some days they warn of dark weather or bad spirits, other days they jus' share their excitement, and some days they jus' want to reassure us that we okay."

The bird in the window chirped loudly.

Windsor glared across at Reagan, and mouthed, "I don't get it."

Phaeole sipped his tea and turned toward his feathered friend on the windowsill. "Their songs comfort us, keep us close to the flower and the sky. We fly with them. You see . . . they sing to us and we are safe. If we don't hear their song, we have fear, and a far-off place shall follow."

Windsor lifted the wooden bowl to his mouth and held it still before sipping the tea. His grip loosened around the koa wood.

"Your mother must love bird songs—they reach to her, fly with her, while her brain scrambles. So beautiful they found each other."

Windsor finished the bowl of tea and sat back into the chair. "But she really wants to end . . . her suffering."

Reagan could tell Windsor was proud he used the right words, the ones his grandfather would have approved of.

"Who is suffering?" Phaeole scratched the side of his face with his deformed hand.

A pulse of trade wind blew from one window to the other, allowing the ambient forest noise to penetrate the silence.

"She didn't even know who I was," Windsor looked at Phaeole.

Silence followed, again. The outside light cast its rays on the wooden slats under their feet. The chirping stopped momentarily, as the breeze halted.

"Do we suffer for ourselves or others?" Phaeole sipped his tea and exhaled loudly with his mouth open. "Do we assume others are suffering—to help us make right choice?"

Windsor looked out the window as tears crept through the edges of his eyes. "My mother has these gray-blue eyes that were always so beautiful. Now they are cloudy. And her skin used to be so soft, especially the tops of her hands, but now they are blackened with bruises." He choked out the next words. "Her smile . . . that is the best thing about my mother."

"Does she have same smile?" Phaeole asked.

"Why, uh, yes she does. That hasn't changed."

"And is she in pain? Who is suffering?" Phaeole leaned toward Windsor.

Windsor didn't answer at first. He took off his glasses and wiped the lenses with his shirt. "I can't watch her die. If I go—" The tears started slowly, then they gushed out.

Reagan moved next to Windsor and held his hand in hers. He withdrew it reflexively before placing it back in her hands.

"Our fear is like fallen tree on path, it stops us. You need to move around broken tree."

"I can't." Windsor looked at the floor.

"If you don't move around tree, no one behind you can go. Now all have fear and all stuck. You must go around tree."

Windsor sat upright.

Phaeole looked back at the bird, chirping loudly. "Yes, yes I hear you," he answered the bird. "I'm not saying I know all, some people say I do . . . I don't, but I do know your mother knows you're there every day. She sings to bird . . . maybe she think bird is you."

Windsor got up from the wooden chair and walked slowly around the room. He stared at the light rays from the open window to the floor. He walked over and stood above Phaeole. "How do you know?" he whispered.

Phaeole's crooked yellow teeth appeared beneath his expanded smile. "I don't know how I know . . . I just do."

Several moments of silence lapsed before Winsor walked to the window. The expansive view from Phaeole's lanai exposed layers of banyan trees over palm trees—green over green. Beyond the green were lines of blue ocean merging with blue sky. Parrots and lorikeets were in plain sight, some flying, some perched.

"Are *you* suffering?" Windsor turned toward Phaeole.

Phaeole chuckled, "Look at my life." He pointed from the stacked paintings to the bird on the windowsill, back to the view of the trees and ocean. "I live with soli bula; the trees and flowers are my family . . . singing humpbacks and seagulls—my close cousins, the wind and rain clean me."

"What is soli bula?" Windsor shrugged.

"Soli means to give . . . and bula means many things . . . so to me, soli bula is to give what I can and live my best life."

"But you're blind and all alone. And your—" Windsor stopped short and cleared his voice.

"What? My hands? My face? None is important anymore. All of this good enough."

Reagan remained in student mode, listening with earnest intent. She contemplated what *good enough* meant. It seemed relevant and somewhat healing.

"What if it's not good enough for me?" Windsor frowned.

"Only you have answer for you."

Trade winds blew the hanging chimes outside the window, creating chaotic tones. They settled while the wind shifted, then gave a hearty encore with a clashing melody surpassing the first one. The bird had left the windowsill and taken flight toward a small flock of lorikeets.

Reagan absorbed the mystical symphony, amazed at the power and the beauty of Phaeole. As his body diminished, his spirit soared. Yes, it was all good enough.

18

THE next day Reagan walked with Windsor down to the dock. He had decided to leave several days earlier than he'd planned. "You sure you don't want to stick around and meet my dolphin friends?"

"It sounds really adventurous, all of this, but I want to go hold my mom's cup of tea. You saved me, Dr. Caldwell . . . and my mom."

Reagan hugged him. "Please, call me Reagan. There's another Dr. Caldwell out there, and that is not me." She suddenly remembered her mother's rapid departure from the hospital when Laura was born. She shook the image loose before it multiplied. "When you're ready for a longer internship, I suggest you go to Sydney Annex, where the root of all healing begins."

"Is Phaeole a teacher there?" he asked.

"No, but you could add on another few weeks after the annex and come here as well. I'd be happy to be your preceptor."

"We'll see if I get into medical school and, more importantly if I can even pay for it."

Reagan gave him a side glance. "Don't you dare let that stop you."

The boat captain waved at Windsor to board.

He took a step on the boat and looked back toward her. "You are a good doctor, Reagan. I hope to do what you do someday."

Reagan released the bowline from the dock cleat and looked at him. "Don't worry so much *how* you say things, Windsor. Just *do* the right thing."

They waved goodbye and the inter-island boat chugged out of the harbor.

The next few weeks were filled with family time for Reagan, Jeremy, and Laura. Roger joined them for most dinners, and once a week Maura and the kids would visit, but otherwise it was just the three of them, together all day, with Atta Boy in tow. The dog followed wherever Little Laura went, living up to his blue heeler traits. Laura was almost four months old and full of new personality daily. They would dip her in the ocean, all the way under and watch her giggle when she came to the surface.

Laying on the sand, at the water's edge, Jeremy traced his fingers around Reagan's protruding belly button, "How is your world coming along?"

"Yah know, it's coming together, I'd say. Close to a perfect world. No more talk of dying from me." She ran her hand through his salt-crusted hair.

"I couldn't have done it anyway. Don't know how you people in medicine handle the death thing so easy."

"What makes you think it's easy?" Reagan sat up.

"I don't know, you doctors and nurses seem to brush off death better than most of us."

"We silently grieve because another patient is always in the next room, and we need to show hope."

Jeremy propped on one elbow, gazing at Laura asleep on the sarong next to them. "This little one gives me hope."

"I wonder what she'll love in life." Reagan kissed her daughter's cheek.

"Everything you do." Jeremy stroked Reagan's upper lip with his finger. "I missed these lips, the way they smile . . . the way they make me feel. Imagine if those boats stopped working and no planes could fly and we had to stay here forever, stranded."

"Yes, if the world stopped now, I would be content with all of it." She laid her head on his warm stomach and sighed.

"And what if—" Jeremy started to say.

"Reagan," a voice from the resort bar interrupted. "Call for you . . . from the States." Roger held up the phone, restricted by the short cord connected to the wall.

She shaded her eyes and yelled back up the embankment: "Who is it?"

After a few moments, Roger hung up the phone and held up his hand toward her. He half-jogged toward them. "Reagan, there's been an emergency in the States. It's your dad." Roger was out of breath as he bent over and propped himself on his thighs. He finally looked up at her: "He's been admitted to the ICU. They're asking if you can go to L.A."

Reagan remembered when she was nine years old and she had fallen off a horse at summer camp. Her concussion was so severe she had to be induced into a short-term coma. When she woke up, all she wanted was her dad, but her mother couldn't reach him. He was on a surf trip in Mexico. Three weeks later when he finally returned, he wept for days knowing he may have never seen his daughter again. Now, with a daughter of her own, the image of his distress came to Reagan like an advancing monsoon cloud.

"Yes, yes, I'll go." She looked to Jeremy, "We'll all go. All three of us."

She thought of her mother's unwelcome surprise in her hospital room, only to find out she wanted to test Reagan's baby for research purposes. The idea of it hurled a deep stab into her stomach. She would certainly avoid her when she went to see her father. Reagan softened, thinking of her dad and the years that had gone by without much contact. She had missed him terribly at first, but communication was difficult from the resort. So as the years passed, she let go of the urgency to talk to him.

"I'll pack our bags." Reagan picked up Atta Boy and held him to her chest. "So much for my perfect world. Guess you get to stay with the girls for a bit, little guy." The dog didn't take his eyes off of Reagan.

19

THE traffic around LAX was filled with yellow taxis, shuttle buses, and horns blaring. A maze of hurried travelers and competitive transport companies prevented a better parking spot, where Lydia would have preferred—adjacent to the baggage claim door.

"Damn it, Mike, we're twenty minutes late. I shoulda jus' went to the airport on my own to get Reagan, but noooo, they all say, bring Big Mike."

Mike shook his head, "You should've seen those fans last time, no way you could handle them, such beasts, those groupees of his."

"Oh, don't you start with me, Suga, no need to question who or what I can handle." Lydia's hand flew in the air, one index finger moved from side to side. "Honey, you got no idea what I've seen and done, up this street or down this alley, tis' nothin' for no one's lazy-ass sorry eyes."

"I'll stay here, you go try to find them." Mike said.

"No kiddin' you'll stay here. Don't you think of moving this here car without—"

Lydia continued to talk as she headed through the sliding glass doors of the airport pickup area. A few minutes later she exited a different set of doors two hundred yards away, walked down the sidewalk, shifted her head from side to side and re-entered another set of entry doors. The circular path repeated for several laps until she walked back to where Mike was parked.

"Come on Lydia, I can't stay parked here, the security guy said to move it or get fined."

"Who be sayin' that to you?" Lydia spoke fast, "You jus' stay put. They be here any time now."

Mike opened and closed the back hatch again, as he watched the airport security man approach his car for the third time.

"Sir, this is the last time I am telling you—"

"Telling him what?" Lydia blurted. Her hands perched high on her hips as she shifted to face the man with a badge. "He's not movin' that car an inch 'til we have our girl and her baby safely in our arms. Sure you be seein' what we're up against . . . the whole fan thing, and you know the paparazzi is minutes away." Lydia inched her way closer to the officer as she launched her lecture.

The security guard froze. His mouth hung half-open and his hands raised, palms facing her. "Whoa, easy Ma'am. What whole fan thing?"

Lydia unleashed her inner powers: "Jus' you give us a moment, they're right here you know, no one's takin' skin off your back for just leavin' us be—"

"But, Ma'am, I'm just doing my job here." The security guard looked toward Mike then back at Lydia, before lowering his arms.

"Yeah, well you can jus' as easy do your job down there too, I reckon." She pointed down the outside corridor.

"Lydia!" the energetic voice of Reagan saved the security guard from the ongoing lecture.

"Oh, sweet Jesus!" Lydia almost tripped as she ran toward Reagan and Jeremy.

Mike looked at the security guard. "Guess we'll be on our way, Officer. Thank you for your patience."

The guard nodded, then added an eye roll as he walked down the sidewalk.

"Where is she? Where is my little goddaughter?" Lydia begged.

Reagan unwrapped Laura from the sarong, snugged against her body. It took several moments to unswathe the little baby from the complicated Fijian wrap.

Lydia covered her mouth with her hands. "Oh sweet, sweet lil' baby girl. You are jus' perfect." Lydia looked at Jeremy. "Seems you're a much better papa than actor-boy . . . good thinkin' changing your job description."

"I'll take the compliment," Jeremy laughed.

"Sorry, we were delayed a bit . . . had to convince our country of Laura's dual-citizenship. It took a bit of explaining since the last-minute temporary passport issued at the airport was questionable," Reagan explained.

"Yeah, I bet. Born in an Aussie hospital, lives on a tiny island in Fiji, parents are Americans—with different last names. Huh, what's not to get?" Lydia smirked.

"Come on, let's get out of here before we're recognized." Mike held open the door to the white Suburban.

"Wow, do I own this?" Jeremy asked.

"No, it's Sara's." Mike kept it short.

"Huh, do I know a Sara?"

"She's a friend who has a reasonable car for an infant." Mike took baby Laura from Reagan's arms and confidently placed her in the freshly purchased infant seat. Somehow he knew just how to adjust the belts and secure the precious cargo. He turned to Reagan, "Now, what do you need?"

Caught off guard, Reagan looked behind her, "Are you talking to me?"

"Of course I'm talking to you. Laura is set, now what do you need?"

"Uh, I think I'm fine."

"What about a restroom or maybe some water?" He handed her a bottled water, opening the cap.

"How did you know? Yes, I'm pretty dehydrated from the plane ride."

Mike reached into his pocket and presented her with three different energy bars. "Please eat. There could be traffic and . . . well, I'm sure you're hungry too."

"Thank you, Mike. I really . . . well, I really appreciate you."

Jeremy closed the back hatch and approached Mike and Reagan, "Got one for me too?"

Mike blushed as he got into the driver's seat, "Buckle up, everyone. Off we go."

As they turned onto Pacific Coast Highway, Reagan picked up Jeremy's hand and kissed it. "Remember the last time we were here, so much stress, so much unknown."

Reagan felt Mike's intermittent stare at them through the rearview mirror.

"Can we go straight to the hospital?" Reagan caught his glance in the mirror for the fourth time.

"Well, your dad's not doing so well. Hasn't eaten in days. They say he just sleeps. But if you can wait a day, your mother is at a two-day conference in Santa Barbara, starting tomorrow."

"How do you know that, Mike?" Reagan glared.

"Oh, don't you start askin' Mystery Man here how he gets his intel." Lydia shook her head. "He jus' seems to get what he needs without any fuss."

"Okay, one more day will do." Reagan smiled at Mike.

20

AT the entrance of the Intensive Care Unit, Reagan was asked to wait while they checked to see if Earl was ready. Reagan found it was strange for them to comment on her dad's readiness, but she didn't question it. As she waited, she couldn't help but notice the hectic movement of people around her. A code was called and she perked up—what if it was her dad, what if she was too late. Several nurses and doctors rushed into a room with a crash cart and Reagan was relieved when she heard: "She needs . . ." It wasn't "he."

The nurse hung up the phone and turned to Reagan. "Yes, Miss Caldwell, he is available now. Room 401."

Reagan walked down the long hallway of the ICU, looking for the correct number on the door. *325, 330, 355, 375.* There were no rooms with the number 400 anywhere.

"Can I help you, Ma'am?" a volunteer asked.

"Yes, please, I can't seem to find room 401."

"What is the patient's name?" the volunteer asked while looking at her clipboard.

"Earl Caldwell."

"Oh yes, Dr. Caldwell's husband. He's on the concierge wing, next floor up. You need access. I'll help. Can I see your I.D.?"

Reagan was perplexed and irritated at the same time with the concept of a V.I.P. section of any hospital. Only her mother would arrange for something so decadent.

"Here you are, Ma'am. You'll need this badge to get through the locked elevator to the fourth floor. There's a guard at the top."

"But I thought he's in the ICU." Reagan raised her hands.

"They've got everything up there." The volunteer smiled.

"But that defeats the purpose of . . . oh never mind." Reagan attempted to smile as she stepped into the open elevator. She inserted the badge, granting her special access to a special floor, designed for the overprivileged. She dropped her shoulders, exhaled louder than intended, and shook her head.

Opening her father's door, Reagan saw a hospital room that resembled a luxury suite. The floral blinds were tightly sealed, with the brim exposing a suggestion of sunlight. Two leather couches formed an "L" around a glass coffeetable with a vase of long-stem lilies overflowing the top. A small refrigerator had a see-through door, showing a variety of drinks in glass bottles and fresh fruits with hardened chocolate smothered on top. And the cappuccino maker smelled of fresh brew.

"Dad, are you awake?" Reagan whispered as she walked toward the bed.

"He hasn't spoken in days." The woman's voice came from the dark corner. It startled Reagan. "He sleeps most of the time. Unresponsive when he opens his eyes."

Reagan shivered, pulling her sweater tight to her body, as she looked at the stranger.

"I'm his private nurse." The woman was in her sixties, professionally dressed, without nurse scrubs, and sitting quietly in a leather chair in the corner of the room.

"I'm his daughter." Reagan countered. "I'd like to visit on my own, if that's okay with you."

"Just let me know when you're done. I'll be right outside." She picked up her handbag and bottled water.

"Don't you have other patients to tend to?" Reagan asked.

"Your father is my only patient." The woman smiled.

"Of course," Reagan whispered.

The door quietly clicked closed as the nurse left the room and Reagan stood still, lost for a moment. Was she too late—just like her dad was years ago for her? She took the Fijian scarf off her neck and wrapped it around her shoulders. The room was cold and dark within the attempted façade of beauty. The smell of antiseptic mixed with cleaning agent was heavy, imbedded in decorative wall coverings.

Reagan walked over to the closed blinds and opened them, allowing full light and warmth to enter the room. She closed her eyes and inhaled the sunshine. If she *was* too late, she would simply sit with him, and wait, like she did with all her patients in Fiji. But at least there would be sunshine in the room—the strength she needed.

Earl's bed was on the other side of the room, near the door. She unlocked the wheels with a flick of her foot and rolled the bed closer to the window. Then she pulled the chair from across the room and sat next to him, touching his hand. She didn't say anything for several minutes.

Stroking his wrinkled and sun-stained hand, she reminisced about the exotic places he had traveled to when she was young, and the surf trips to Mexico when she was finally old enough to join him. Reagan remembered the big grouper he had speared—too heavy to lift over the gunnel of the boat from the water, so she had to get in the water and hold the sixty-pound fish in place, while he got into the boat to haul it in. With one hand on the side of the boat and her other fingers intertwined through the gills of the grouper, a big harbor seal came and stole the fish from her grasp. Reagan had screamed for help and her dad had just laughed.

"Well, a seal's gotta eat too." It's just the way he was.

"R.C. Is that you?" Earl opened one eye, shielding the other from the sharp rays of sunlight.

"Yes, Dad, it's me." She hadn't heard her nickname in years.

"How's the surf down under?" There was a scratch to his unused voice. His tongue was dry and it stuck to the roof of his mouth, making a clicking sound when he talked.

Reagan filled the water cup from the glass pitcher. She helped him drink. Windsor and his mother came to mind, the cup of tea being held for hours, with such love.

"The surf's real good, Dad. You'd love it. There's a long left at my reef, and it pops up with a fast barrel. You've never seen such clear water. Although, come to think of it, you probably have."

"That's my girl. I have . . . missed you . . . so, so much." His words were labored and difficult for Reagan to hear. He looked toward the window.

Reagan held back tears. She hoped her daughter would never leave her for so long. "You must be tired." Reagan's voice matched his tone.

"No, no, this is the best I've felt . . . in a long time. My baby . . . came home. I feel alive all of a sudden." He opened both eyes, blinking several times and focused on her.

Tears seeped from Reagan's eyes.

A new nurse walked in the room, went straight to the windows and pulled the blinds closed. "Can I get you anything?"

Reagan looked to her dad, who had closed his eyes and dropped his head. "Oh, are you talking to me?" Reagan asked.

"Well, you're the only person in the room, aren't you?" the nurse commented, shutting the final blind tight.

"What happened to the other nurse?" Reagan asked.

"There are several of us assigned to Mr. Caldwell. Naomi is the watch nurse." The woman had a sharp tone and moved fast around the room. "Did you move this bed?" She faced Reagan with her hands on her hips and eyebrows raised.

Reagan wiped the remaining tears dry and looked to her dad, who was asleep, mouth open with a subtle snore.

The nurse removed the empty IV bag and hooked up a new one.

Trying to ignore the nurse's abrupt demeanor Reagan asked, "What are you giving him?"

"Morphine. It helps with the pain." The nurse kept her eyes on the IV bag.

"I understand my dad hasn't been talking much."

"Yep, not a word since he was admitted." She adjusted the line to the nasal cannula attached to Earl's nose.

"Then how do you know he's in pain?" Reagan stared at the woman.

"It's in the order. They're all in pain at this stage."

"What stage would that be?" Reagan stood up.

"Look, sorry if they haven't told you, seeing as you just arrived and all, but the patient here isn't faring well. It won't be long, so the morphine helps."

"His name is Earl." Reagan raised her voice.

The nurse pivoted and walked out of the room, but before the door closed, she turned back to Reagan. "Please don't move the bed again. Hospital policy."

Reagan leaned forward with her head in her hands, *unbelievable*. She walked back over to the windows and opened the blinds with a shove, once again allowing the light to enter.

"R.C., is she gone?" Earl whispered with one eye open, lifting his head off the pillow.

Reagan raced to his side. "I thought you fell asleep."

She lifted his hand and brought it to her cheek. "Dad, what's going on?"

"Not sure, my girl. But I think I'm dying . . . or else I wouldn't be here, right?"

Reagan nodded her head in disbelief. "Dad, do you remember our conversation before the nurse came in?"

"Of course, you told me about the left hander at your reef. I bet it's beautiful. Tell me more about it."

"And do you remember where I live?"

"Of course . . . Fiji . . . the land of everything beautiful and simple. Bula, Bula."

"But wait . . . I thought you couldn't hold a recent memory, that the dementia had worsened." She stood but kept his hand in hers.

"Well, if so, I certainly don't remember." His laugh was hearty, with several deep coughs in between the laughter.

Reagan laughed with him, keeping her concerns disguised. "Dad, I need to go . . . gotta go talk to someone who really knows what's going on with you. I'll be back this evening, I promise. I've got a few people for you to meet."

"Okay, my dearest, can't wait to see you again. But you better close the blinds so we don't get in trouble, eh?" Earl winked, maintaining a coy grin.

"I love you, Dad." She kissed him on the head and proceeded to partially close the blinds, before walking out heavy-hearted.

Passing the nurses' station, Reagan saw Earl's nurse at the front desk. She stopped momentarily to say something, but the nurse had her head down, texting on her phone. Reagan looked around and saw the same pose with several other nurses at the station. It was deathly quiet—highly unusual for a hospital. Her gaze shifted from the long-stem tulips in vases to the reclining chairs with individual television sets and the concierge medicine sign perched high over the threshold of the hallway.

A deep wave of nausea enveloped her. Reagan looked back toward her dad's room for a moment. Her pull to him was magnetic, but her emotions took over. She needed to get out of there.

21

REAGAN dropped her over-the-shoulder bag at the entrance of Jeremy's home and headed to find Laura. Her visit with her dad at the hospital was short and with a quick twenty-minute drive home, she wasn't close to missing a feeding. She halted at the entrance of Jeremy's bedroom door. In the few hours she was gone, the staff had whipped up an infant room decorated in pink and yellow flowers, with seahorses dangling over a polished oak crib. Reagan was momentarily flustered—she didn't even have a real crib in Fiji, rather a handwoven hammock with flotation devices from the boats to cushion the mattress.

"We ordered a few other things, but they won't be here for two more days," George said somewhat apologetically. In addition to being Jeremy's chauffeur, George was in charge of the household affairs.

Jeremy had a towel wrapped around his waist as he walked out of the bathroom, freshly showered. His hands were in the air. "It wasn't me . . . told you they'd be excited to meet her."

Reagan surveyed the room—a dangling array of pastel greens, pinks, and yellows, musical ornaments playing carousel music, and gifts on the counter in baby-themed wrapping paper. Reagan placed one hand over her mouth, "Oh my God, this is too. . . ."

"I know, I know. I told them we were only staying until your dad got better." Jeremy walked over to her and kissed the back of her hand. He leaned over her, "It's okay, my love. Just 'til he's out of the hospital."

"And who knows if he will." Her voice trembled. "I need to find out what's going on, but the only person who really knows is in Santa Barbara at a medical research conference."

"Did he recognize you?" Jeremy asked.

"Who?"

"Your dad, did he know who you are?"

"Of course . . . no problem at all, short-term and long-term memory intact. Not exactly classic Alzheimer's condition. They also said he hadn't spoken since he'd arrived, but he had a regular conversation with me."

"Didn't your mother say he was in and out of awareness?" Jeremy asked.

"Yeah, but he was fully there, the whole time, even after the nurse—"

Reagan stopped midsentence, her eyes dilated. "I think my dad might be playing them all. I think he's just escaping my mom . . . and well, possibly the whole charade."

"Smart guy," Jeremy smirked.

"In many ways, yes . . . in so many ways."

"Can I meet him?"

"I'm going back tonight. Maybe nights are different than mornings and I'm hoping the staff may be different," Reagan said.

"Lydia wants to meet with us tonight, something about info on the power plant."

"You know it's gonna be *good* info if she wants to meet us in person." Reagan drew out the word *good*.

"Yeah, and get this, she tracked down the doctor who signed off on all the patients—the ones who worked at the power plant, who got so sick."

"How'd she find him?" Reagan was only half-surprised. She knew Lydia was a stickler for getting the job done and making sure justice was served.

"Well, I think Mike may have helped, to some degree. He found some odd connection with—"

Baby Laura's cry was a familiar interruption.

"I got her." Jeremy walked over to the crib.

"No, let me. I miss her."

Jeremy smiled, "Nice."

George tapped on the bedroom door, "Phone call for you, sir. Sounds important. It's the hospital."

Reagan shot up. "Is it my dad?"

Jeremy took the phone from George.

"Yes, this is Jeremy Black. Yes, she's right here. I can put her on—"

Jeremy turned his back to Reagan and whispered into the phone, "I see, uh huh . . . I don't understand . . . how'd it happen?"

"What?" Reagan's voice was frantic.

"Of course . . . we can get there right away. Is there anything else you can tell me—" He turned to face Reagan with the phone still fixed to his ear.

Her face became ashen. Reagan dropped onto the bed as she watched Jeremy end the phone call. Had she left her dad too soon? So many years of not coming home, and now she might be too late.

"It's your mother. She's been in an accident. They're airlifting her to High Point Hospital now." Jeremy said.

Reagan went numb. "My mother? But how . . . what happened? It can't be . . . she's the strongest woman on the planet . . . nothing bad ever happens to her." Reagan slowly sank to the edge of the bed, "I don't understand."

"Let's go, I said we'd meet them at the E.R." Jeremy stood with his hand extended to Reagan.

"But what about Laura?" Reagan glanced at the five adults who had congregated in the room—all competent staff and more experienced in childrearing than her or Jeremy.

"Please, Reagan, let's go. They will take good care of her. There's still two bottles of your pumped milk in the fridge," Jeremy urged.

Reagan was torn apart. She strained to look at Jeremy and then back at her daughter. The conflict weighed her down like a crushing wave.

Jeremy kissed her wet cheek. His hands cradled hers. "I'll drive. We'll face this together."

George swaddled the baby into his chest and smiled at Reagan. "My dear, I have seven grandbabies. Until you know what has happened, you must go."

Everyone in the room focused on Reagan. The nudge of nonverbal encouragement helped her move forward. She hesitantly slipped on her sandals, then kissed Laura on her head and followed Jeremy out of the house.

22

WHEN Reagan was young, she was often in situations where she had to explain to adults why she was home alone. Her dad often traveled abroad, and her mother worked late hours at the hospital. So when a stranger at the door asked if a parent was home, Reagan had excuses, none true. Once, when Reagan was twelve, a previous patient of Roz Caldwell's, who had recently been denied his fifth refill of oxycodone, appeared at their front door early one evening. As he stood there, staring down at preteen Reagan, the man accosted her with questions.

"I'm here to see Dr. Caldwell. Is she home?" The man had a gruff voice, overgrown facial hair, and a nervous way of scratching his neck.

"My mom's in the shower. Best way to see her is at the clinic. I'll tell her you stopped by."

"No, I can wait." The stranger forced his way into the house. He looked down the hallway and up the stairs, intensely scratching his neck.

"She's getting ready for a big meeting." Reagan held fast to the banister, trying to think of something that would stop him.

"I said I'll wait." The stranger sat on the edge of the couch, in between the living room and stairs.

Reagan never forgot the man's coarse dark stubble on the lower half of his face. There was also a strong odor that she didn't know—a cross between wet towels left in a corner for days and cabbage that had gone bad.

"Mom!" Reagan called out to no one, in the direction of the staircase.

"Someone's here to see you." Reagan perched her hip on the banister and crossed her arms.

The man sat on the edge of the new leather couch—the one that no one was supposed to sit on. Reagan had greeted her mom's colleagues before, but this guy looked and smelled different.

"She's really in a hurry. She's gotta leave for the meeting, like I said."

The man looked at Reagan, unhinged.

"My dad's on his way home . . . any minute, actually." She paced, "And Hitchcock doesn't know you. He's our pit bull." The lies got deeper and deeper. She only wished she owned a dog.

"Where's your watchdog now?" The man fell into the crease at the back of the couch and propped his dirty work boots on the fresh upholstery. Clods of dirt fell onto the couch. Then he reached for the pillow with hummingbird needlepoint, the one clearly not to be handled, and Reagan flew into a rage.

"Why are you here?" She yelled at the man. "What do you want?" Reagan moved closer to him, grabbing the pillow and putting it back in its place.

"Your mother took my meds from me. She's a bad doctor." His clenched fists were about to explode.

"Yeah, well she's a bad mom too. She's never here for me . . . she's not even here now." Reagan's fury matched his and their eyes met.

In an instant, the man was on his feet and lurching toward Reagan. His whole body resembled an inferno about to engulf her.

Reagan ran to the kitchen and clutched the first things she saw—a meat cleaver and a dirty knife with butter on the edge of it. She darted back to the entry—ready to attack, but the screen door bounced shut and the man was gone. She dropped to her knees, piercing the two utensils into the wooden floor.

When her mother got home that night, around ten p.m., Reagan watched her pour a glass of bourbon and hurl it down her throat. "What a day at the hospital. You wouldn't believe what I have to deal with. Someday you'll understand."

Reagan stared at her with sunken eyes. She dropped into the chair as her mother rambled on about a patient, and this and that, and how she saved so many lives that day. "Reagan, dear, whatever you do, don't be a doctor. It's too taxing."

As Reagan remembered those years of loneliness, the admitting nurse asked if she was Dr. Roz Caldwell's daughter. She stared in the same state of bewilderment as years ago.

"Yes." Jeremy answered for her. "This is Reagan Caldwell, her daughter."

"Sign here, please. We'll let you know when the doctor can bring you up to speed."

Reagan looked at the page with a blank stare: Medical Power of Attorney to declare. . . .

"Do I have to sign this?" Reagan asked.

"Only if you want control over what happens to your mother." The nurse looked up from her clipboard.

"I don't."

Jeremy looked at her squarely. "What if something bad has happened?"

Reagan declined the pen, and pushed the clipboard away.

The nurse leaned in, "Your dad is incapacitated. Don't you think you have a responsibility to—"

"No, I don't." Reagan didn't feel the need to explain.

"We cannot disclose all pertinent info to you if you don't—"

"I don't need to know." Reagan interjected. She closed her eyes and thought of her dad. He was across town with concierge treatment and here was Reagan in a position to help her mother get the same care and the same privilege. "I'm sure there's an advance directive somewhere."

The admitting nurse shook her head and walked away.

"Reagan, why is this so hard? What has your mother done to you?" Jeremy's hand was on hers.

"It's not just me, it's what she's done to everyone in her life. It's her world and her way. I guarantee you, whatever I do will not be *her* way."

"Reagan? Reagan Caldwell?" The portly doctor called to her.

"Yes."

"It's Tal, Tal Gourtz, your mother's doctor. Do you remember me?"

Reagan tried to jog her memory for any Dr. Gourtz—it did not register.

"You used to visit us at the lake house, up in Arrowhead."

Reagan couldn't remember any lake house or any man who looked like him. "I'm sorry, I've been gone a while and may have forgotten."

"Yes, I understand. Well, in any event, I'm your mother's doctor and friend. We've induced her into a medical coma. She was sideswiped on the 5 freeway, car went flying over the embankment . . . unconscious when medics arrived and she was airlifted here because of L.A. gridlock." The doctor glanced at the clock on the wall. "Follow me."

They walked into Roz Caldwell's ICU room together.

Reagan was silent. Her fingers fastened securely to the side pockets of her drawstring pants.

The doctor looked at the various numbers on a screen while continuing, "She was leaving a conference in Santa Barbara, you know . . . she had just received the Tyrell/Reneau Award. We're all so proud of her latest research. And some guy, no lights on, probably passed out at the wheel." The doctor shook his head and looked away. "Firefighters said the guy reeked of tequila. He was dead at the scene and your mother's here. Injuries are critical—life support fully implemented."

Reagan stared at her mother's body hooked to the various forms of life-support machinery. The ventilator clicked and clunked rhythmically as it breathed for her. Lifelines in both arms balanced her chemistry to give her a chance of survival. Several reddened abrasions and deep scratches led to bandages in many places on her arms and face. Reagan looked away from the screen, not wanting to know how bad it was. Two bare feet extended out of the sheets, and Reagan, for the first time, noticed the similar foot shape her mother and she had—same arch with an inward reach of the big toe with a slight bunion. It had never dawned on Reagan how similar her physical body was to her mother's. Then she looked at her fingers and compared the shape of her mother's nails to Reagan's. She quickly closed her hand into a fist.

"We'll keep her quiet until the inflammation goes down—maybe another day or so. I'll repeat her scans in the morning. Then start some cryotherapy." The doctor scribbled notes on a clipboard while Reagan surveyed her mother's physical body.

"Why cryotherapy?" Reagan looked at the doctor with sunken eyes.

"It's Roz Caldwell." The doctor snickered. "We're not sparing anything. You never know . . . most people in this kinda accident would've already died."

Reagan picked up her mom's hand and turned it over. They both had the same lines and the same distended veins on top. It was eerily familiar. She held it for a few more moments as Jeremy exited the room.

He re-appeared moments later with the clipboard and pen, and handed it to Reagan.

Taking the pen, she rolled it between her fingers a few times before signing the Medical Power of Attorney release form. Her watery eyes clouded over the words. It didn't matter.

She handed the doctor the clipboard and pen. "Please do what you think my mother would want."

Walking to the car, holding hands, Jeremy asked, "Home?"

Reagan shook her head, "I really want to see my dad. It's not far from here."

Jeremy faced her and pushed the stray locks of blond hair behind her ear. He nodded, "I can't wait to meet him."

Reagan's glassy stare brightened, "He's a character, for sure."

23

EARL'S eyes were shut as Reagan and Jeremy entered the dark hospital room. The blinds were drawn again and the lilies freshly replaced on the glass table.

With a quick glance around the room, Jeremy grinned, "This isn't too shabby. Is that a mini bar?"

"Dad . . . are you awake? It's Reagan. I'm back."

Jeremy opened a glass bottle of sparkling water and handed it to Reagan.

"I'm not paying for that," she said.

"Yeah, I doubt anyone here is."

"Dad?" Reagan tapped his arm. She was careful not to touch the many bruises on his arms. The road map of darkened flesh led up into the hospital gown sleeve.

"Maybe we should let him sleep." Jeremy stood behind her.

Reagan walked over to the windows and pulled the blinds back exposing the final rays of sunset. The day stretched forever in the late summer. It was close to seven-thirty p.m. Reflections of yellow and orange brilliance bounced off the wall and projected onto Earl's bed, casting numerous spotlights across his face.

"Oh, Reagan, you're back." Earl startled both Jeremy and Reagan.

"And you have a friend. Hi, I'm Earl." Reagan's dad sat upright and extended his hand to Jeremy.

Jeremy leaned forward to meet his outstretched hand, almost tripping into the bed. "Jeremy, Jeremy Black, so nice to meet you, sir . . . I mean Mr. Caldwell."

"Relax, son, no need for formalities. Call me Earl. You look familiar. You surf?"

Jeremy smiled, "Uh, no not really."

"Yeah, but I know you from somewhere." Earl scratched his chin with overgrown jagged nails, leaving a red streak on his skin.

Reagan took her dad's hand. "How are you feeling, Dad? Are you in any pain, anywhere?"

"No, no pain here. Just weak and old."

"Have you been out of bed today?" Reagan picked up his sheepskin slippers from across the room.

"Oh, yeah, I get up all the time. I was at the gym this morning."

Reagan smirked, "Come on, Dad, let's get you up."

"But they said I can't . . . supposedly I'm bed-bound. See the sign." Earl pointed to the whiteboard above his bed.

"Why?" She placed her dads' slippers on each manicured foot as he slowly sat at the edge of the bed. "Nice nails."

"Oh, that. You know that's your mom's doing."

"Dad, why do you think you can't walk?"

"Not sure, but I just figured they were right." Earl looked back at the sign over his bed. "Bed-bound! That used to be code for 'I'm taking a girl home from the bar.'"

Jeremy laughed while Reagan rolled her eyes.

Reagan helped her dad sit at the edge of the bed. Rather than monitoring his vitals on the machine, she focused on his eyes and face color. "Looks good to me." She supported his arm.

Jeremy joined on the other side and matched Reagan's lift.

"Just take a step or two." Reagan engaged her legs, ready to rescue his fall.

Without hesitation, Earl shuffled around the room, with Jeremy and Reagan on each arm. He looked up periodically at both of them, giggling and shaking his head simultaneously. He glanced at the words over his bed, *Bed Bound, Nonambulatory,* then flipped his middle finger toward the sign.

"Not so hard, huh?" Jeremy grinned.

"I think it would be easier if you both weren't grabbing me so much," Earl said.

Slowly, Reagan let up on her grip and then nodded at Jeremy to do the same. She kept her hand under her dad's arm a few inches.

"Now there, that's better. Oh yeah, feels great to be above ground." Earl stretched his arms toward the ceiling and yawned. The dried cracks at the edges of his mouth only allowed for a partial yawn.

The click of the door preceded the nurse's footsteps, which were seconds from Earl dropping to the ground. Jeremy caught his head before it hit the floor and Reagan yanked his arm upward.

"What the—" the nurse threw her clipboard on the couch and ran to them.

"What are you doing to this poor patient?"

"He wanted to take a walk—" Reagan tried to explain.

"He is practically comatose. He can't walk. What were you thinking?"

Two other nurses joined them in the room, helping to lift Earl back to his bed.

Jeremy and Reagan stood and watched, unable to respond.

The nurses moved quickly removing slippers, the extra gown and readjusted his nasal cannula, all in a short order.

Reagan moved in. "Dad, Dad, wake up. What's going on?"

"We got this, dear. Please step outside while we handle this incident."

Reagan raised her arms upward. "What incident? He's fine, we were just—"

"Like I said, dear, let us get this situation handled. This man obviously is not able to walk. He's not even conscious, for God's sake."

"He was just awake and talking to us. He walked on his own." Reagan's eyes glazed over.

"This man has not said a word since he was admitted. You must be hearing things, happens a lot when family members miss their loved ones."

Jeremy chimed in with an elevated tone, "He *was* awake, and he *was* talking. Don't tell my wife she's hearing things."

Reagan noticed one word.

"It's time for you both to leave. Visiting hours are over." The nurse pointed to the door.

Jeremy took Reagan's arm and led her out of the room. Holding her close, he kissed her head. "What just hap—" The sound of the blinds being closed abruptly, interrupted Jeremy's question. They both walked to the elevator without saying a word to each other.

Getting in the car, Jeremy broke the silence. "Think we should check on your mom?"

"No, not tonight . . . let's get home to Laura."

Resting her head against the car window, Reagan gave into the rumble of the car's engine. Her breasts ached—Laura must be hungry. *He called me his wife.* So much had happened with both of her parents in the last twenty-four hours, she needed to figure things out. *I wonder if he really meant the word wife, maybe girlfriend was too cheesy.* It was dark out but the oncoming car lights on the other side of Pacific Coast Highway stole her attention. One after another, the glaring lights shot at her. When Reagan was ill, she would cower from bright lights and shield her eyes from the stimulus. Now, driving at night with oncoming headlights, she did the same thing—cover her left hand over her eyes, and hide from the light.

Phaeole came to mind. How did he manage with his age muddled with his disability? The forest and waterfall spoke to him, the sunlight guided him. He found his way with the warmth of the sun's rays giving a blind man sight. *Things aren't always what they appear. The brain—*

"Wait," Reagan shot upright and gripped Jeremy's arm. "Turn around, go back."

"But I thought you—"

"No, I need to get back to Dad, now. I figured it out."

"Figured what out?" Jeremy slowed the car.

"Please, Jeremy, just turn around and go back to the hospital."

Reagan reached for the steering wheel, but Jeremy stopped her hand from grabbing the wheel.

"Okay, okay. Let me get to a safe turnout."

Making several illegal turns, Jeremy was back en route to the hospital.

The car had barely stopped in a parking place, when Reagan bolted toward the hospital entrance.

"Reagan, wait for me." Jeremy chased after her.

24

REAGAN pushed the elevator button again and again until Jeremy had caught up, out of breath.

"How'd I miss it?" She stared at the numbers overhead on the elevator.

"Miss what?" Jeremy panted.

Reagan had learned new ways of healing—not traditional, to say the least, but this was easy. The stress of her mother's accident had gotten in the way. She pushed the fourth-floor button again, harder this time.

"That floor is private. Elevator won't open without access." A woman behind her explained.

Jeremy turned to find an elderly woman in a white jacket with the word *volunteer* embroidered under the lapel. She was stooped over, yet lifted her head as she spoke to Reagan. The woman's nametag was hinged to the side, obscuring the name. He made out what he could. "Gwenn, could you help my wife and I? Her dad is on that floor and we forgot the card they gave us to get up there."

"I know you, of course." The woman reached into her side pocket retrieving a laminated card with barcodes on it. She swiped it across the access pad and the doors opened on demand.

Jeremy touched the woman's arm. "Thank you, young lady."

She blushed while covering his hand with her crooked fingers.

"Thank you," Reagan pulled Jeremy into the elevator.

"Good luck," the woman held her arm where Jeremy had touched her.

Reagan squeezed Jeremy's hand, "I need to remind myself your access is much better than mine." She stared at the elevator numbers lighting up overhead.

Jeremy turned her face toward his, "Tell me what's going on, please, tell me."

"I shouldn't have missed it." She bit her lower lip, "it's just so obvious."

"What is?" Jeremy couldn't hold her any longer. The door opened and Reagan pounced through the threshold, in the direction of her dad's room.

"Wait, Ma'am. Visiting hours are over . . . hey." The voice echoed as Reagan made the final turn toward his room.

Jeremy picked up his pace, struggling to keep up with her.

Reagan entered the room and propped open the door with a chair. She ran to the blinds and whipped them open, leaving the metallic pieces bouncing off each other in a chaotic dance. *Nothing, it's too dark.*

Two nurses and a security guard entered the room. Jeremy was right behind them. "Reagan, what's going—"

"Wait!" Reagan held her hand outstretched in their direction. The quiet was eerie. No one made a sound. Reagan walked over to the wall and switched on the overhead lights and waited. She rolled Earl's bed to face them, one hundred and eighty degrees from the position it was just in.

"Watch!" Reagan whispered.

Seconds passed before he spoke. "Reagan, my dear. Back so soon?" Earl's voice was soft but audible.

One of the nurses gasped, "What?"

The other nurse interrupted. "Mr. Caldwell?"

"Well, hello there. How are you gals?" Earl smiled, cracking the side of his lip for the second time that day.

Jeremy exhaled deeply and put his hand on the security guard's shoulder. "I think we got this."

One of the nurses stepped forward, and inspected the monitors above Earl's head. She placed two fingers over Earl's wrist and looked up at the clock. The other nurse picked up the phone on the wall and said something that neither Reagan nor Jeremy could hear.

"He must have had a middle cerebral artery pinch . . . not quite a stroke, but enough pressure to eliminate his vision and hearing on one side of the brain." Reagan walked across the room to the light switch and flicked it off and back on. "When the light comes on or the sun comes in the room, the rods in his eyes are activated and jumpstart the neurons in his brain. But his good side faced the wall and he can't hear so well out of his surfer's ear, so he never acknowledged anyone in the room."

Jeremy turned to the nurse. "Fascinating, huh? She does this all the time."

Earl's doctor entered the room. "What's going on here?" He flipped through pages on the clipboard at the end of the bed, reading the short list: *bed-bound, unconscious, failure to thrive*. He looked back at Reagan, with his hands in the air.

Reagan explained, "When he hears the door click open, he shuts back down, maybe a breakdown in the processing or something. Maybe the psychotropic meds trigger an automatic response. His brain is nonsensical on those meds."

"Can I go to the bathroom?" Earl asked.

The nurses rushed to his side, but Reagan pushed back. "Of course, Dad, it's right over there."

Reagan put the slippers on each of her dad's feet. She unplugged the IV from the port and took off the O2 saturation monitor from his index finger. After lowering his bed, she took three steps back. "The rest he can do on his own."

Earl stood up and contorted his spine in a circular manner. He looked at the whiteboard and raised one eyebrow. Then he shuffled with small steps to the bathroom. He glanced at each nurse, before shutting the door behind him.

The questions in the room started firing in unison:

"Why hasn't he. . . ."

"When did you. . . ."

"We must get a hold of. . . ."

The doctor faced Reagan. "How could you have known, without an MRI, CT or brain scan? It seems . . . well, rather impossible."

She smiled, thinking of all the lessons from Dr. Yiung's clinic—all the patients worked for their purpose, understood their own symptoms and partnered with the physicians and staff to change their prognosis. And, of course, the way Dr. Yiung listened intently to every patient.

"It took me a bit to see the whole picture. Sure, I know this patient, quite well, he's my dad, but I also saw what he needed."

Earl shuffled back to his bed. "Now, what's all this commotion about? He leaned to smell the flowers. "Nice tuberose, by the way. I smell them every day."

"So he can smell fine?" The doctor looked back at Reagan.

"Olfactory is deeply imbedded, unaffected by middle cerebral artery. In fact, if you would have put a tray of food in here each day, he may have sat up and turned to face it." Reagan huffed.

"But he wasn't conscious. Why would we have brought him a tray of food?" The nurse answered unapologetically from across the room.

Reagan sighed, so much for her father's concierge care. She wondered if he had been on a regular floor with other patients if he would have smelled the food from the hallway and . . . she stopped her nagging regrets.

"Can we work out a discharge plan?" Reagan asked the doctor.

"Well, no, it's not that easy. The hospital has strict guidelines and procedures to go through. Benchmarks must be—"

Jeremy jumped in. "I'm sure you can cut through some of that red tape. After all, this is Dr. Roz Caldwell's husband."

The room got quiet.

"Where *is* my wife?" Earl looked at Reagan.

"I will work on that discharge." The doctor said as he walked out of the room, with the nurses and security guard close behind.

The harsh reality set in. Years of Earl putting up with being Dr. Roz Caldwell's husband—a post he held loyally without the need for recognition, would now pay off.

A nurse walked back in the room and handed Reagan a bottle of meds. "We were told your dad needs to take these daily."

"What're they for?" Reagan tilted the bottle up searching for a name on the nondescript white pill. "There's no label."

"We asked the same thing and were told to just make sure he took them when he woke up." The nurse had a blank look on her face.

Reagan didn't know what to say—the sense of loss was palpable. From the concierge care and almost losing her dad, to an urgent discharge, with someone handing her unknown pills that must be taken. She hoped she wasn't too late.

Jeremy stood next to Reagan. "Earl, you have a granddaughter. Would you like to go meet her?"

25

THE final descent along the cobblestone walkway reminded Lydia that her knees were in no shape for this kind of obstacle course. She wasn't even forty years old, yet her heavy stature and years of being on her feet with patients all day bore down on the mainframe of her body. She faltered over each rolling rock, avoiding several close calls of going down.

Lydia glanced at her phone to check the map—the directions were gone. "Great, no service, and not even close to some old brick building. What the hell have I gotten myself into, and why'd I wear these stupid heels?"

Hours earlier, she had dropped everything and agreed to meet Jean Michael at this off-the-grid location to hand over more critical information on the power plant. Lydia clutched the set of files under her elbow, securing them as she turned in a circle, hoping to see a sign. Her weak knee buckled for the third time.

A sudden honk blasted behind her and Lydia jumped, dropping her purse. She turned to see Jean Michael and then let out a sigh before picking up the contents of her bag now strewn all over the ground.

"What the hell was that?"

"Sorry, Lydia. Just trying to get your attention." Jean Michael had a childish grin. "Did you bring the file?"

"Of course, I brought the file. What kinda stupid-ass question is that?"

"Well . . . you know, I just—" Jean began.

"Come on now, I'm not one for forgettin' somethin' like that. It's why we're meetin' out here in the middle of nowhere."

"No service out here, so no tracking. Hop in." Jean leaned across his seat and opened the passenger door for her.

"You're kiddin' me, then why'd yah have me plug in the address?" she asked.

"It got you close enough. Did anyone follow you?" Jean looked in his rearview mirror.

"Of all the preposterous ideas . . . you think someone's gonna follow me and take my work." Lydia clutched the paperwork to her chest. "This stuff's classified!"

Jean laughed, "You're one of a kind. You do all the special ops, uncover the evidence—plea bargain, bust up the bad guy, all to protect your patients. You're a mix of Shaft and Mother Teresa, but more on the saint side."

"Saint, my ass. Doin' the right thing is all I be doin'. I expect no less from you, movie man." Lydia handed him the manila file filled with pages upon pages of incriminating evidence of the power plant's coverup.

"I'll try not to disappoint." Jean was sincere. He wanted to expose the truth as much as she did.

"Turns out, them scumbags paid six figures to each of them lowlife, bottom-feeding docs to get them to stay tight-lipped. Get 'em to be confidential . . . to the power plant boys, that is . . . like they needed to be reminded."

Jean smiled. "You know, you can make a good living as an actor if you are ever interested."

Lydia chuckled, "Yeah, it's my good looks you'd be stammerin' for."

"Tell me something, Lydia . . . could any of these people have been saved?" Jean held up the file of medical information. "You know, these guys who were so sick with radiation poisoning?"

"You mean the ones who were never treated? The ones that this doc neglected because he was in so deep that he couldn't find his way out?"

Jean bowed his head, "Are you telling me, yes?"

"Reagan got treated. She lived."

"Why didn't these employees go to another doc, you know, outside of the power plant?"

"Well, I'm no genius, which I know is a surprise to you, but my guess is they was all runnin' scared. They probably was sold a bag o' goods that turned out to be hogwash."

"Lydia, why don't people question their docs more?"

"Not sure when the doc-on-a-pedestal thing started, but maybe pain drives it, or maybe it's fear."

"Explain." Jean leaned toward her.

"Well, take the whole pain thing. A patient is hurtin' and the doc has the drugs needed to take the pain away."

"And fear?"

"That's a big one. Fear drives everything. You either freeze or run an' hide; fight-or-flight, you know." Lydia's hands were in the air. "Fear makes a person crazy, makes yah question reality, makes yah believe and do stupid-ass things."

"So, doctors are the pain-and-fear experts."

"Maybe pain, but not fear. The only experts for treating fear are those close to yah. Those that know yah and can reassure yah, love yah. You know, jus' tell yah it's all gonna be okay."

Jean pointed to the medical file again: "What are we gonna do about these patients? These workers?"

"You, movie man, have to tell the story. Do the right thing. Get it out so it don't happen again."

"That's the plan. Want a ride back to your car?"

"Hell yes."

26

ROSEMARY, thyme, and a scent of burnt orange wafted into the entryway as Reagan followed her dad into Jeremy's home in Malibu. Natural light oozed from the floor-to-ceiling expansive windows, blurring the boundaries between outside and inside. The design features were a striking combination of block glass and travertine stone, sharp lines and soft edges. Earl stopped momentarily, with a blank stare, then looked toward Reagan.

"Dad, this is Jeremy's home."

"Excuse me, this is our home," Jeremy added.

Earl looked at her and then him, "I see you've done well for yourself."

"Jeremy's an actor, Dad. A pretty good one, at that."

"I know." Earl got closer to the window and turned side to side. "You can see Point Dune from here. You see it, R.C. You used to boogie board there when you were three." He grinned, then sighed. "That was some time ago, huh?"

"Yeah, Dad, some time ago."

Earl stood motionless; his gaze was outward, toward the open Pacific. He swayed slightly, then his knees buckled.

"Dad! You okay?" Reagan moved closer to him.

"Whoa, I feel like the Scarecrow. No legs. Guess it's better than the Tin Man, eh? Imagine that, no heart."

Reagan placed her hand on his bony shoulder. "I agree, easier to work on wobbly knees."

Earl looked directly at her. "I missed you for a long time. Then I just figured you weren't coming home. Something had a hold of you—which I understood. The ocean, it always wins, huh, my R.C.?"

Reagan did understand, not just her pull to the island, her ocean, and all of its inhabitants, but why her dad stayed away for all those years.

"Did you forget about meeting your granddaughter?" Jeremy held Laura on his chest as he approached them.

"Oh yes, of course, we come then . . ." His words were jumbled. "I mean . . . then, that . . . that's what we came for, right?"

It wasn't hard to see the lapse, the correction and the coverup. Not just the hindered search for words, but his sharp wit was also gone. Initially Reagan figured it was the effect of the sedatives in the hospital, used to keep patients calm and nondisruptive. Now as she observed the subtleties, she realized the deterioration.

Earl stared at baby Laura. He touched her cheek with the back of his wrist. "Should I wash my hands?" He looked to Reagan.

"No, you're fine. She's hardy." Reagan recalled her mother's obsession with everyone washing their hands in their home growing up.

"She's got my feet." Earl wiggled Laura's toes.

"If we're lucky she's more Caldwell than Black." Jeremy added.

"Well, I hate to be the one to break it to you, but she looks pretty white to me," Earl whispered.

"No, I mean Black, it's my last name."

Earl stared beyond them.

"Dad?" Reagan touched his arm. "Let's get some food. Come into the kitchen."

The smells were enticing and a welcome distraction. They sat along the marble counter, adjacent to the open doors facing the ocean. Bamboo trays of fresh turkey and Swiss cheese, smoked salmon on homemade croissants, and an array of warm nuts, figs and cheeses were placed in front of them.

"Is that Brie?" Earl overfilled his plate with the blooming cheese. "And are those Mission figs?" He took an oversized bite of the black fig and closed his eyes while he chewed. "Oh my God, this is the best fig I've ever tasted." A trail of juice seeped out of the corner of his mouth. He glanced at Reagan and Jeremy periodically but kept trying different bites of food.

Reagan wondered what had happened to him. No solid food for close to a week, he was over-medicated to sedate him and deprived of the care he needed. Was this really dementia? Or maybe the effect of the stroke? Or the years of being under Roz's control? How long had it been? Reagan didn't realize her fork was suspended in the air.

"Well, are you gonna eat that or let it escape?" Earl pointed to the cheese and fig on Reagan's fork.

Reagan popped the food in her mouth.

When Earl loaded his plate with his second serving of food, Reagan intervened. "How about a walk around the property? The gardens are amazing."

"But I thought we were gonna have lunch. I'm starving."

Reagan and Jeremy glanced at each other.

"Come on now, can't you take a joke?" Earl popped another big slice of turkey in his mouth.

She half-smiled and took his arm, leading him out the kitchen door to the garden. Rows of teacup roses flowed along the walkway. A dozen or so monarch butterflies fluttered in and around the south-facing slope. Purple cone flowers held their petals open for the gentle landing of the butterflies.

Earl watched the flying dance and grinned at Reagan. "That reminds me of the mountains in Mexico, just west of Mexico City. What was the name of that place?"

"I don't remem—" Reagan started.

"Oh, yes, Michoacan," Earl stopped walking. "It's a living statue. All the monarchs gather, I think mid-November. They find a resting spot on the oyamel fir tree—on the trunks, then up the empty branches. Layer upon layer of beautiful monarchs, disguised as leaves. Then something sets them off, maybe a shadow, or a bird, and off they go, all at once." Reagan's dad looked out in the distance. "Then the tree just disappears. Huh . . . kinda like—"

"Like what, Dad?"

"A . . . a story of some sort, I can't quite put my finger on it."

Growing up, Reagan cherished the stories her dad told of his many adventures around the world. Earl described every detail, from the mysterious blue coral in the Tasmanian Sea, finding lost treasures in the Pacific, to the hidden underwater pyramids in the Mexican Caribbean. Earl had a subtle life lesson in all his stories, but there was one story in particular that he told over and over. It was one of Reagan's favorites.

"Dad, do you remember the story of the octopus with seven arms? I think you said you met him in New Delhi at an aquarium, on your way home from the India conservation summit."

Earl nodded.

"How do you think his life went in that big aquarium?"

Earl walked over to the bush of roses. He picked a red petal from a fresh bloom and brought it to his nose.

Reagan noticed the intention tremor in his hand, which settled as he inhaled the scent.

The breeze picked up and Earl opened his eyes and looked straight at Reagan with a blank stare. He opened his mouth to speak, but no words found their way.

Reagan felt the sudden drain in her own energy, as the reality unfolded before her. She reached for her own rose petal and brought it to her nose the way he did. *Does he smell this? Or has he forgotten?*

Reagan felt the cell phone in her pocket vibrate. She dropped the rose petal, and seeing the name of the caller she answered it quickly.

"Yes, this is Reagan."

"Hello, Miss Caldwell. This is Dr. Grunow from your mother's medical team. We need to inform you, her vitals are shifting rapidly, in the wrong direction . . . and well, we feel that you should get here as soon as you can . . . to discuss her directives."

Reagan looked at her dad, who was picking a small weed out of the rose garden. Her grip tightened around the phone. A multitude of feelings swarmed as she whispered to the caller, "I'll be there within the hour."

As she ended the call, she noticed her dad staring at her. "What is it?"

"His missing tentacle, the one that was stuck in the sea cave, it should have ended the octopus's life. He would've died if he didn't pull away— amputating it. It was a good decision."

"Yes, you remember." Reagan was surprised.

"How could I forget? You gotta do what you gotta do . . . to live."

27

AN intricate web of emotions tangled Reagan's heart as she climbed the last flight of stairs to the ICU. She needed the steps, instead of using the elevator, to clear her head, whirling with concern for both of her parents' health. Reagan chose not to tell her dad why she had to leave him with Jeremy and baby Laura so abruptly. Reagan shook off her dad's odd stare as she left the house with Mike. Jeremy had insisted Mike drive her. Her quads burned as she climbed another flight of concrete steps in the hospital stairwell.

Reagan reached the top of the last flight of stairs and hesitated. Pushing back the long strands of sun-bleached hair, she opened the door. She missed the salty crust usually at the edges of her long locks. She'd been out of the surf way too long, but her ocean life would have to wait.

"As you know, Reagan, we've induced your mother into a medical coma so we could control the edema on her brain. The blunt impact from the accident created a bleed in her brain that we had hoped to prevent. But now. . . ."

Reagan leaned back into the wooden chair with both hands on her lap, legs crossed at the ankles. She listened closely to the doctor, as she would with a patient she didn't know.

"The advance directive she . . ." the doctor's voice faded in and out of her focus. Reagan glanced at the top of the doctor's desk, beyond the multiple piles of paper. "Her directions and wishes are very clear in writing. She preferred . . ." The words came at Reagan in an even, rhythmic flow like the islanders' chants after a death. She pictured Maura's face turned skyward as she rocked side to side and sang to the heavens.

Reagan strained to remember, before her appearance at Sydney General, when was the last time she had seen her mother. She started to feel something. It was small at first. Jeremy and Laura came to mind, then Maura and the kids, Phaeole, the chief, Roger. . . .

A childhood memory jolted her attention, of her mom desperately hugging Reagan after she went missing one afternoon, when she was twelve. Reagan had simply lost track of time and had stayed in the surf all day then fell asleep on the beach until sunset. She had missed the last bus home. The police had searched for her endlessly, until Reagan hitched a ride home and walked into a house full of concerned adults. Her mom wouldn't let her go. The memory was vivid now, as the pounding in Reagan's head grew.

The doctor's words became louder. "It is really up to you, Miss Caldwell. What do you want us to do?"

"I need to see her," Reagan stood. She wiped the side of her wet face with her sleeve. "Please, I need to see her now."

"Of course, right this way." The doctor stood and put on his lab coat.

As the door to the private ICU room opened, the air was still. Reagan saw numerous IV's hooked up to her mother's arms, and the slow rise and fall of her chest, in response to the ventilator's push. After checking the heart and pulse rates on the overhead monitor, she let her gaze shift to her mom's face. Her features were peaceful, no furrowed brow or drawn cheeks, just a relaxed, still body.

A nurse put her hand on Reagan's shoulder and handed her a cup of water. "The doctor will be right back. He needed to grab some paperwork."

Reagan gulped it in one sip. She held her mother's hand and stared at the perfectly manicured scarlet-red nails. Strangely they shared the same small bulbous protrusion at her knuckle—Reagan had never noticed. She found herself breathing, continuous with the ventilator's hiss and huff, matching her mother's rate of inhale and exhale.

The door opened and the doctor walked in. He had short gray hair that curved upward, a groomed mustache and icy blue eyes.

"Your mother is a personal friend and colleague of mine. We . . . uh, traveled together . . . to conferences, sometimes." The doctor put his hands on his hips and stared at Roz.

Reagan kept her mother's hands in hers. She didn't want to move, as it would require her to act—make a decision that she wasn't prepared to make.

"Sometimes, we'd have dinner together . . . at these conferences. She spoke so highly of you . . . she was so proud, really." The doctor's gaze stayed fixed on Roz as he spoke.

Reagan had a hard time processing the doctor's words. Her heartbeat was palpable and stayed in rhythm with the breathing machine.

"Her directives are very clear, succinct in fact: *Do not keep me on a ventilator more than thirty-six hours.*" The doctor read from a page of Roz's chart, then looked above the rim of his glasses at Reagan.

"Pretty specific alright." Reagan blurted out, louder than she had intended.

The doctor stared at her. "Your mother always knew what she wanted."

"So when will you wean her off all this?" Reagan pointed to all the tubes, lines, and machines attached to her mother.

"We started an hour ago, when we called you." The doctor's voice softened.

A sudden blip in the heartrate changed, sounding an alarm. Rather than Roz's heart rate slowing, it was increasing. It shot from eighty-two to ninety beats per minute in only a few seconds.

"Maybe just an accelerated rush of adrenalin. Her coma level isn't that deep." The doctor moved toward the ventilator.

The door flew open and a nurse rushed in. "What seems to be the problem?"

"Not sure, but it hasn't been this high since we started to wean her. Let's see where it stabilizes." He put his two fingers on the inside of Roz's wrist.

"Machine working fine?" the nurse asked.

The doctor nodded. "Neural activity decent also."

Reagan stood motionless. She attempted not to be a doctor. That would have been easier. She'd been that doctor taking a patient off life support, as well as delivering the lethal injection. It was predictable.

The rate stopped at ninety-five and held for minutes.

"Huh, as I was saying," the doctor kept his eyes on the monitor. "Your mother had so many great things to say about you and your research on those islands."

Reagan glared at the doctor. "What did you just say?"

"You know, the work you're doing with the Hansen's patients . . . so admirable."

The alarm set off again, this time louder, and the number flashed in red—one hundred and five. Her pulse shot up ten more counts. The nurse was back at the patient's side, adjusting the IV attached to Roz's arm.

The doctor laughed, "Okay, Roz, we get it, you need to be in on this."

"She can hear us?" Reagan blurted.

"Come now, Miss Caldwell . . . I mean Dr. Caldwell, you must have known all along she was listening. She's your mother; she can't be left out of anything."

Reagan looked back at her mother, eyes still shut and tranquil. She'd never seen her so peaceful. There was no strained forehead, no tight lips or slanted look, no judgment in her eyes—just quiet. As Reagan was about to let go of her mother's hand, she felt a firm grip. "What's happening here? Is she waking?"

The doctor and nurse adjusted many of the lines to the machine connected to Roz. The alarm kept sounding, higher pitches than the previous, as the heartrate and pulse continued to escalate. More clinicians entered the room, and Reagan released her mother's hands and stepped back. They worked on her for five minutes, calmly focused on the moment. The nurses moved around Reagan's mother in a choreographed slow dance, each knowing their parts, bowing and dipping.

Then silence.

There was a heavy pressure on Reagan's chest. She couldn't expand it . . . she couldn't breathe. Reagan swallowed, feeling a slight release in the oppressive squeeze. Chief Toro came to mind; his last breaths arduous and fatigued, and then she pictured her other patients, who she had helped pass. Another gulp for air. Her lips were dry and the swallow didn't help. She pictured the mottled skin of Chief Toro and others and the change in heartbeats, the singing and humming of the islanders, the full acceptance of their fate, all jumbled in her brain as the dance in front of her came to a stop.

"Time of death . . . twenty-one hundred: twenty-two."

28

REAGAN pushed open the exit doorway and gripped the cold metal handrails. Everything moved in slow motion as she tumbled into the wall and attempted to hold on.

Above her, out of sight, she heard the bang of the heavy hospital door slam shut, followed by rapid footsteps down the flight of stairs toward her.

"Dr. Caldwell, are you okay?"

Another slammed door and Reagan heard more steps approach her.

"Get her back upstairs."

"No, give her a moment."

None of the faces or voices were familiar to Reagan. She barely heard their words, but she could feel people pulling at her arms to lift her. Her body was upright for a moment, then she collapsed back onto the hard concrete floor. She recognized the man crouched over her. He was the doctor in her mother's room, with the gray hair—with the fold in it, like a wave.

"Look at me Reagan, breathe through your nose. Inhale slowly . . . yes, another one . . . again." The doctor held her head off the ground.

Reagan watched his nose flare and mimicked the same movement to help the air move in and out. Her trance-like stare let her hone in on just his nose. She opened her mouth to attempt to speak, but no words came out. Moving her lips side to side, she tried again. Nothing.

"She's in shock. Let's lift her. . . ."

"No." the voice was gruff and direct.

It was familiar to Reagan. She tried to turn her head to see who it was, but she froze, unable to move on her own.

"No!" he ordered again, this time with more authority.

The group of helpers stopped.

"I got her . . . back off. Give her space."

Reagan watched as a heavy stare came within inches of her face. She knew him.

"Mike?" Reagan heard her own voice speak.

"I got you, Reagan. Hold still, I got you."

"You said you were going to stay in the car."

"Shhh." Mike lifted her into his arms and carried her back up the stairs. The precious cargo was secure—no need for medical intervention. She was in shock—the sensation before grieving and loss sets in, and Mike knew what was needed.

He carried her to a bench near the outside garden of the hospital. It was under a sweeping jacaranda tree and right beneath Reagan's mom's room. Mike had been sitting there after he dropped Reagan off earlier. Although it was dark, the lights cast from the hospital perimeter allowed full view.

"Did you hear?"

"Yes," Mike whispered.

"I just didn't think I would react so—"

"Me either . . . when my men died."

Reagan watched Mike's eyes soften; the hard edges around his face also let go. They had discussed loss before—their own experiences so similar, yet under very different circumstances. She knew he understood. Suddenly, the memory of what the doctor in her mother's hospital room had said, repeated: *She spoke so highly of you . . . she was so proud.*

The words stung with a fierce reminder. As her tears flowed and her body trembled, Reagan half-choked in panic.

"Slow it down . . . slow that breathing." Mike had both of her hands in his. "Shh, Reagan, let it go."

"I didn't . . . even tell her. . . ."

Mike wrapped his arms around Reagan and moved in unison with her sobs and shaking. He tucked her head into the crook of his shoulder and whispered into her ear. "She knew. You showed her through your work, and she just knew." Mike kissed Reagan gently on her head and continued to rock her side to side, with his face against hers.

Between the shudders and regrets, Reagan felt safe in Mike's grip. She breathed in his musky scent and was well aware of the kiss he had just placed on her head. She welcomed it.

"Can we go home now?" She wiped her face.

"Would you rather sit for a few?"

Reagan shook her head and attempted to stand but buckled into his hold.

"Let's stay put for just a few more minutes." Mike brushed loose strands of drenched hair out of her eyes.

"She was so stoic, my mom. Nothing ever budged her, not even a happy tear. I used to think her muscles were steel and her veins rigid like pipes."

"I bet she had a soft side." Mike's voice was monotone. It soothed and calmed her.

"I think you're right. I just never saw it."

"She was lucky you were there." Mike repeated what Reagan had once told him about his men passing in his arms in Iraq. "You held her hand. She knew you loved her."

"How am I gonna tell Dad? He's just coming around and getting strong. I don't know what—"

"Hey, look at me. It will be okay."

Reagan focused on Mike's eyes. The deep brown, almost black hue, was enhanced by the expansive white surrounding his pupils. Subtle creases lined the outskirts of his eyes, similar to a set of waves lined up on the horizon. She felt a layer of grief peel away—surely more grieving would follow.

Purple flakes of jacaranda flowers scattered the ground and bench. Two squirrels hopped about as Reagan leaned into Mike's chest. A man in scrubs walked by, followed by another couple with arms linked.

"It feels good just to sit here, like you said, just a few more moments." Reagan's eyes followed the couple down the walkway.

"We can stay as long as you need," Mike added.

"Yes, just a few more, please."

29

MIKE'S call was ahead of their arrival, so when the car pulled up to the driveway, Jeremy was there to open Reagan's door.

"Reagan, I'm so sorry. How—"

Reagan put her hand up. She buried her face in his chest. There were no tears left. As she lifted her head to look at Jeremy, she noticed her dad standing in the entry, eyes wide open—knowing. Before walking over to him, she tightened her lips and nodded in his direction.

"I'm sorry, Dad, I didn't—"

"My R.C., we'll be alright."

Reagan searched for any signs of his suffering. She questioned whether he realized his wife had just died. Reagan's mother was the stoic one, not him. He usually cried at the death of their small animals, or the loss of the neighbor's beloved cat. But now there was nothing.

"Dad . . . do you . . . um . . . Mom's gone."

"Yes, I know."

"How did you know?"

"Just knew, that's all." Earl replaced a lost strand of Reagan's hair behind her ear. His hand settled on the side of her cheek.

"Dad . . . what if . . . what if you came with us to Fiji?" Her surge of enthusiasm brought a new look on her dad's face.

"Well, I don't think . . . I mean I have to . . . wait, what am I saying . . . there is nowhere else I'd rather go."

"After a memorial, of course." Reagan slowed down.

"What memorial?" he asked.

She didn't let his dementia overtake her. It would be fine. He was strong enough, even though he was just discharged from the hospital, but the idea was a good one as far as Reagan could see. She would introduce him to Dr. Yiung and start holistic treatment for his memory loss. There were plenty of herbs she could get on the island that would help boost his immune system, and then there was the ocean—

She looked around for Jeremy to share the news and found him talking to Mike in the shadows of the carport. Jeremy's hands flew up in the air gesturing about something. He leaned in close, while Mike stood at attention. Not hearing any of the conversation, Reagan led her dad into the house. "Let's go find Laura."

George was rocking Laura in the glider, humming softly.

"Oh, my sweet little girl. Just the medicine I needed." Reagan picked her up and kissed her cheek. "Your grandma's gone, but at least she got to meet you."

George placed the infant blanket over Laura's body before gently touching Reagan's shoulder. "My condolences."

"We're gonna be just fine." Earl spoke to no one in the middle of the living room.

Reagan walked toward her dad, nodding to George. "I got him. And thank you, George, for being here . . . for all of us."

Earl's back was to Reagan and his hands were out to the side, "Really, there's plenty of money."

"Dad, you okay?" She got right in front of his face.

"Oh, sure, R.C., we're all good. It's gonna be just fine."

"What is, Dad?"

"Your mom has plenty of money, you know. She hid it for us."

"Why would Mom hide her money?"

"So those guys don't get it." Earl had turned away from her and spoke to the wall. "She had to hide the money . . . she told me . . . she found the answer, but they wanted it. . . ."

Reagan walked in front of him again. "Dad, who are you talking to?"

"Well, your mother of course. We've talked about this before, you know . . . but maybe you weren't there . . . I can't remember who . . . let me think. It was on Blanco Street . . . maybe we were in the kitchen. . . ."

George walked over and handed Earl a glass of water. "He gets confused, talks to someone here or over there." George pointed across the room. "Not sure how many extra houseguests there are. I offered to feed them all, but your dad just laughs it off."

"Probably the meds they have him on. Hallucinogenic effect." Reagan rocked Laura. "Is he eating okay?"

"If they feed me anymore food, I'll have to start exercising." Earl faced them both.

"Dad, do you know where you are?"

"Sure, at the actor's house. Your boyfriend, right?"

A subtle wind blew through the side windows clinking the blinds together, breaking the tension.

"And you know about Mom?"

"Can't forget that now, can I?" Earl walked out of the room.

"Are you going to bed?" Reagan trailed him.

George followed. "Let him go, Reagan. We all need to get some shuteye."

The next few days were spent memorializing Reagan's mother. The only specifics in Roz's directives were about not being on life support for more than thirty-six hours. There was nothing mentioned about what she wanted after she had passed. Reagan decided to spread her mother's ashes off of Leo Carrillo Beach, the place Earl had taught Reagan to surf. Jeremy, Mike, Earl, baby Laura and her stood ankle-deep in the ocean. Reagan came up with a few nice things to say about her mother—she focused on her accomplishments in her career and all the patients she had helped. Then she opened the urn of ashes and let them fly. The rising high tide would do the rest.

"That's my kinda send-off . . . when it's my time." Earl commented.

"Anything else?" Reagan asked.

"Well, maybe you catch a few waves with me before you throw me off into the Pacific." Earl smiled.

"That's what I'll do." Reagan held her dad's hand as they watched waves bounce off the main rock. An outside set approached—the water walled up and turned into a beautiful right hander, with several surfers paddling for the wave. There were celebratory hoots from the surfers, and both Reagan and her dad joined in their surf tribe language, sending off Roz Caldwell.

Messages from numerous colleagues flooded Reagan's voicemail. She listened to several and then decided to save the rest for another time. The hospital had given Reagan a bag of her mom's personal belongings that were delivered after the car crash, but the nondescript plastic bag sat in the corner of the room, untouched. She would also have to deal with her parents' personal items at their home, but later. For now, Reagan wanted to get back to Fiji.

Jeremy brought her a cup of tea. "All booked. We leave tomorrow at eight a.m., direct on New Zealand Air. I know you're tired, and George has offered to put together Laura's items. So maybe just take a moment and drink this tea."

"What about my dad's stuff? I need to help him—"

"Mike's on it, probably already done."

"Oh, I see, but what about his passport and other—"

"Mike handled it all."

Jeremy sat next to her at the edge of the bed. "We got it all, except for you." He stroked her hair and turned her face toward his. "What else are you concerned about?"

"My dad might need a window seat." She took a sip of the chamomile tea. "He's more comfortable looking out at the ocean when possible."

"I got two rows in first class so he can sit wherever he's comfortable."

"That will be a first for sure."

"What, his own row?" Jeremy got up and threw a few shirts into his luggage.

"No, first class. It's not in his pay grade or mine."

"Well, it is now." Jeremy zipped up his bag, "Done."

"I bet that's a first for you, too." Reagan said.

"What, first class, are you kidding me?"

"No, packing your own bag."

He walked back to Reagan and bent to kiss her. "Okay, you're sitting in coach."

She smiled back lovingly, "You spoil me."

They kissed more deeply for several moments until loud voices caught their attention.

"Is that my dad?"

"No, I think it's Mike." Jeremy peered down the hallway.

Mike supported Earl's arm while walking toward Reagan and Jeremy's room.

"I don't need their approval." Earl pulled at his arm.

"Let's see what Reagan has to say about that." Mike looked up at Reagan, standing in the doorway.

"What's up, Dad?"

"Well, this guy here says I can't drive over to my home. It's real close. I think we have the same view? Kinda."

Jeremy appeared in the doorway and stood next to Reagan. "Earl, what's up? We're packing for our flight tomorrow. Everything okay? Long flight in the morning. You may want to get some shuteye."

"Oh, yeah, you again." Earl looked from Mike to Jeremy. "So, which one of you is her boyfriend?"

"Dad! Please, this is Jeremy. He's my—"

Mike interrupted, "Easy mistake, sir. We kinda look alike."

Reagan's cheeks burned red. "Dad, what do you need? I'm sure we can order it and have it delivered to Fiji."

"I need to bring my meds with me, the ones your mom has me on . . . some sort of research thing." Earl moved his head side to side, nervously.

"Maybe we'll try you on some new ones, Dad."

Earl protested, "No, no, I have to stay on the special ones . . . she said so . . . or my brain will be totally gone . . . the research said so. The drug company said so."

"Dad, do you remember the name of the med? Or maybe what marking or letter is on the pill?"

"No, no markings, it's all white . . . yeah, that's it, all white, nothing else. Only it's not the placebo, your mom made sure of that. It's the real thing." He paced in front of Reagan, then turned and paced a few more steps. "Really, Reagan, I have no choice . . . I must be on those . . . or . . . I . . . I just really need them. Even if there's no markings or no name . . . they're all white, but I just . . . can we go get them now?"

Reagan was exhausted. Her body ached from the stress and adrenalin, the emotions of loss and grief had set in. The last thing she needed was to drive across town.

"I'll go." Mike asserted.

"I'll join you." Jeremy jumped in, "Reagan, you need to get to sleep, way too much on your plate."

Reagan nodded. “Thank you, I really am—”

“We’ll be back,” Jeremy grabbed his jacket off the coat rack. “My cell’s almost dead, but we’ll be quick.”

Mike nodded at Reagan as they left.

30

THE final turn onto Reagan's parents' street changed from asphalt to concrete—a newly paved entrance, not far from the other private roads. Roz had claimed she needed her privacy and Earl needed enough breathing room away from chummy neighbors. They had moved into The Woodland Estates two years earlier, deep in Malibu canyon.

Jeremy searched his phone for the map showing which way to turn next. There were no street signs and only a few dozen private homes, without addresses posted. According to Google maps, their home was only twenty minutes away from Jeremy's, but the development was so new that the GPS directions didn't line up with the actual streets. "Crap, I hope we find it before I run out of charge."

"Turn left in five hundred yards, your destination is on the right," the automated voice announced.

"It's a dead end; just go to the next street and we can backtrack it." Mike knew his way around a nonfunctioning GPS system. "Yeah, turn here and then the next left."

"How the hell?" Jeremy put a hand up.

"Just lucky."

"It's just ahead—" Jeremy started to say.

Swirls of smoke entered their path and Mike slowed the car to an idle.

"What's going on?" Jeremy choked.

An ominous wind funnel launched bits of charred paper into the sky, littering the driveway with embers. There was no one in sight and the next closest house was about a half-mile away.

Mike stopped the car and rolled up his window blocking the smoky fragments and an odd chemical smell from entering the car. "Look, we should call 911 and get the hell out of here."

"No, just a sec, there's no flame, just a weird—" Jeremy got out and walked up the long brick walkway toward the entrance. He looked in a window then turned back to Mike and shrugged his shoulders.

"Jeremy, for chrissake, get back in here, the whole place could be rigged. Get the hell away." Mike opened the car door.

"I'll be quick. Earl needs those meds, you heard him." Jeremy yelled back at Mike.

"Oh no yah don't, Jeremy, wait . . . stop." Mike got out of the car.

"He said the meds are right on the kitchen counter. I'll be quick. It's just some smoke." Jeremy unlocked the front door and disappeared in the entry.

"Don't go in—" Mike urged.

Dropping to his knees behind the car door, Mike shielded his face from the massive blast. The sound jolted him back to the trenches—the haunting memory flashed through him. Severe ringing in his ears preceded the immense pain in his head. He covered his ears with both hands. "Nnooooooo, get out."

Billowing smoke fogged his view. Crackling sounds of trees igniting surrounded the entrance of the house. Then a hissing sound and a second *POP* sent Mike into the stress zone. "Mayday, Mayday." He yelled.

After several seconds of holding his breath, he came back to the realization of where he was. Standing up, he let go of the car door, "No . . . No . . . Nooo."

Another loud explosion. Mike heard the echoing cry of pain. "Jeremy!"

The front door was on fire, black smoke and debris shot in the air. There were no discernable objects, just chaos, and flames, and smoke . . . and no Jeremy.

Mike covered his head with his jacket and crawled through the flames. "Jeremy, Jeremy." His voice trailed as he dove to the ground.

Between the black smoke and the intense heat, he wasn't sure what hit him. Mike looked up and caught a brief glimpse of a man with a two-by-four coming at him. There was a final crack on his head.

"What could be taking them so long?" Reagan asked George for the third time, hours after Mike and Jeremy had left. "It's after midnight." She paced the long travertine hallway. Her cell phone was fixed to her hand and she kept looking at it, hoping for a response to her four previous texts and six phone calls.

"Maybe call them again," George pleaded.

"I just did." Reagan was irritated, not wanting to dial one more time and get Jeremy's voicemail once again. If he would just answer her texts or pickup the phone and call her. If only—

Ring.

Reagan dropped the phone she was so startled. Picking it up off the floor, she yelled into the phone, "Jeremy?"

"No, Hun, It's Lydia, got your text. What's got you all riled this late at night?"

"Jeremy and Mike went to my parents' house to—"

The beep of another caller stopped Reagan midsentence. She clicked over without saying another word to Lydia. "Jeremy?"

Silence.

"Hello. Who is this?" Reagan yelled into the phone.

There was a long silence on the other end, yet Reagan could hear breathing. The screen on the phone said *Unidentified Caller*.

She attempted to calm her voice. "This is Reagan, who . . . who . . . is this?"

The call dropped.

"Wait, wait!" Reagan shouted into the phone.

The phone rang again and she picked it up abruptly. "Don't hang up."

"Reagan, it's Lydia. What's going on, girl?"

"I don't know . . . I don't know where they are . . . or what happened . . . he won't answer. He always leaves his phone in the car." Reagan spoke fast as she looked out the front door—searching.

"Did you try Mike?"

"Yes, both, and neither pickup."

"You stay put, on my way. Don't you move an inch. I'll be there in—" Lydia's call clicked off.

Reagan's vision got blurry, before she fell onto the hard concrete driveway. Flashes of Earl nonresponsive in the hospital, Reagan holding her dying mother's hand; it was all too much. The sense of something ominous descending on her was palpable. Her gut spoke—it always had and it was always right. She struggled to stand, no one was there to help her . . . not George, Jeremy, or Mike . . . no one.

31

THE fluorescent light flickered and danced on the bricks as Mike opened his eyes. His head throbbed in rhythmic agony. He could smell dried blood and knew it was his. Was he in Iraq? Or Afghanistan? Did he remember how to speak Pashto? He couldn't orient himself—the pain and trauma penetrated deep. Where were his men? Were they okay? What battalion was he with?

A bright light stabbed at his eyes. Mike reoriented. *I'm here. I'm in L.A. with Jeremy. We went to get the meds for Reagan's dad . . . their house . . . the explosion . . . Jeremy.* He couldn't see who was on the other side of the silhouetted shadow. At first there appeared to be several men, but as he kept his head straight, only one came into focus. The stranger wore dark glasses and a bandana covered the lower half of his face. There were no other distinguishing marks.

"What's your name, big guy?" The man had a gruff voice with a slight accent.

Mike looked at the shadow of a man.

"Why were you at that house?" The hoarse voice spoke slowly.

Mike's survival instinct kicked in, "I'm Sergeant Mike Peters, fourth battalion south brigade, sir."

"Save it." The man put his hand up in the air. "What do you know about the people who live at that house?"

Mike wasn't about to submit. "We were on a mission, second interlude off Kabul." He stuck to the script . . . knew how to stay in the trenches. "My men and I were crossing the Isleca bridge when we were attacked. I'm not sure they all got out. . . ."

"The guy's a nut case. Probably homeless, living in the canyon." A second voice beyond the shadow said.

"We threw a rescue flare, hoping you would see us." Mike continued.

"Get rid of him. He doesn't know anything . . . we got the wrong guy."

Mike stayed quiet.

"What about the other guy?"

Mike kept his head low and kept talking in military jargon.

"He's as good as gone. Get rid of this guy." The man with the bandana spat a wad of tobacco onto the floor near Mike.

Mike swayed and rocked his head back and forth, and periodically looked at the flicker of light above him.

"Come with me, Sarg. You're dismissed," the second voice said.

Mike was thrown into the back of a Cadillac Escalade and after ten minutes on a rugged road, the car stopped. The driver got out, opened the back door and pulled Mike out of the car by his shoulders. "Here yah go, Sarg. I'm sure your cavalry is gonna show up any minute, asshole." The driver kicked him in the gut, got back in the SUV, and churned his wheels as he drove away.

Clumps of mud and gravel showered Mike. His head pounded with a growing lump and caked layers of mud-laden blood matted his hair. Mike rolled to his side, propped his elbow in the mud and got to his knees. He pushed himself up slowly watching blood drip and pool around him. *Christ, what hap—Gotta get to Reagan.*

A rare Indian summer had developed along the Southern California coast, bringing with it short bursts of rain on the coast of Malibu. Reagan knelt in the driveway—her tears mixed with the sudden rain squall. A shiver of disbelief held her captive, unable to move in any direction.

George ran to Reagan's side with a blanket. "Reagan, please . . . please come inside. He probably just lost cell with the storm, my dear. Come, let me help you."

"Something's happened, George. I can feel it . . . that last phone call . . . Jeremy . . . he's . . . he's in trouble, something bad—"

Earl appeared at the entry in an oversized robe. He walked with caution down each step toward his daughter. There was no rail to assist his unsteady steps. Stopping momentarily, he looked around. The rain drenched his velvet robe, creating a train of fabric dragging behind him. He reached Reagan and put his hand on her back.

"It's the drug company, they want my meds," Earl said.

"Dad, what are you talking about?"

"Those young men, your boyfriends, didn't they go to the house to get my meds?"

"Yes, Dad. Jeremy and Mike went to get your meds." Reagan stared deep into her dad's eyes. They were glassy and dull, yet he seemed focused.

"It's why we moved so much." Earl looked away.

"What do you mean, moved so much?" Reagan stiffened.

"So, they can't find her . . . and her secret meds."

"What secret meds, Dad?" Reagan clenched her dad's shoulders.

Earl continued, with a clear voice. "They altered your mother's research for FDA approval and funding. They shifted the shares before it went public."

Reagan looked at her dad, confused. "What do you mean . . . the shares?"

"It's hard to fathom . . . the things your mom struggled with . . . what it's like to walk in her shoes. All those regulations and roadblocks to make headway, to get a drug to market, to help rather . . ." Earl paced back and forth.

"Stop, Dad . . . stop. What does any of this have to do with Jeremy?"

"Maybe they thought he was your mother coming back to the house . . . or maybe me, not sure. Either way, they want her research . . . they want the new data. There's often a suspicious car on our street. Last house was broken into twice. She doesn't even keep anything at the house anymore."

Reagan stared beyond her dad, toward the distant sky, "Who are they?"

32

MIKE willed his feet forward, sloshing through mud in the darkness. A faint glow projected off the streetlight and guided him toward a paved road. He calculated how long a ten-minute car ride would translate to walk time. Jumbled numbers added to his confusion. The pain in his head added to his loss of direction. *Where am I . . . one foot in front of the other . . . no man left behind. . . .*

When the second street lamp appeared—dangling off its post, Mike picked up his pace. He was close. *Stick to the plan . . . stick to the plan.* Thirty minutes passed before he saw another glimmer of light. *Where is that third streetlight? Must have miscalculated.* He looked behind him—pitch black. A light ahead was dull but still there. He trudged onward, hunched over in pain.

Desperate memories drew out more pain, which stabbed at the back of his neck. He stopped for a moment, thinking he heard something.

Mike stumbled toward the light. *Left, left, left, right, left . . .* He wiped the sticky blood from his eyebrow. He wrestled with low hanging eucalyptus branches that snagged at his neck and shoulders, threatening to choke him.

Clearing the last few branches, Mike saw a small house with two cars and a truck parked in front. He could hear laughter and every few seconds a shadow of a person walked past the curtained window. There were no fences or other obstacles, so Mike approached the front door and knocked three times.

"Hello, can I help you?" The elderly woman, bent over a wooden cane, answered the door. Her eyeglasses dropped below her eyes, while she peered above the rims. "Oh, my dear, you in trouble, son?"

"Yes, Ma'am, some guys jumped me, stole my phone. I just need help getting a hold of . . . um . . . my friend. Could I use your phone?"

The woman tilted her head, staring at the blood on Mike's face.

"I promise, I mean no harm. I'm U.S. Air Force. Just need a phone."

A man with thinning gray hair pulled back in a ponytail appeared at the entry to join them. "What do we have here?"

"Says he got in a scuffle, needs a phone. Says he's Air Force." The woman pointed her cane at the gash on Mike's head.

Mike added, "I was jumped, sir."

"That's quite a wound." The man with the ponytail kept his eyes on Mike's hands at all times. "We heard sirens earlier tonight, down the road. Did you see firetrucks go by?"

"No, sir, I didn't see anything." Mike lied. He had heard sirens hours ago. He assumed they were for Reagan's parents' home, but there was no need to add more detail for this group. "I tried to fight back, the guys who jumped me, but—"

With arms crossed, the man nodded his head in the direction of the kitchen. "Phone's on the wall."

Mike followed the woman with a cane into the kitchen. Three more people sat at a table, playing cards, with a stack of cash in the middle of the table. Mike nodded toward them. They all froze. He could easily identify the earthy smell in the smoke-filled room. Everyone in the room seemed wary of the stranger.

"Phone's in here, honey." The woman held the receiver toward Mike.

Mike tried to recall any phone number . . . any one number . . . an area code, but nothing came to mind. All the eyes in the room held him hostage or possibly vice versa. "Uh, seems I've gotten used to my cell keeping all the numbers for me . . . I don't remember—"

"Well, where do you live?" The man with the ponytail asked as he placed his pipe down on the ashtray.

"Not far from here, but I really don't know the address."

"Huh, so you're jumped late at night, no phone on yah, big ol' goose egg on your head and no idea where yah live."

"Yes sir, that seems to be correct, sir."

Everyone in the room remained silent. Wafts of sweet smokiness held the group motionless. A straggly haired card player coughed out, "Try 911. They'll help yah . . . eventually."

Laughter broke out with a blend of hacking coughs and wheezes.

"Look, I'm sorry, I mean no harm. I really can't remember exactly—" Mike stared at the pile of cash, half-smoked joints, and a small mound of pot in the middle of the table. "I really just need to get home."

No one spoke. One of the guys at the table swept a bunch of marijuana buds into a bowl and walked out of the room.

"So, if *you* don't know where yah live and *we* don't know; I don't think we can help yah," the woman said.

"Well, Ma'am, you're right, but do you know Jeremy Black? I live with him."

The room erupted in laughter, again.

"Sure you do. We all know Jeremy Black. We have dinner with 'im every third Wednesday, and play cards. He loves us!" Another white-haired lady laden with Mexican jade jewelry threw everyone into fits of belly laughter.

"Probably just trying to find out where he lives," another person added.

"Maybe you should have downloaded *Homes of the Rich and Famous* app."

More laughter with rings of smoke filled the air.

"I swear if I don't stop laughin', I'm gonna pee in my diapers," one of the men at the table said.

Mike scanned the room full of giggling seniors and remained silent.

The man with the ponytail put on his raincoat. "Come on, son, let's go. It's not far from here, I'll take you." The man opened the door, exposing his military tattoo on the inside of his right forearm—dagger and all, similar to Mike's.

Mike walked in the door and saw Reagan wrapped in a blanket, shivering. George and Earl stood simultaneously, and all three stared at Mike.

"You're okay?" Reagan leapt to her feet.

Mike drew a painful breath noticing Reagan's swollen eyes. "Where's Jeremy? Did he beat me back?"

"He's not with you?" Her voice strained.

Mike looked at Reagan's father and George, who both faced him with the same unspoken question. He looked back to Reagan, who was ashen and shaking.

"We got . . . uh . . . separated. I hoped he was here." Mike looked away from Reagan. A sharp pain stabbed at him.

"But he's not . . ." Reagan swallowed hard. ". . . not here. Where were you guys?"

Mike stood with his hands in his pockets. Finally, he looked at her—he couldn't help but notice the way she swayed from one foot to the other, as she would on a boat. Her shirt hung loosely off one shoulder, draping off the side of her arm. In her right hand, clenched to her chest, was the black cell phone. He froze, mouth dry, silent.

Earl got closer to Mike, "So you went to the house?"

Mike stared at Earl, "Yes, sir."

Reagan looked to her dad, who paced slowly across the threshold, away from Mike. "Dad? What's going on? Is there anything else you know?"

Earl shook his head. "Not that I remember."

Mike looked at Reagan, then to George and Earl, "There was an explosion. . . ."

Part 2

33

DREARY shades of wet fog seeped through the cracks of Reagan's bedroom window. Bleak layers of gray consumed the view. There was no need to move. It had been ten weeks since Jeremy went missing and the season was changing in Malibu. Extensive police and private detective searches led nowhere. Media attention dwindled and the Hollywood community grieved the loss of a beloved actor. Reagan didn't allow herself to see any of it—no TV, internet, or newspapers. Even Jeremy's staff protected her from all the stories and speculation. She saved her energy for Laura and her needs—nothing else mattered. Her nightmares had returned, and when they didn't include morbid scenes of Jeremy, there were crushing images of her falling off a cliff or almost drowning, or simply not breathing. Death surrounded her.

There was no evidence of a body at her parents' house, demolished in the fire. It had been combed for any trail of foul play or human remains. Numerous private security and investigative services were hired to figure it out. Mike also worked diligently to piece together what had happened—he returned to Reagan's parents' property a dozen times, always leaving empty-handed. He barely slept most nights, on the phone with different agencies, gathering any relevant info and retracing that night.

Reagan never asked him how it was going. She assumed if there was any positive news, Mike would have told her. Days moved in and out, with Reagan unaware of the calendar or time of day. Earl played the ukulele, repeating the chords too many times, but neither Reagan nor Earl had noticed. Jeremy's staff came and went, dropping off plates of food several times a day, only to be taken away an hour later, with most of the meal untouched.

Looking around the modern-decorated room, Reagan realized every piece of it belonged to Jeremy. She stared vacantly at the Roche leather armchair. Reagan had never intentionally moved in to the Malibu mansion. The plan was to set their roots down in Fiji, with Jeremy commuting to film shoots when needed. Laura was seven months old, and Reagan needed to decide soon what to do—just not at that moment. For now, she wanted to stay put, in his bed, buried in the damp gray air. Until Laura needed her, there was nothing else to get up for.

"Good morning Reagan," Mike knocked on her door. "A special nurse is here to see you."

Reagan pulled the sheets over her head. She put her earbuds in and turned up the volume of cascading waterfall sounds. A few minutes later, a gentle hand rested on her arm. Reagan could sense Lydia's presence and her warmth. She withdrew her arm, "Uhuh."

"That's what you said yesterday, and the day before yesterday." Lydia pulled the sheets back and placed her hand on Reagan's again, just like yesterday.

"Please, Lydia. Give her a minute." Mike's voice was low.

"I know it's too much for anyone to do on their own. But you got me and Mike here to do the heavy lifting. Jus' need your input and—"

Mike cleared his voice, interrupting Lydia's same speech from yesterday.

Reagan knew what they wanted. She just couldn't come to grips with memorializing Jeremy. Pressure from Hollywood producers, friends, admirers and the media, all wanted to know the details of the tribute. Jeremy had no living blood relatives, so it was Reagan who needed to make decisions. The list went on and on of all the things Reagan could no longer do. She was lethargic with deep bouts of depression. The only respite from her grief was taking care of Laura. Even then, she would catch herself saying: "Daddy would be so proud of you sitting up" or "Daddy misses burping you, but he'll be back soon."

Lydia reached over and gently pulled out Reagan's earbuds. Stroking her cheek upward, Lydia forced a shallow smile. "Hello, hello, anybody home?"

Reagan stared at Lydia, before blinking several times—a sort of Morse code for *I'm here*. The lightness in her eyes had been gone for weeks. There was none of the positive energy that usually filled the room when Lydia greeted Reagan, before Jeremy went missing.

"Mike and I have been talking." Lydia brushed Reagan's hair off her face. "We want to go visit your island in Fiji. I've never been that far, and Mike assures me he will be our guardian." Lydia lifted Reagan's chin toward her. "Hello . . . do you hear me in there?"

The slight whimper from the crib prompted Reagan to move. She got out of bed without hesitation, leaving Lydia's hand in midair. Reagan lifted Laura into her arms and walked to the changing station to start the day. Essential tasks got her to take the first step. She changed Laura's diaper and got her in an outfit in less than a minute. Moving to the rocker, she adjusted the pillow under her arm and proceeded with her morning feeding.

Lydia had seen Reagan's routine often—she came by each morning before her work shift started, in search of her friend. Lydia waited a few more minutes before trying again. "What do you think of going back to Fiji? Mike and I . . . we really want to go . . . and well . . ." Lydia was cautious. "Jus' so cold here and winter's 'round the corner." She smiled between certain words and made sure she waited before going on, until Reagan shifted her stare from Laura to her. "We could go Tuesday, two days from now. It's a good day for getting 'round . . . and well . . . its jus' a good day overall. Don't yah think?"

The cool ocean fog penetrated the room. November weather could go any way in California, but lucky for Lydia and Mike, today it was especially cold and damp, and convincing. She waited for Reagan to reposition Laura to her other breast. "It's awfully chilly in here. Here's another blanket." Lydia looked in the direction of the open windows.

Reagan propped Laura upright on her chest and gently tapped her back—the way Jeremy did. She stood and held her daughter tight into her chest. The ground had a distinct coldness that had been stored all night in the hardwood floors, ready to penetrate bare feet in the morning. Reagan shivered slightly as the breeze whisked through her shirt and ran down her legs. She covered Laura with a sheepskin blanket, bundling her, and then handed her to Lydia. Their eyes met.

"I'll pack." Reagan looked at her without emotion.

Lydia curbed her smile.

Standing in the threshold, Mike bit his lower lip and smiled under his full mustache. "I'll make the arrangements."

34

ROGER rechecked the weather data on the airport screen for the fourth time. Nadi airport was on the map, yet updates were often sluggish.

"How much longer?" Lelei whispered to Roger.

"You know how it goes here, trades are shifting again, could be another cyclone. No update yet."

"I'm not sure how much longer that one can stay fixed to the window." Lelei pointed toward Joni.

"How about some breakfast, honey?" Roger held out the guava juice box toward Joni.

"Or I have lemon gobs," Massina shook the box of candy. "Your nose is gonna be stuck to dat window forever if you don't give it a break." Massina popped two lemon drops into her mouth and made a loud sucking noise.

Lelei shook her head at her younger sister, "No candy this early."

"You haven't eaten a thing all morning, Sweetie." Roger held his arms open. "Come sit with me and eat these banana chips."

"No!" Joni kept her nose affixed to the window.

"Okay, I'm giving them to Atta Boy," Roger threatened.

"I don't care." Joni glanced at the pup for an instant and then back to the window. "I only want to see Reagan . . . and Lit . . . tle . . . Laura . . . noth . . . ing else." Like a magnet, her nose was back on the glass.

Massina mimicked her quietly, "Lit..tle Laura, noth . . . ing else."

"Now, now." Roger half-scolded.

"There she is . . . I see the plane . . . I see it, I see it . . . told you, told you." Joni jumped up and down as her voice shrilled.

"Calm down, little one," Roger jumped up next to Joni, almost tripping over Atta Boy. It had been months since Reagan had left so urgently to be with her dad at the hospital. Now after the death of her mother and the loss of Jeremy, he was more anxious than ever to see her.

"Why is dat plane moving so slow?" Joni stomped her foot hard onto the ground, knocking over the box of juice. "Stupid juice, outa my way." She kicked it further, and Atta Boy took chase.

"Ah, ah, Miss Joni . . . Mama would not like that behavior at all. And you know she said I was in charge, since she couldn't come." Lelei held Joni's shoulders down.

Atta Boy retrieved the box and brought it back to Joni, leaving a trail of fruit juice across the floor.

"But why's it taking so long? He moves slower 'dan green sea turtle." Joni had her nose scrunched back into the window, "Doesn't he know how to drive a plane?"

Roger grinned at Joni. "She's almost here. I know it seems to be taking forever, but you should see her any—"

Joni shrieked as Reagan appeared at the top of the flight deck stairs. "There she is, it's Auntie Reagan. I saw her first . . . I saw. . . ."

Reagan couldn't see through the one-way glass, but knew Roger and the girls were watching. She waved vaguely in their direction, keeping one arm under Laura. Although the deep undertones of sadness and loss were still palpable, she edged a smile in their direction. "We're home, little one." She squeezed baby Laura into her chest.

Mike carried the overfilled personal bag, with an assortment of baby diapers, wipes, bottles, pacifiers, infant toys, books and snacks. He insisted Reagan only carry Laura. Earl carried his worldly possessions in a surfer's pack on his back. They stayed within a few steps of Reagan.

"Too bad Lydia changed her mind at the last minute, huh?" Mike made small talk. "She woulda loved this heat."

Walking across the stifling asphalt seemed to take longer than Reagan remembered. The humidity was thick and her lungs were slow to adjust. She took off her sweatshirt and loosened the sarong holding Laura. A sudden emotional rush swept over her. She longed for Jeremy—the man she had grown to love, the man who had crossed oceans for her—was still missing. Would she ever really know what had happened? Maybe it was better not to know the finality of his days. The emotional memories drew her into a deep crevice, with the walls closing in on her. Her steps slowed as she approached the entry door to the waiting area. She choked on the harsh reality of it all—her knees buckled for a split-second, before she straightened.

"It'll be okay." Mike placed his arm under hers, and led her up the final steps into the airport. His firm touch lingered.

The door opened and several passengers ahead of her rushed through. Mike's reassuring grip helped her regain her composure to greet Roger and the girls.

"Auntie Reagan, Auntie Reagan." Joni was the first to rush out of the crowd to Reagan. She squeezed between Mike and Reagan, breaking his hold.

Lelei and Massina followed and joined the group hug. Reagan touched all three of them, intermittently with her one hand, while securing Laura, who was crying inside the sarong.

"Can I take her?" Lelei extended her arms.

Reagan forgot for an instant the magnitude of her own loss as she breathed in the three girls' salty smell and tangled sea hair. Atta Boy scratched at her leg and attempted to jump into her arms. Mike and her dad chatted in a familiar way. Collectively, the family armor would do its work.

Then Roger came into view, and after handing her baby to Lelei, Reagan ran to him like a small, vulnerable child seeking safety.

"I know, I know," he stroked her hair. "You're home my dear. We got you."

Mike pretended to struggle with the infant chair. He re-adjusted the bags on his arms and looked away from Reagan and Roger, clearing his throat.

"Everyone, this is Mike. He's a good friend of Jeremy's and helped us all get here safe and sound." Reagan held her dad's arm, "And this is my dad, Earl."

"Wow, you're big," Joni stretched her neck upward to Mike's six-foot-two frame.

"Yah wanna ride on top?" Mike pointed to his shoulders.

"Up high, yeah," Joni giggled and placed her foot on Mike's bent knee and then was lifted up onto his shoulders. "Sooooo good up high. I can see all da' clouds. I'm the big one now, ha ha to you down there." The giggling was perpetual and healing for everyone.

"Hey, what kinda bird is dat?" Joni touched Mike's tattoo on his forearm.

"That's a Watchover Eagle. Keeps an eye on people when they're lost." Mike winked at Lelei and Massina, who stared at the tattoo.

"You watch over Reagan?" Joni touched Mike's forearm, stroking the image of the eagle with a dagger in its mouth.

Mike looked up at Joni. "Aren't we all? I mean you too . . . aren't you gonna help watch over Reagan and Laura?"

"Oh yeah, Auntie Reagan family, baby Laura too . . . we all watch for each other, silly. But I don't put bird painting on my arm. Bird is always with us." Joni patted Mike's head.

Mike looked at the three girls and Roger beaming over Laura. His glance fell back to Reagan. "This looks like a fine place to spend a life."

A sense of calm surrounded Reagan. The sincerity of Mike's words struck a chord. She only wished Jeremy had felt that way about Fiji.

Joni looked down from Mike's shoulders. "Auntie Reagan, why your cheeks the color of hibiscus flower? All pink and puffy?"

Reagan wiped her face with her sarong and was surprised how wet it was. "Come on, guys. Let's get to the boat. I want to see Maura."

35

A WEEK had passed since returning to Fiji and in between intermittent waves of depression, Reagan felt a pull toward her surf break. Mike had insisted she go, with him and Roger tending to Laura as long as she needed. But as she slow-motored away from the resort, Reagan felt a tug of guilt leaving her daughter behind. She turned the boat back toward the resort, but straightened at the last minute. They knew what Laura needed, what Reagan needed. This was her moment to move forward or she could get stuck. The thoughts tangled with her distraught emotions. She throttled forward.

Traces of golden algae bloom danced on the surface of the ocean. The gentle moving trade winds would move it offshore soon enough—for now it pirouetted and twirled the floating foam, landing it softly until its next lift. Reagan let her whaler drift into the shallows near the edge of her surf break. The reef's outcropping was out of harm's way of the propeller. Local trevally, angelfish, and grouper gathered to explore and feed on the algae-laced chain as she lowered the anchor. A black-tip reef shark appeared, inspected the line, and cruised onward with no meal to entice it to stay. Reagan watched the brilliant spotted shark weave its way through the broken crystals of light piercing the sea.

Landing the anchor with a surgeon's touch, the sand wrapped around the precious metal. Reagan looked around the perimeter; the reef had expanded since she was last there. The long fringing coral castles were alive and thriving. Pink, purple, and orange appendages reached for the sun. She arched her back, rolled her shoulders, and lifted her face toward the sun's warmth. A smile eked through.

Reagan waxed her board, repeating the circular motion, lap after lap to create the perfect raised paraffin bumps. She dangled her feet in the water and looked in all directions for a familiar movement, a splash, or any sign that her sea friends would join her. A few more circles of wax, another spritz of sunscreen, leash strapped onto her back leg and then, finally, the modulated whistle, expressive squeaks and a train of clicks signaled their arrival. The coded communication from the two bottlenose dolphins was easy for Reagan to translate.

"I've missed you two." She felt a sudden unexpected lightness in her body. Reagan tossed her surfboard a few feet from the boat. She slid into the water, letting her skin and soul absorb the ocean. Holding her breath, she descended several feet and felt the texture and warmth of the ocean embrace her. Her exhaled bubbles seemed to rise in slow motion. She saw Jeremy's smile within the downward angled sunrays. It hurt, until she realized she needed air. Breaking the surface, Romeo and Juliet were right there to greet her.

"Thank you," she spoke out loud as the dolphins rubbed their noses into her side. She stroked their sleek skin and a layer of grief peeled away. Her smile grew, matching their perpetual smiles, as they circled her, coaxing more play.

"Let's go catch some waves." Reagan hopped on her board.

She paddled out to the reef with the dolphins leaping around her—unraveling another layer of loss. Every stroke she took was a dose of medicine. The white water was another fifty yards ahead and she would soon be in the lineup. A brief memory of Jeremy's smile snuck into her being—the first time she watched his childish way of jumping off the boat into the ocean. She envisioned his sculpted arms against the backdrop of the sun and another time when he— *Stop it!* She lifted her head, bent one leg, and propelled forward. She needed to catch a wave.

Since childhood, Reagan had turned to the ocean to heal, listen, figure things out. The answers came easy out there. The ocean was her sanctuary, and riding the waves—her refuge.

Finally in the lineup, a set of waves headed her way. Numerous indicators around the reef let her know what was coming. The symmetrical lines preceded the drop in the horizon, and then an upwelling of energy gave the wave its personality and shape. She turned her board, paddled three strokes, and hopped to her feet. The memory of the motion was embedded at an early age, regardless of how long she had been away or how much her body had been through.

The fast-moving wave guided her as she dropped her knees in a low squat and ducked into the crystalline barrel, exiting without a whisk of whitewater hitting her face. There was a quick burst of adrenalin, almost undetected. She kicked out of the wave and dropped down to her stomach on the board. The moment seized her, shook her, then purged like an erupting volcano, "Ahhhhhhhhhh!" She yelled it again, "Ahhhhhhh!"

The primordial sound had been pent up for weeks and surfaced without warning, cracking her wide open. Her hands trembled, making it difficult to hold onto her board. She looked around in case anyone had heard her. There was a distant boat, far enough away, so she belted another liberating, "Ahhhhhhhh." So much loss—Jeremy, yet so much beauty in baby Laura, "Ahhhhhhh."

A low-flying V-line of pelicans swooped in her direction, gliding effortlessly. She watched a few of the birds divide momentarily, then flapped their broad wings rapidly before rejoining the procession. Reagan remembered what Phaeole had said about pelicans symbolizing love, sacrifice, and motherhood— that a pelican would save its young before itself.

She bowed her head and the memory of Jeremy reappeared. This time she let it stay. His smile and eyes lingered. She reminisced about their first kiss, first lovemaking, and then she couldn't recall the last time she had seen him—what had she said or done, did he kiss her goodbye? It was a blur—nonexistent. As hard as she tried, there was no memory of her last moment with Jeremy. She felt the wet rubbery nose of Juliet nudge her thigh. Opening her eyes, she stroked the dolphin's long nose.

"You've kept it so simple. We have so much to learn." Reagan stared into the intelligent eyes of her mammal friend. She sensed her dolphin-friend's compassion. Another set approached, and she made a fast pivot to paddle and catch her second wave. This time she made a steep drop, arms flying behind her, until she caught up with the force of the wave. She clenched her jaw, bent her knees and cranked a sharp bottom turn, more forceful than needed, and the nose of her board flew skyward meeting the lip of the wave. She held on as the wave tossed her over the whitewater, floating seamlessly for several seconds while she gained control and dropped back into the wave. She carved a few more turns with her board and finally landed in a deep, long tunnel of thundering ocean, until it swallowed her.

Coming up for air, more exhausted than previous surf sessions, Reagan hooted in celebration. She'd made it, in so many ways, from almost dying to surviving, from suffering the unimaginable loss of her lover, falling into a deep and dark depression and now, here she was, back in the ocean. A necklace of kelp entangled her hair. She left it in place and paddled back out to the lineup.

36

IDLING back to the resort after two hours of surfing, Reagan longed to see her daughter. She threw the lines around the dock cleat and left all her gear on board while she jogged up the ramp to find her.

Mike and Earl stood at the top of the ramp. Reagan caught their glances and waved at them. The two of them, side by side with their eyes focused on her, resembled each other from her perspective. She caught Mike's smile and hesitated for a moment before she realized she was smiling back at him.

"How'd it go?" Earl asked.

"Really good, Dad. Wish you could've come. New swell's here, out of the south." As she got closer to them, she slowed down. Mike's piercing gaze halted her. She tugged on her shirt from the back, revealing less of her chest. "Where's my baby girl?"

"Roger has her and won't give her back. When you leave the dock, it's a custody battle around here." Mike lowered his sunglasses.

Reagan felt a flush of warmth in her cheeks. She squelched Jeremy edging his way into her consciousness again. The surf had helped. So had the dolphins, the pelicans, and simply being back in Fiji. She caught Mike's smile again.

"Lunch is ready." Earl came off the rail, arched his back, and stretched his arms upward. "Ahi's freshly sliced and those mangoes won't eat themselves."

A surge of hunger pulsed through Reagan. Tropical fragrances—plumeria, tuberose, and jasmine, surrounded her. Her senses were alive. "Yes, lunch sounds perfect."

The sashimi-style tuna was served rare on the inside and crusted with fresh herbs on the outside. Shaved coconut spirals topped the salad with slices of mango and avocado, and a papaya-banana smoothie rounded the menu. Reagan ate more than usual, thanks to her surf session. Her hunger had returned.

After lunch, Roger brought Laura to Reagan. The baby was wearing a blue and green tropical print outfit with a matching headband. "For the record, Laura said she wanted to be with me this morning." He looked over at Mike and winked.

"What about the yellow dress I had her in earlier?" Mike asked.

"Many costume changes around here. You know how it goes." Roger chuckled as he adjusted Laura's diaper. "This little one knows how to eat."

Reagan took it all in—the doting uncles, her dad's attentive look, the birds of paradise and ginger blooms as centerpieces. She watched her daughter's eyes glisten and stare at her, which brought a mixture of feelings, none of which included loss. It was the most joy she had felt in months. Reagan was fully aware—the beauty and belonging, and the satiated feeling of not needing a single thing in the world.

Mike placed his hand on her arm and tapped it lightly. "What do you think?" He asked.

"Sorry, what?" She stared at his hand on hers. His fingers were long and muscular. There was a gentle and warm sensation to his touch. She followed the defined lines to the edge of his tattoo.

"We were just talking, your dad and I, that we'd love to join you on the boat tomorrow and get a lay of the ocean, yah know, see what you do out there." Mike left his hand on her forearm.

Staring at the colors of his tattoo and edge of the image, Reagan froze. "Yeah, yeah, whatever you guys want." She pulled her arm away and looked to Laura, "You too, my big girl, time for you to meet some ocean friends." She shifted in her chair, noticing the eyes at the table on her. "I think it's time for us girls to go nap."

Earl added, "Me too . . . my second one today."

"No need to keep track here, Dad. Sleep when you want, do what you want."

Reagan stood with Laura and bent to kiss her dad on his head. She sensed Mike's eyes still fixed on her. As she turned to leave, she knocked over a glass of water, but Mike caught it inches from landing on the ground. "Definitely time for some rest. See you guys tonight. Maura and the kids are coming over for dinner. Finally got their boat fixed."

"Do you need my help?" Mike stood.

"No, I got it." Reagan shifted Laura to her hip and picked up her water bottle.

"How 'bout I carry her to the room?" Mike held up the infant bag.

"We got it, I mean . . . I got it," Reagan fumbled her words.

"But it's no—"

Earl jabbed Mike with his elbow. "I think she's got it, which means she wants us to stay here and have another beer."

Mike shifted his glance from Earl to Reagan and back to the table. "Oh, okay, then. See you for dinner."

Leaving the restaurant, Reagan focused on her steps. There was a familiar yet distant sense of longing. She shook it the best she could, but couldn't resist turning back one more time to see where his eyes were. This time Mike and Earl faced each other and chatted casually, each holding a Fiji Bitter. Relieved, Reagan made a quiet escape.

37

DINNER at the resort restaurant was usually casual and simple. Fresh fish and vegetables were laid out banquet-style and guests helped themselves. As Reagan approached the entry to the restaurant, she stopped and took in the scene. Festive lights of green and orange hung low across the stanchion poles. Lilac and plumeria blooms floated in conch shells on the long family table. A trail of red ginger petals were strategically lined up from the entrance to the table.

Joni skipped in alternate leaps and jumps to meet Reagan at the entry, presenting her with a homemade lei. "It's a feast, Auntie Reagan, a big feast."

Reagan bent down to meet Joni and let her place the lei around her neck. "Who for?" She whispered.

"It's a surprise." Joni giggled as she skipped away.

Laura immediately snatched the fresh blooms of Reagan's lei and pulled them to her mouth. "Oh no you don't, my precious. Those aren't the edible kinds of flowers." Reagan placed the loose flower behind her left ear, automatically, as if she was with Jeremy. Then slowly, she switched it to her right ear, as she glanced around the lanai.

Joni skipped back to Reagan and pulled her hand toward the decorated room. Maura sat at the head of the table, across from Earl, Lelei and Massina. Roger carried out platters of tuna and yellowtail, decorated with mangos, papayas, and sugar bananas. Mike extended his hand to Reagan as he pulled out a chair for her to sit next to him.

She stood still for several moments staring at him. A gust of wind swept through the open-air restaurant and swirled thick strands of Reagan's hair in her face, temporarily blocking her view. The single plumeria flower blew off her ear and landed on the ground. After putting the lost strands of hair back in place, she searched for the bloom, before giving into Mike's outstretched hand.

Mike lifted Laura out of her arms and propped the infant on his hip as he had done hundreds of times. "Please sit, Reagan." He stood behind the chair, waiting for her to sit.

"What's this all about?" Reagan hesitated before sitting down.

Mike raised his glass and nodded to the others, "To Reagan, for bringing us all together."

Earl lifted his beer, "And for breaking me out of jail."

Everyone took sips of their drinks but were quickly distracted when Joni mistakenly took a sip of Roger's white wine, then coughed it out, spraying the table.

"Yuck! That's not apple juice. Pew, pew, pew."

Roger cleaned up the wine as others began to mingle and eat.

A soft shade of yellow and orange illuminated the side wall of the restaurant. Reagan noticed the blended rainbow and fought memories of Jeremy. He had loved the way the colors danced on that same wall when they had dinner together at this same table. She stuffed the feeling deep down.

"How about that sunset?" His hand was next to hers; their pinkies touched.

Reagan jolted back to the conversation as she heard Mike's words. "Yes, those colors—" She stopped. His hand was on top of hers, holding her captive. She glanced at Maura's eldest daughter who was busy helping the girls dish up their food. Maura was partially blind, and Earl and Roger were comparing sunburns from the day. She was alone with Mike for the moment. His hand was heavy and warm, possibly reassuring, like it belonged. His other arm held her daughter who was asleep—content and settled. Her heart raced.

"How about some wine?" Mike reached across the table for the bottle of Shiraz.

"I don't really—"

He filled her glass halfway. "I know you don't usually drink. But you might enjoy this."

She was surprised Mike knew this about her. What else did he know? She and Mike had only met a few times before Jeremy went missing and now they seemed to be together most hours of every day. Reagan felt the dampness in her armpits and the water glass felt slippery in her grip. She inhaled; his smell was musky. Confusion and indecisiveness surrounded her as she watched the movement of everyone at the table—eating, drinking, laughing, more drinking, more laughter. His hand landed on hers again. The back of her neck pulsed with tropical heat. She shifted in her chair and took a sip of water.

"Relax, Reagan." He whispered.

She kept her eyes on Maura, who was looking in her direction. Reagan reached for the wine glass, hesitated to lift it, but then took it to her nose. Closing her eyes she brought the glass to her mouth—the aroma was nutty and sweet with a hint of blackberry. She took a sip and let the wine slow dance in her mouth. The liquid swished and rolled from one corner of her mouth to the other, letting her tongue play with the tempting Shiraz. She swallowed. It was delicious.

Mike arranged a makeshift bed for Laura on the end chair, then snugged it to the table. "Perfect timing, little one." He kissed her forehead and tucked a blanket around her.

"Impressive," Reagan smiled.

Mike took Reagan's plate and dished up small amounts of food, each item not touching the other. As he added fresh ginger shavings, some of it dropped onto the fish. "Oops, let's get that out of there." He moved the delicate slices to an empty area on the plate.

"It's alright, I don't mind the food all mingling." Reagan said.

"Just not sure how you like it." He placed the plate in front of her and rotated it so the fish was in front of her.

"Huh," she smiled. "I never considered how I like it. No one ever asked me that before."

"Well, how do you like it?" Mike held her glance.

"I . . . I'm just not . . . sure." Beads of sweat accumulated then trickled down the back of her neck.

"Cheers." Mike lifted his beer bottle toward her glass of wine. He was more clean-shaven than necessary for the tropics, yet a missing top button on his shirt gave him a casual and relaxed appearance.

"Yes, cheers." She clinked lightly and took another sip. This time she swallowed immediately.

Reagan was distracted the entire meal. Between his hand near hers, and Maura's girls asking her questions, she found it difficult to focus. Mike offered to refill her wine glass and Reagan covered it with her hand, embarrassed that it was empty.

"Auntie Reagan, which one you want?" Joni was at her side.

Reagan jumped, "What do you mean?"

"Ice cream, silly. Which one you want?"

"Oh, um, either . . . one."

"You talk funny, Auntie Reagan." Joni handed Reagan an orange creamsicle.

A slight squeal from Laura rescued Reagan from responding. She propped her on her chest and turned to Mike, "I think I'll turn in."

"Okay, but this time I need to help." He stood up and took the squirming baby from Reagan.

"Okay."

Reagan hugged Maura and the girls in turn, saying the Fijian word for *much love*, "loloma bibi."

"The dinner was really special." Reagan said as they walked back to her bure. She kept her hand on Mike's forearm while Laura was enfolded in his other arm. "Oops," she bumped into Mike, swaying a bit. "Sorry, I'm not used to drinking. When Jeremy and I—" she stopped midsentence, remembering when she and Jeremy had long intimate dinners with a taste of wine, followed by a night of lovemaking.

Entering the bure, Mike placed Laura in the cradle and kissed her on the head. He adjusted the sarong window coverings and turned on the reading light next to Reagan's bed. "Can I get you anything?"

The effect of the wine was obvious to Reagan. She poured a glass of water and tried to find words—any words that would help slow her pulse and lower her heartrate as he walked toward her.

"Thank you for caring so much . . . for Laura . . . and . . . well—"

"Good night." Mike whispered, before he kissed her on the forehead.

Reagan noticed his broad shoulders as he left the bure. She stood motionless for some time, feeling the dampness of his kiss mingle with the breathless night air.

38

REAGAN tossed all night with short bouts of sleep and long stretches of despair. Remnants of sugar and alcohol held her down, making it difficult to decipher what was real. Her body finally gave into exhaustion. She dreamed she was driving a boat toward the reef, chased by ominous black clouds. She knew not to leave the resort with an impending storm bearing down, but she needed to get to the reef. There was a sense of urgency. The clouds broke open, and a torrent of rain pelted her. The cyclonic winds overpowered the boat forcing her off course. The engine backed off on its own, pushing against her downward thrust. She was headed toward the exposed coral reef with no control of the boat.

"Reagan, you up?" A familiar voice penetrated the wall between consciousness and sleep.

She shot up, vaguely holding onto the dream. It was as vivid as the voice she now heard. Sweat saturated the thin cotton sheet on top of her.

"Hey, I got some fresh coconut milk and a full French press."

"Mike?" She used the sheet to dry her drenched face and grabbed her sarong. "That you, Mike?" She wrapped the Fijian sarong, island-style, around her naked body.

"You expecting someone else this time of morning?"

He had been there every morning, same ritual, except today was the morning after something had changed.

"Give me a moment to—" Baby Laura's cry interrupted her. Reagan lifted Laura out of bed while fussing with her sarong.

"Here, I got her." Mike walked in and placed the fresh plunger of coffee on the table. He took Laura and in exchange handed Reagan a small mug. It resembled a half coconut, shaped to hold a hot beverage. The smell of the strong brew filled the bure.

Reagan took it with both hands. "Hmmm. I need this." Bringing the mug to her mouth, the barely tied knot in her sarong released, sending the fabric off her shoulder. It now lay stranded on her hip, exposing her breasts.

Mike stared and they both froze.

She felt a sensation of pleasure—long forgotten, but recently found. She bit the edge of her lower lip and slowly brought the sarong back in place, covering her body.

Mike moved closer, with Laura clinging to his chest. Their faces were within inches for a second. She felt his breath and smelled his familiar scent.

"I don't know—" She attempted to talk.

"I do." He countered.

"But—"

"What?"

He kissed her with hesitation and tenderness.

Reagan let it happen—she surrendered, as she did in her dream. She let go of the throttle. After their lips parted, their gazes met. She saw Jeremy's eyes within his, although Mike's were dark brown with a soft orange around the iris. Jeremy's were— She stepped back, mouth closed and lips tight, then she took Laura from Mike and walked back to the changing table.

"Uh . . . so are you with me . . . on the boat today? You and Dad, that is." Reagan went to the corner chair to feed Laura. She never bothered to cover her breast while nursing. Since Jeremy had been gone, Mike had been around, always ready to help. Her modesty had left weeks ago. Yet as she nursed her daughter, she pulled the edge of her sarong over her breast.

Mike stood a few feet away, motionless. "Uh, yeah. Yeah, we're coming."

They had crossed over that imaginary line of intimacy—similar to the beginning and end of the horizon line, not knowing where one ended and the other began, but the line had been crossed.

She handed Laura to Mike to be burped and refilled her coconut husk mug with the rest of the brew in the press. Walking out to the lanai, he followed, with Laura in one arm and the coffee cup in the other. No words were said, no movement, just stillness. She sensed his need to talk but smiled when he didn't.

Reagan heard the familiar whistling and looked up to see Earl headed toward them. The dirt path was uneven, yet Reagan's dad walked dexterously as a surfer would, cross-stepping to the nose of his longboard. He carried a small dive bag with sun-bleached fins, a mask and snorkel, and a canteen. His straw hat, freshly woven a few days previous, appeared tattered, since the ends of the fronds had yet to take hold to secure their place within the frame of the hat. The untethered strands wandered back and forth with each step Earl took, giving him the appearance of a scarecrow.

"Morning, Dad." Reagan welcomed the distraction from Mike.

"Ah, Mike, you beat me to it. I was gonna get you both coffee."

"Ready for a boat ride?" Reagan asked.

"As ever. Just wish I was bringin' my board too."

"I have a longboard." She answered.

"Oh honey, don't tease me. . . ." Earl waved his hand in the air.

"Hey, who's that?" Reagan pointed toward the dock at the small roundabout approaching.

"Maybe new guests?" Mike asked.

"No, they come and go on Sundays. It's Tuesday, right?" She looked toward her dad.

"You're asking me? I hardly know where I am, let alone what day it is."

"I think Roger's on board. But it's not one of our boats." Reagan squinted as she walked toward the edge of the lanai to get a better view.

A light rain weaved through the rays of sunlight, typical for the time of year. The seasons were slow to change gears south of the equator. The sprinkles sat lightly on Reagan's eyelashes, causing her to blink several times to clear her view. Scents of deep ocean bloom weaved through the rain and rode each droplet of water. Reagan walked toward the ramp. She was a few steps ahead of Earl, Mike, and Laura.

Roger waved from the boat as they docked. There was another passenger with him and an unfamiliar boat driver. The sprinkles picked up yet the clouds were nowhere to be seen—a strange phenomena in the tropics that occurred before an impending storm. There was no wind so the air sat thick, slowing even the most energetic person. A good rain would be welcomed.

Roger waved again, this time more frantic. The three passengers got out of the boat and steadied their legs on the dock. Roger held the arm of one of them, while the driver fastened the lines to the dock cleats.

Watching the whole scene, Reagan figured someone from another island was injured and was brought here to see her, as happened from time to time. She hoped it wouldn't interfere with their boat plans for the day. It had been a while since her dad had journeyed out to a reef break, and even longer since he'd seen her surf.

Roger helped the man walk up the dock.

"Oh great, sorry guys, an injured bird is coming our way. We may have to wait a few—" Reagan was unsure what came first—the gust of wind that blew her hair in all directions, the hovering clouds that suddenly appeared with a steady flow of rain, or her quiet scream from within. *It can't be.*

39

"JEREMY!" Reagan's scream escalated to hysterical. She ran to the top of the plank and stared at the man, who bore no resemblance to the Jeremy she had last seen. His head was shaved, he was twenty-five pounds lighter, and the deep burn scars on his face made his features unrecognizable, except to her.

Pulling Reagan into his chest, Jeremy embraced her with all the strength he had left. "I didn't believe Jean Michael. He said you got away, but the thugs convinced me you were gone. They said—" He buried his face in her neck and cried a deep and haunting animalistic cry.

Reagan touched the deepest of the burn scars on his right cheek. The fascia had already thickened and turned outward. A light pink stretch of skin between darker pigmentation connected one scar to the next, leading to the bridge of his nose. The sockets of his eyes drew inward, hollowing out the lower edge of his eyelids, yet they were clearly Jeremy's eyes—hazel green and blue with yellow lines, like the water's edge meeting the sand.

Their lips met. Reagan immediately felt the irregular surface of another scar—the jagged edge of skin cut into her bottom lip. Their connection was real and painful. She didn't dare pull back. She tasted his blood, or was it hers? There was palpable pressure on her shoulders as he dug his fingers into her skin.

Jeremy spoke fast. "The explosion . . . at your parents' house. Mike tried to get to me . . . I saw him . . . in the doorway, he was so close, but they hit him, hard."

"You're . . . alive." Reagan's voice was barely audible.

"They dragged him away. I couldn't—"

"You're alive." She repeated.

"Yes. They told me—"

Reagan pulled him in and held him, more like an injured child than the man she loved. Her tears flowed.

The cackle of baby Laura finally detached them. Reagan jolted back to reality and turned to face Mike, who had Laura in his arms. Then she felt Jeremy's arms drop and move toward their daughter.

As Jeremy took Laura from Mike's arms, Reagan swelled with mixed emotion. A turbulent wave held her down.

"Oh my God, Jeremy, it's really you." Mike's face was white.

"Yeah, it's me, alright. Well, kinda. Jeremy pointed to his face.

"What hap—" Mike started.

Laura fussed more than usual. The confusion of the moment had all of them alarmed.

Mike reached for Laura, "Want me to take her?"

Jeremy pulled his daughter back, "No, I got her."

Reagan's eyes landed on Mike then glanced toward Jeremy and Laura, then involuntarily back to Mike. Her chest tightened. Opening her mouth, a trickle of blood landed in the corner of her mouth. There were no words.

"Well, what do we have here?" Earl joined them.

"Hi there, Earl." Jeremy hugged him hard, creating an outburst of cough from Earl.

"Easy, I'm an old guy. What happened to you?"

"Some bad guys—" Jeremy halted.

"The guys at the house?" Earl had no problem remembering.

"Who were they?" Reagan's voice was subdued.

"Still not sure about that, but I know they were determined to find something in your folks' home. The place was torn apart before the explosion."

"They want the secret ingredients." Earl spoke casually. "That's why we moved so much."

Mike chimed in, "You mean the ingredients for your memory meds?"

Earl nodded, "It's all there . . . in the patent."

"Lydia has a lead on them. Said some German company is in line for that patent when the date expires. It's already been eighteen years." Mike had both hands in his pockets and stood several feet away.

"What are you guys talking about?" Reagan held onto Jeremy's arm.

Mike avoided looking directly at her: "Your mom has a pharmaceutical patent on a med for Alzheimer's. Somehow, she kept it out of the FDA's hands and locked it up in a German pharm company." He turned to Earl. "Earl, do you know why she kept it out of the U.S. market?"

"Oh, that's none of my business." Earl picked at strands of palm fronds that escaped his hat.

Mike faced Jeremy. "What'd they do to you?"

Jeremy rocked his daughter side to side and kissed Reagan on her cheek. "After the blast, they drove me somewhere and put me in a garage, fed me crappy oatmeal for breakfast and a cold soup for dinner. It was a total surprise that they let me use the bathroom in the house. They wanted me alive for some reason. Several weeks passed, and one day some old woman who was changing the bandages on my face left the door unlocked when she left. I escaped that night . . . and ran, for days."

Mike walked over to Jeremy and patted his back. "I'm glad you're alive, bud. Just glad you're alive . . . and here." He glanced at Reagan.

A tidal surge of emotion reappeared as she closed her eyes. Air was trapped in her lungs. It wouldn't take long for the carbon dioxide to build up and take over. She would have to breathe sooner or later.

"Yeah, me too, Mike, me too." Jeremy stood between them.

Reagan sensed a deep and troubling dread. She cringed thinking of Mike that morning, and the last two months of despair and hopelessness.

"Let's get you a shower and a beer." Roger slapped Jeremy's back. "You must be exhausted."

"Honestly, I'm just relieved . . . and happy. I'm back with the love of my life." Jeremy kissed Reagan on the lips. "For good."

There were several moments of silence, until Earl made a move, toward the restaurant. Roger followed.

Mike held out his arm in a sweeping manner to Reagan, "After you two."

40

PLATES of fresh mango and pineapple, muffins, granola, and all the tropical condiments were waiting for them at the long family table. Reagan wasn't hungry. There were so many questions she had for Jeremy—what happened? Who did this? Why hadn't he called when he was rescued? She stared into his hazel eyes, the one feature that hadn't changed. So many thoughts, but she started with, "It must've been awful."

"I had no idea where I was. I circled the hill for days. Some strangers gave me food and sometimes I ate out of . . . well none of that matters. George got a call from a neighbor saying a strange man had been wandering around." Jeremy looked away. "They had no idea who I was." He pointed to the new etchings on his face.

Blocking a new surge of tears, Reagan held Jeremy's hand. "You can tell me more later. You're here now, that's all that—"

"When I finally remembered, I found my way home and George was there. He handled it all, said I needed to get to you in Fiji, right away. He got me on a plane and here I am. He said whatever's in this envelope might explain something."

Reagan stared at the envelope that Jeremy handed her. Her name had been crossed out and *c/o Jeremy Black* was handwritten above it.

"It arrived at the house last week." Jeremy leaned toward her.

"I don't know of any Franzenchor Banke." Reagan pointed to the return address. "Dad, have you heard of these guys? Maybe Mom mentioned them?" Reagan held up the envelope toward her dad, who sat at the other end of the table.

Earl stared blankly for several seconds holding his index finger over his upper lip. "Uh, maybe." He lowered his hand and tapped his fingers in a melodic pattern, the same way he played a CGE chord over and over.

"Dad?"

The fingers stopped. Earl looked at Reagan, then back at the sky. Finally, he gazed back at her, "Yeah, I heard of them, maybe." Back to the finger tapping, "Germans. Huh. Who woulda thunk?"

"What do you mean, Dad?"

"Well, you know, they just always think they're the first ones to be on to something. You and I know it was your mother's idea." Earl shook his head.

"What idea?" Reagan asked.

"You know, the DNA profile piece, the data about your genes and forgetting—"

Jeremy chimed in, "You mean Alzheimer's?"

"Yeah, whatever, dementia, Alzheimer's . . . it's all one in the same to me. Your mother figured out how to bypass the damn connection. No one would ever have to suffer again," Earl explained.

"But, what does it have to do with this bank in Germany?"

Earl picked up his beer and looked across the restaurant at Mike, who sat at the bar. "Hey, stranger, you gonna join us or what?"

"Dad, focus. What does a bank have to do with this?"

"Not really sure. I know she had a bid from another Pharm company and then this German company said they'd pay eight figures, so she did some fancy footwork to make it happen. You know, R.C., like walking to the nose and back on your longboard." He smiled.

Mike walked over to the table and sat next to Earl.

Reagan kept her eyes on her dad, although the presence of Mike at the table was unsettling. Her neck started to sweat. She opened the envelope and read a single piece of paper to herself.

"Well? What do they want?" Earl asked.

Reagan's head moved side to side in a steady manner, reading the paper. When she looked up, all eyes were on her. She looked back at the paper, "Who is Slider C?"

Earl raised his hand, "That'd be me."

Reagan chuckled, "Surf name?"

Earl shook his head, "Haven't heard that name in years. Huh, clever."

"Seems like you, me, and Slider C are the three names on the account. Someone from the bank is trying to get a hold of us." Shifting her glance for a brief moment, Reagan was relieved Mike wasn't staring at her. The quandary between Jeremy and Mike weighed heavy on her heart. She had fallen for Mike's chivalry and kindness, he had rescued her, and Jeremy was presumed dead. Of course, Mike wouldn't fight for her; after all Jeremy was here. He was alive.

Her chest tightened as Mike pushed his chair back to get up. Reagan flinched and got back to the conversation. "Did Mom owe money?"

"Oh, who knows? Could be something, or maybe nothing. Maybe they're just closing an account or asking for my permission to pay for something." Earl picked up the ukulele and strummed a familiar tune.

"I will call them for you and—" Reagan put the letter back in the envelope and leaned back in her chair, exhausted.

"No, no, don't bother, dear. I get letters from them all the time and just toss 'em."

"Dad, it's labeled *urgent*. Looks pretty official to me."

"Nothing urgent here, R.C., except for this beer that's getting warm."

Jeremy and Earl touched beer bottles and sipped their Fiji Bitters.

Reagan watched them attempt to bond. It wasn't the same natural relationship that Mike had with her dad—two old friends clicking with every topic and conversation. Jeremy strained and tried too hard to get chummy with Earl.

"Well, is it okay with you, Dad, if I call the bank and find out?"

"Oh, sure, do whatever you like, but don't let them upsell you. They usually just want you to open more accounts."

Reagan held still as Mike walked away. A strange north wind blew through the restaurant, disheveling a stack of napkins across the table. She felt Jeremy's gaze on her and their eyes met. "I need to go feed Laura."

Jeremy touched her shoulder and she jumped.

"Why so startled, my love?" He stroked Reagan's strands of windswept hair.

"Just want to find out about this bank. That's all. I'm . . . a . . . little concerned, uh, for Dad . . . I gotta go feed Laura. I'll be right back."

Walking back to her bure, Reagan strained to see Mike leaving the harbor in a small boat, by himself. She slowed her pace and turned back to see Jeremy standing, eyes on her, hands in the air. She mouthed, "Be right back, I promise." She turned back to the path and focused on walking slowly. *He knows. He must know.*

41

THE harbor's wind shifted easterly and Mike pushed forward on the throttle. The speed helped to center his thoughts. He had been attracted to Reagan the first time they had met, but she was off limits. Holding back for weeks of telling her how he felt and days of touching her intimately, the timing seemed perfect, maybe too perfect. Never intending to fall so hard for her, Mike couldn't resist any longer—when Reagan's sarong fell off her shoulder, exposing her left breast—ever so slightly. Her lips begged him. He had to kiss her so she would know.

Mike choked at the headwind, rapidly draining his energy. He would have to leave them all. He would miss baby Laura and, of course, Earl, who reminded him of a platoon sergeant from years ago. He'd suffered a head injury and also had trouble remembering. Maura and the girls had become second family in such a short amount of time. He'd made plans to build a treehouse for Joni and her gaggle of parrots. Then there was Roger and his staff, the islanders, Phaeole. They had all taken him in as family. And what about Reagan? She was the reason he was here.

A *clunk* snapped Mike's attention. He slowed the boat and looked back at the floating tree branch. Turning the engine off, he drifted for a moment before raising the propeller, exposing a slight ding to the metal blade. He could easily pound it out later. If only he could do the same for his own coat of armor.

He stood looking at the edge of the reef—the low tide exposed teeth-like projections of coral. The intricacies of each appendage reminded him of flying the Black Hawk over a deep canyon ravine, looking for his men in the trenches. He strained his eyes. The coral design set off his PTSD. Emotion overtook him as the waves sloshed over the coral landscape. He dropped to the deck in a crouch and held his head in both hands. Trying not to let the demons take control, he kept Reagan's eyes in his focus. Flashes of incoming mortar crept in—his buddy waved both arms frantically and yelled from the trenches. The scene blurred and the teal water eased its way back into his sight. *Stay cool, don't wander. Think of her, those lips, that kiss.*

His struggle to wall off the scene was desperate—Mike was back in Afghanistan, flying overhead, looking for his target pickup. "Where are the flares? I don't see them." Mike buried his head in his hands. "Incoming, clear the air . . . clear for landing . . . someone show me the flares, where do I go?"

Splashes of seawater landed on Mike, gently at first, then with more power. Drifting back in the ocean world, he got up to see where the spray of water was coming from, but all he saw was the boat floating in the clear glassy sea. Like an apparition, two bottlenose dolphins peered up at him from beneath the surface. Both sets of eyes stared at Mike.

"Oh, you two. You're Reagan's friends, huh." Mike laughed. "Figured I needed some rescuing, eh?"

The dolphins dropped back into the depths and circled the vessel, creating a draft of current that rocked the boat. They came back to the edge and held their position, glaring at Mike.

"Oh, you wanna play, do yah?" Mike dangled his feet off the edge.

The dolphins circled several more times, creating a surge of current. The side of the boat dropped several inches from the water.

Mike reached for the rail but missed and slipped into the ocean. His thrashing underwater drew the dolphins in for play. As he came up for air, one of the dolphins rubbed against him and Mike stroked the long rubbery body. The other one moved in with its nose.

Several minutes of interaction left Mike fatigued—he floated on his back to catch his breath. This was what Reagan talked about. Her dolphins, her friends, who were always there for her healing. Memories of his lost comrades—taking their final breaths in Mike's arms sat heavy with him while the dolphins nudged at his forearm. He wept in the middle of the ocean, with two bottlenose dolphins as his guardians. The whirring of his rescue chopper entered his mind; it was overhead. The *chuff, chuff, chuff* of the helicopter blades was often calming for Mike while transporting a fallen brother. Yet as he gazed upward, there were only pillows of cumulus clouds and a few seabirds.

Still floating on his back, Mike noticed several pelicans in V-formation, similar to his men in combat, with one leader up front. He let his head roll to the side to watch them glide in an arc, staying in line with the wingtip vortex, then soar back toward the sun. He stretched his neck to follow them, admiring their teamwork and efficiency. The calm blanketed him.

Drawing a deep breath, Mike submerged. There was no noise, no birds chirping, no dolphins clicking, just his bubbles heading to the surface. Mike watched them diminish as the streak of sun projected downward. He let his fingers dance in the rays in slow motion. A small school of sardines swept through his vision, and the sun's rays penetrated his skin. Maybe he could just stay there. It would be easier than coming up for air. Reagan's eyes appeared and his chest tightened. Mike needed air but didn't want to give in. He had the discipline. He would make himself wait, in the quiet. It was much easier than having to face her.

42

THE wind-blown palms carved a natural path toward Reagan's bure. Years of relentless trade winds forced their curvature into a permanent deviation. Struggling to straighten her spine from fatigue, Reagan contemplated telling Jeremy about Mike's kiss—it was harmless, really. She looked up from nursing baby Laura, and captured his eyes.

"Why did you run off?" Jeremy wiped his brow, while holding his sun hat in his hand.

"Just needed to feed Laura, that's all." Reagan looked down at her daughter.

"Talk to me, Reagan. Please. What's going on? You seem to be not saying something. I know this isn't who you signed up for." Jeremy waved his arm up and down his body, landing on the deep scars of his face. "Is it me?"

Reagan grabbed at hope. Maybe he didn't know. She brought Laura up to her shoulder to be burped and stood in front of Jeremy. "No, it's not you. Something inside me died, when you went missing." She kissed him.

Warm winds blew in fragrances of plumeria bloom softening Reagan's concern. The strain across her forehead released its hold as she put Laura in her crib. "It's been such a shock . . . after all these months; I'd convinced myself you were gone. I had to accept. . . ."

Jeremy held her hands before dropping his face into her palms, "I know, I know." He hesitated, "But you and I . . . are we okay?"

At a loss for words, Reagan kissed him. She held her lips to his for moments, until they both softened their grips.

When their lips parted, Jeremy continued, "I asked George to get a hold of you since I didn't have a phone . . . tell you I was coming, so you wouldn't be too alarmed. I take it you didn't get that call?"

She shook her head, "You saw the look on my face. I had no idea."

Jeremy shook his head, "Makes sense now, why Roger was so surprised when he saw me walk toward him at the Fiji airport. The guy looked like he'd seen a ghost. He just stared at me, and repeated my name, over and over. Said he was there to pick up a guest, which turned out to be me. Thought he was gonna break my back when he hugged me. We tried to call you from his phone on the way."

"You know how phone service goes around here." Reagan whispered.

Jeremy scratched his face, drawing more attention to the long scar on his cheek. "Your dad, he seems to be okay. How's he handling all this?"

"It's complicated, but Dad appears to fit in here, so far." Reagan convinced herself that Jeremy had no idea about Mike. "This stuff about the bank . . . it's all so strange. I don't quite understand . . . I'll call in the morning."

"Let my assistant deal with that." Jeremy walked over to his sleeping daughter and stroked her head. "Mike's been helpful?"

The breeze in the room went still. Reagan hesitated to answer or move. She caught a side glimpse of a speckled gecko crawling along the wall. It stopped, looked around, and moved up to the ceiling. Reagan's gaze returned to Jeremy's loving hand on their daughter. She walked over to him and touched his shoulder, "Yes, he's been very helpful."

Their eyes met.

Reagan stroked his cheek, slowing down at the stretched sclerosing effect of the burns. She lifted his chin to face her. "I missed you. The nights were the hardest, lying there wide awake, terrified I'd never see you again. I tried to make sense of why this was happening, why now . . . none of it made sense."

"It never does." He lowered his head.

Reagan half-smiled, "You sound like Phaeole. It's just . . . well . . . I couldn't remember our last kiss, or even saying goodbye, when you left that night. That was the hardest—"

"I'm here for you. And, obviously, I'm done as an actor. Who wants to watch this face on a big screen? I'm an outcast, but anyway, I'm finally home for both you and Laura."

Reagan let his words embrace her. For the first time, in a long time, she could breathe—a complete breath, without choking. The wind chimes outside her bedroom performed a soft melody of clanking and tinkling—the polished seaglass colliding with tubular bamboo, suspended by a piece of koa driftwood, gently soothed her mind.

Moving to the bed, Reagan kissed him deeply. They stayed close for hours, exhausted and content. Reagan only glanced out the window once, as she heard the sound of an outboard approaching the dock. She rested her head on Jeremy's chest, giving into the thoughts that tried to assail her.

43

"HEY there, you awake?" Massina yelled from the side of the boat. "Lelei, get closer."

"Mama, it's Big Mike." Joni had the bowline in her hand, while she stretched her body over the siderail.

"Hey, Mike. That you?" Massina threw the boat fender toward him, creating a splash.

Mike sucked in a breath while thrashing in the water. "What hap—"

"The dolphins chase us down, squealing 'bout somethin', so we follow them." Maura was at the stern putting out the short ladder. "Come, up yah go."

Mike held onto the fender and let the girls drag him to the stern. "Where's my boat?"

"You forgot anchor, silly. Boat goes way over there." Joni giggled and pointed to the outer reef.

Maura handed Mike a towel and sip of her tea. "We comin' your way for dinner and Reagan's dolphins jump high out of water, telling us, somethin' wrong."

"Thank you, girls. Good timing."

"Why you float alone?" Lelei stayed at the steering wheel but looked back at the others now huddled over Mike.

"Don't know, must have fallen out of my boat somehow." Mike clearly remembered. He wasn't coming up. His daunting military past, so many deaths, being homeless and lost, then Reagan, the kiss, and now Jeremy was alive. The quiet beneath the surface was so enticing.

"We get you to Reagan. She take care of you." Maura waived to Lelei to proceed.

"No, no, don't tell her. Please. I mean . . . I don't want to trouble her. Jeremy just returned and all. She doesn't need to worry about me. Please, Maura."

Maura listened and hesitated. "I see . . . we let it go."

"I've been through much more than a little fall off a boat." He glanced at Joni. "You'll keep our secret too, Joni?"

"I'm quiet like lizard. I keep secrets." She twirled in circles at the back of the boat.

Lelei drove across the open reef to Mike's boat and dropped him off. "Massina take you back."

"Not necessary." Mike shook his head. "I'm all good here."

But as he started to push off, Maura nodded toward Massina and she hopped on board with Mike. "She's our Kōkua, she guide you home." Maura raised her eyebrows.

He nodded back at her, hoping she didn't see the sadness in his eyes.

After securing both boats, Mike followed Maura and the girls up the ramp toward the restaurant. He saw Earl overhead, leaning into the rail.

"Sir." Mike nodded as they approached.

"Son, you okay?" Earl asked.

"Of course, just bringing the girls for dinner." Mike looked away.

"You sure?"

Joni skipped up to join them. "I don't tell about secret." She tugged at Mike's arm. "Can we tell him?"

"Tell him what?" Earl looked down at Joni then back at Mike.

"It's nothing, really. Just a little surprise for dinner." Mike lied.

"Well, it's been a long day . . . missed my siesta, got a little worried, but I see we're all here." Earl had watched Mike on many mornings hustle down to the restaurant before dawn and prepare coffee and croissants for Reagan, or go out in the boat midday to catch fish for her dinner, or hike up the lava hill to get passion fruits for the tea she loved.

More than once, Maura had asked Roger for theobroma leaves to soothe Reagan's loss, and Mike would be there ready to find the leaves; "I'll get it." He'd hike an hour each way along the back trail in deep mudflats infested with mosquitos to reach the delicate tree. Roger told him many times one of the resort staff would do it, but Mike insisted.

Maura glanced at Earl, nodding in silent agreement—their secret was safe.

Joni squealed, "Auntie Reagan, Auntie Reagan, we have a secret."

Jeremy, Reagan and baby Laura entered the restaurant. Atta Boy trotted over to Joni. He licked her fingers—sticky with leftover sugar bun from the boat ride over.

"Really, Joni. What kinda secret?" Jeremy lowered down to her level.

"Can't tell, can't tell." She sang as she jumped on Jeremy's back. "Hey what happen to your face? You get in big pig-fight?"

"No pig-fight, but I can tickle the secret out of you." He threatened.

"No, I'm a lizard." She shifted back and forth squirming out of Jeremy's reach, unfazed by his new scars.

Jeremy won, as usual, and proceeded to tickle Joni until she forgot what she was saying moments earlier.

Reagan looked to Maura. "Secret, huh? Now what have you done?"

Mike walked over to the bar and opened a bottle of beer. Finishing it in two gulps, he opened another.

Earl sat next to him. "Slow down there, sailor."

Their eyes met.

"Got it," Mike's sallow cheeks and sullen eyes said it all.

44

THE long-distance static made it difficult for Reagan to stay on hold with Franzenchor Banke much longer. The periodic recorded voice blended with the repetitive elevator music. Reagan stretched across the bar and picked out a ripe mango. She started to peel it when a real voice came on the line.

"Miss Caldwell, sorry to keep you on hold. I have our senior vice president, Allan Ross, on the line."

"Hello, yes, this is Reagan Caldwell."

"Thank you, Ma'am, for holding while we retrieved your file. Your advisor is on an extended leave and . . . well . . . it appears that I will be your new advisor."

"What's this all about? I've received two calls and several ambiguous letters."

"Well, Miss Caldwell, this is all quite confusing to me since I usually deal with your mother. I'm . . . I'm so sorry for your loss."

"Yes, and thank you, please call me Reagan. What's all the urgency?"

"As you probably know, we have to ensure top security for our customers, and we pride ourselves in the utmost confidentiality with all matters such as these. Therefore, we had to attain copies of your P.O.A. from the hospital with the Health Directive."

Reagan put the mango and knife down. "Matters such as what?" She clenched her hand on the phone, glancing across the restaurant.

"Again, Miss, I mean . . . Reagan. With transfers of this size, we want to assure you that we value your business and want you to know if there is anything we can do to convince you to stay with Franzenchor Banke. Your family has been a loyal customer for thirty-two years and. . . ."

Reagan leaned against the lanai railing with one hand fixed on the bamboo and the other clenched to the phone at her ear. "I'm not following. What's going on? What transfer?"

The line went static for a few seconds before the voice came back, ". . . which is why we need you to come in person. . . ."

"Say that again. You broke up. Hello?" Reagan waited.

The line went dead. Reagan dialed the same number several more times, but was empty-handed with plenty of questions unanswered.

Walking out of the restaurant, Reagan spotted Mike hoisting bags onto a transport boat. She raced down the dock ramp, tripping on uneven planks she had managed to avoid every day, for years. "Wait!"

Mike looked up, with two large duffle bags in one arm and the boat line in the other, halfway between coming and going. He froze.

"Wait, Mike. Are you leaving?"

The captain tapped his wristwatch and waved him on board.

"Mike, please. We can talk."

"There's nothing to say, Reagan. Nothing." His eyes were fixed on the intricate twines of rope in his hand.

"But there is something to say or you wouldn't be leaving. Please stay."

Mike's chest expanded. His eyes met hers. "It just wasn't our time."

"But—"

"Shhh, there's nothing to say. Jeremy's alive. Let it go." He shook his head, stepped onto the boat and gently pushed off from the dock, away from her.

Reagan had no words; she swallowed the deep emotion she felt for him and let him go.

The only farewell wave came from the boat captain, signaling his departure. Mike had disappeared.

Standing at the end of the dock, Reagan watched the distant trail of his boat wake diminish. The wooden platform had stopped swaying and the stillness became heavy. She waited until the wake had passed the outer buoys then lowered her hands off the top of her head and walked back up the ramp. A dull ache seeped into her left shoulder blade, behind her heart.

Roger and Earl were at the bar as she entered the restaurant. Reagan caught their glares and turned back toward the path but was halted by Roger's words. "Mike said it was time to go. He had matters to attend to back in the States . . . seems odd, I thought he loved it here."

Reagan turned back toward them, eyes cast downward, and entered the bar.

Earl stared beyond her, out toward the ocean, "What's not to love?"

Reagan sat next to her dad and opened a ginger beer and held it against her cheek before taking a sip. Only last week, Mike had brought her one every afternoon. He always seemed to know what she needed. She closed her eyes and let the tart drink take its effect. The slight burn in the back of her throat was welcomed. She felt a hand on her shoulder, and keeping her eyes shut tight she placed her hand over her dad's hand. "Thanks, Dad."

"For what?"

"For being here."

45

"I'M not leaving to go see bankers in Germany. I don't care what they do with her accounts." Reagan had another sleepless night filled with warped dreams that had no meaning. She strained to open the coffee canister.

Jeremy flipped the metal lever and popped it open with ease. "Here, let me make it."

Reagan paced the room. Laura was still asleep, but five a.m. was Reagan's time to get a start on the day regardless of how many hours she did or didn't sleep. "I mean what do they want? We've talked on the phone three times and they won't disclose anything specific."

Jeremy placed both hands on Reagan's shoulders and stopped her pacing. "Hey there, let's go back to bed. Take the morning off." He kissed her lips. "I'm sure whatever it is, can wait."

Baby Laura whimpered and rolled toward the edge of the crib.

Reagan lowered her voice. "Did you say you have someone who can take this on? Don't I need a lawyer? Dad said he'll go, but that makes no sense." She broke his hold to retrieve her coffee mug.

"Yes, I'll talk to George."

Laura opened her eyes and yawned, loud enough for Atta Boy to hop up into the crib.

Jeremy scooped the baby up and smothered her with kisses. "You'll go back to bed with me, won't you, my little one."

Reagan took her coffee, a banana, an ocean bag, and headed for the door, "I'm gonna go surf for an hour or so. You two go back to sleep."

Jeremy waved his hand toward Reagan while humming into Laura's ear. Atta Boy snuggled up to both of them while the bure door slowly shut.

Lowering the anchor over the edge of the boat, Reagan watched for a clear landing. The cloudy sediment rose and fell. She waxed her surfboard and called her friends. "Click, click, click," she imitated their sound. Romeo and Juliet appeared within moments. She stroked their wet noses and slid into the ocean.

The clarity was better than usual—at least fifty feet of visibility. Below her she could see shadows of sea bass and tarpin. Everyone was awake. She paddled toward the surf break, pulling at the water, clearing a path. Schools of fish, displaying their tropical colors, darted out of the way. Juliet stayed at her side, as usual, while Romeo was several feet ahead of them.

A variety of emotions scattered along the way, like bait fish. *What does the bank want from me? Dad can't go on his own. Why is Jeremy so needy all of a sudden? He won't leave my side. Where is Mike?*

Juliet nudged at her arm with her nose.

Reagan noticed a set wave a few yards ahead of them. "Oh, thanks, girl." She duck-dove through the first wave. It pushed her back a few feet. Taking another breath, she dove through the second one. It was bigger than the first wave and she was thrown off her board.

Romeo was at her side and Reagan hopped back on her board. "I don't know what's up, boy." She paddled harder and made it through the last wave, out of breath. Reagan looked for her dolphin friends—they had left the lineup.

The next set was already building. Reagan hesitated and turned her board back toward the boat but then switched direction to head out to the oncoming waves. The newly arrived swell was unexpected—the size of the surf had doubled from the previous day.

This time she dove deeper than usual to clear the power of the impending whitewater. Reagan tried to surface but was tugged downward. Still underwater, she was stuck several feet from the surface. She looked down and could see her leash wrapped around a coral head. She knew better than to dive so deep here.

Reagan pulled at the quick release on the leash, but it held fast to her ankle. After several failed attempts to detach the leash, she finally pulled herself hand over hand to its end and broke the coral branch, releasing its stranglehold. Catapulting out of the depths, she barely got enough air before another big wave crushed her downward and stripped the surfboard away. She swept her arm blindly and the rail landed in her left hand. She clutched on tight.

This time as she surfaced, Juliet was there. Reagan held onto her dorsal fin. The surge of the dolphin's acceleration pulled her out of the pounding waves. Clear of the big surf, she finally let go of Juliet's fin and floated, exhausted. Her ankle pulsated and she felt a large hematoma rising beneath her leash strap. Releasing the Velcro, she discovered blood seeping through her fist with large reef cuts tracking up her arm.

Both dolphins circled around Reagan. A green sea turtle appeared and stayed beneath her. Schooling fish gathered and a line of cormorants landed on the surface.

"Nice pit crew," Reagan spoke out loud to her sea friends. "I get it. Heed the warning."

Driving back to the resort, the entourage of animals stayed close. Pelicans and seagulls led the way, a humpback whale with her newborn were several boat lengths away, and Romeo and Juliet were in her starboard bow wake. The trade winds circled up wisps of saltwater as she turned toward the resort. "Thank you, all of you." She gazed upward.

Jeremy waved as Reagan entered the channel. Laura was in his arms and she bobbed on and off Jeremy's shoulder in response to the boat sounds.

After fastening the lines, Reagan ran to Jeremy and hugged them both. She stroked his face, "I'm so sorry . . . I didn't think you were coming back, I just—"

"Shh, my love."

The kiss lasted several moments before Laura pulled Reagan's hair.

Jeremy stroked Reagan's head. "I had a bad feeling about you out there, today. Everything okay?" He glanced at the bloodstain on her hand and the deep scratches up her arm, before resting his eyes on hers. "What happened?"

Reagan inhaled and took Laura from Jeremy's hold. She contemplated telling him more. "Just a run-in with a stray reef. I'm fine. These scrapes will clean up."

Baby Laura reached out to the pelicans on the rail as they flapped their wings.

"Wow, look at that." Jeremy pointed. "Never seen them up close before."

Reagan helped Laura wave to them. "They're just keeping an eye on us today. Could be ancestors, you know. The chief, my mom, your mom. Those that have left this world and moved on to the next."

Jeremy smirked, "Sounds pretty quirky."

Just as the words left his mouth, one of the pelicans flapped his wings excessively, and squawked loudly at Jeremy.

"That one's your mom, for sure," Jeremy said as he stepped back.

"Yeah, well which one's yours?" Reagan stepped closer to the other two birds. Neither flinched. One dropped down low, while the other stood up at attention. "I guess you're the chief?"

"What if we really do have another life after this one? I've never really considered it." Jeremy walked closer to the birds. They stayed still.

"Well, you know what the islanders believe, as well as Dr. Yiung. They say the circle of life is neverending. The same soul moves around in different guises with different purposes. It just assumes new roles and personalities."

Jeremy, Reagan, and Laura sat at the end of the dock for another hour, talking and dreaming out loud about the *what ifs* of the world. It became a competitive game of outdoing each other.

"What if you could be a cloud during the day and a star at night?" Jeremy pointed to the sky.

"How about if you could swim underwater for hours without needing air?" Reagan proposed.

"What about coming back as someone who could hear all thoughts?"

Reagan laughed off his comment, and shoved it away quickly, "How about . . . what if this moment would never end for all of us?"

46

MIKE arrived at Jeremy's house in Malibu. George greeted him and waved him into the kitchen. After mixing him a gin and tonic, they sat together at the granite counter.

"How's the baby?" George asked.

"She's an angel. Her eyes and cheeks, oh my God, and those little fingers—they wrap around your heart."

"And Reagan and Jeremy? Must have been quite a surprise—Jeremy showing up, unexpected."

Mike looked at George, not answering. He downed his drink.

George turned the barstool to face him. "The neighbors were talking about some homeless guy walking about, lost in the canyon. I never imagined it could be him. We were all so shocked when he showed up at the gate. Then his profile appeared on the security camera. I wasn't even sure it was Jeremy until he started talking."

"Must have been quite a surprise, to say the least." Mike poured a second drink, this time no tonic.

"I tried calling Reagan, but no connection. I got Jeremy on the first direct flight to Fiji," George explained.

Looking toward the living room window, Mike pressed the cool glass of gin against his forehead. There was nothing to say.

George cleared his throat. "There's been several calls from a bank asking for Reagan."

Mike took a long sip of the drink. "Yeah, they called her in Fiji too."

"What do you know, Mike?"

"Not much. Something about her mom and a bank account. She may owe some money, some outstanding debt, maybe to some pharmaceutical company."

George finished his drink. "Jeremy called, asked if you could get some intel on them."

Mike's ears perked up hearing Jeremy's name.

"I got all the names and numbers, even got Roz's account and pin. He asked if you could backdoor the info." George handed Mike a short stack of papers.

Mike swallowed the last bit of alcohol and poured another. The burn in his throat was a subtle reminder of *her*.

"Hey, you alright?" George leaned back in the chair.

"I'll give it a look. But no guarantees. Probably need a collections agency and a good attorney. These doctors are always going in the red." He gulped the third drink. It took effect quickly.

"I bet it was . . . strange . . . having him show up, after all these months." George kept his voice low. "Don't get me wrong, I'm elated that he's alive, really."

Mike looked west at the Pacific Ocean. The windows allowed a broad view north, south and west, but he kept his eyes due west. Sipping remnants of his drink, he kept an ice cube in his mouth and tossed it around. He spit it back in the glass. "I accidentally fell in love, George."

George shifted his chair to look at the same view as Mike. A brief lapse of time went by until he broke the silence: "We all do, from time to time, that is if you're lucky. You can't help it, when you meet those special people. You just can't help it."

"It hurts." Mike whispered.

"Yes," George choked up. "It does . . . hurt . . . to lose someone you love. But she's not gone. She's just not here."

Mike placed the glass down and turned toward George. "Oh . . . sorry, sir, I didn't mean to—"

George held his hand up, "No, no. I'm fine." He finished his drink and handed it to Mike for a refill. "I just wish my son was still here, alive. Instead, I try to honor him the best I can."

Mike bowed his head, as the last rays of sun dropped over the ocean. They both stayed silent for some time. Kitchen staff came and went, with plates of food put in front of the two men. Few words were spoken and a few more drinks were consumed, until Mike stood up: "I'll work on those bank numbers."

Four days later, Mike was in Germany and in the executive office of Franzenchor Banke, awaiting Roz's account manager. He had never seen such exquisite furnishings. Mike stroked the elegant sixteenth-century credenza. It matched the rest of the décor in the office—all of it was a little ostentatious for Mike's taste, but it was comfortable.

A short man with salt-and-pepper hair walked in the office with an outstretched hand to Mike: "Hello, I'm Allan Ross."

Mike was surprised by the American accent. He shook his hand, "Mike Peters, here to represent Reagan Caldwell."

"Yes, I know. Sit, please sit."

Mike obeyed and waited quietly while the man looked through a document in his hand. A strong tobacco smell seeped across the desk. Mike contained his cough and looked around at all the antiques in the room.

"So, what's your relationship to Miss Caldwell?" The man lowered his glasses down his nose.

"A friend." Mike stared at the man.

"A close friend, I take it?"

Mike tilted his head to the side before answering. "Yes, sir, a close friend."

"Huh." The man went back to reading the document, mumbling something that Mike couldn't hear. Then he lit a cigarette and took a long draw before blowing smoke upward.

Mike placed his hand over his mouth for a few seconds, then finally coughed.

"This bother you?" The man held up his cigarette.

"Just not used to it, sir, you know, being from California."

"Yeah, definitely not in the no smoking section of the world, here in Berlin, huh?" He snorted a slight laugh.

The portly man continued to crinkle and turn pages. "I . . . I mean we . . . really need Miss Caldwell to sign all this, with a notary."

"Can't that all be done electronically?" Mike needed to cough again but held it in.

"No, this isn't America. We need it all in writing, in person, with a notary." The man tapped the extended cigarette ashes into a paper cup.

"Yes, I heard that part."

"Just so you understand, Mr. Peters. This is highly unusual we're even talking with you. You're only a . . . close friend." He looked directly at Mike. "This usually doesn't fly, even here in Germany."

Mike's voice got louder. "Then why'd you confirm our appointment? I traveled sixteen hours to get here 'cause you said we could straighten this out in person." He coughed at the financial advisor, twice.

The man extinguished his cigarette and poured a glass of scotch. "Care for one?" He held up a crystal tumbler.

"It depends. Are we doing business or am I walking out of here?"

The man filled the second glass with Dewar's gold-label scotch and handed it to Mike.

47

STALKS of green kelp floated up against the side of Reagan's boat. Last week her emotions held her back and she practically drowned. This was a new day and as the ocean guided her. She glanced at the dolphins and nodded in the direction of the lineup.

The first wave jacked up high and pitched its peak forward. Reagan repositioned and paddled deep for the next wave. She stroked hard and caught the head-high wave. Tucking into a crouch, she gripped the rail and kept her eyes open. The small barrel spit her out—unscathed.

The next set expanded from the horizon line to her boat. Mirror-like glass allowed her to stroke effortlessly. The wave lifted her and launched her forward. The exhilaration breathed new life into Reagan. She leaned into the speed and momentum of the wave. The sound from inside of the barreling freight train was a deep roar. Its vibration was a shock wave to the depths of her soul.

Exiting the long-fragmented tunnel, Reagan found her moment—the deep bond and connection to the ocean. She took it all in, before paddling back for another wave. She surfed for another hour until a boat from the island showed up.

"It's Phaeole. He got high fever, even Lelei can't get it down." The boatman yelled to Reagan out in the lineup. He patted his glossy sweat-soaked head with a small rag. "What do we do?"

Reagan paddled to her boat and up-anchored swiftly. Arriving at the islanders' dock, she felt ashamed she hadn't seen Phaeole more frequently. She had sought him in her mind, while under the dark cloud of thinking Jeremy had died. She even dreamt of Phaeole a few times. It dawned on her that maybe he had snuck his way into her subconscious, to check in, to remind her how to live her life.

Exiting her boat, several people grabbed her lines and coaxed her up the dock to the steadfast donkey.

Maura stood holding the reins. "Please be quick. Lelei say it no good this time, no good. He be leaving us soon."

Reagan hugged her friend. "I'll go see about that."

The small donkey trotted up the long dirt path to Phaeole's house, as if he was part of the rescue brigade.

"Slow down, Lil' Helper. He'll be okay. I know what to do." Reagan said.

Phaeole's entry took on a new look. The normal overgrowth of vines had been cut back. The broken stairs—repaired, and a fresh koa-wood door, with a working hinge, was propped open. Reagan figured Mike had stopped by a few times. She walked in and found a clean and organized room with paintings hung throughout his home. They were his paintings, which used to be stacked against the wall three frames deep. Fresh-cut flowers hung loosely out of mason jars and, most surprising, the peaceful steel guitar of traditional Hawaiian music infused the room.

"Is this Mele Oli or Mele Hula?" Reagan asked.

Phaeole straightened from a slouch like a waking snake and sat upright in the wooden chair. "Mele Hula, of course."

Reagan smiled at Lelei, who was at his side.

"I see you've cleaned things up around here." Reagan looked

toward Lelei, but Phaeole couldn't see, his blindness had shut down everything, including the direction people faced.

"Now, now, Reagan. You be nice, you know I can't go 'round cleaning things. Besides messy is okay."

Reagan raised her eyebrows to Lelei. The room was impeccable.

Lelei shrugged back, "Maybe another day."

"What brings you up the mountain, my friend?" Phaeole shifted toward Reagan's voice.

"I thought I could pick some of your cocoa leaves." Reagan placed the back of her hand on Phaeole's head.

Lelei held out a thermometer, which Reagan declined.

"Yes, you take all you want. Hard time sleeping?"

Reagan took his hand, raised it overhead and pushed on his fingernail beds.

Lelei held her hands up.

"Tissue perfusion and circulation. To monitor dehydration." Reagan answered. "I put pressure on the nail bed 'til it turns white. It's called blanching. Then let go and see how long it takes for the color to return."

More than ten seconds later, the color slowly turned pink.

"Phaeole, are you drinking all the water you're supposed to drink?"

Tilting his lips downward, Phaeole grunted and shrugged.

Lelei chimed in, "He takes small sip then waters the plants."

Reagan filled a coconut husk with water and handed it to Phaeole.

"You girls too bossy." He sipped a quarter of the small mug.

"More." Reagan took his pulse while he complained.

"You don't know what it's like. Too much drink, too much pee, such a pain to get way over there." The knuckle of his gnarled wrist pointed across the room. "And someone moved my path, so I hit big toe, yell big words and almost fall to ground. I can't find my way, so forget the water, damn toilet too far."

Lelei and Reagan smiled at the same time.

"So, how 'bout you just pee off the lanai. It's right here." Lelei giggled as she said it.

"Nice job, little Kōkua. Get the job done. That's good medicine." Reagan beamed.

Phaeole managed to drink three mugs of water in fifteen minutes, and Reagan repeated the fingernail blanch test. It worked. Not perfect numbers, but enough to verify dehydration.

"I'm going to pick my cocoa leaves now. Be back soon, I promise." Reagan gestured to Lelei, pretending to hold the mug to drink, more and more water. As she left the bure, several of the islanders put their hands together and bowed their heads. "Come on, this was an easy one. You guys have to stay hydrated."

Reagan felt light and relieved as she sauntered down the trail on foot, leading the donkey behind her. A fleeting moment of relaxation and sincere happiness infused her body. She trotted the rest of the way down to the landing.

Back at the dock, Maura waited for Reagan, propped against the lean-to shelter. Her spine bent to one side, pitching her head sideways. She strained to lift her head as Reagan approached.

"Is he gone?" Maura's voice had diminished. Her skin was pale, and much effort was needed to stand on her own.

"No, Maura. Phaeole's fine, just dehydrated." Reagan's upbeat answer didn't seem to help.

"How could . . . that . . . be? I dreamt he was saying . . . goodbye. It seemed so real."

"Are you okay, Maura?" Reagan could see the look of despair and loss on her face—the layers of sagging skin underneath her eyes and sunken cheekline, the forgotten smile and misplaced hope.

"Just tired, my friend, very tired." Maura attempted a smile.

Reagan propped against the makeshift building, matching Maura's stance. She looked seaward and waited. A hummingbird buzzed around the wooden rail and several seagulls flew by. "When Jeremy came back, you didn't flinch at his scars. Why's that?"

"He's same person, only better now."

"How so?" Reagan asked.

"Las' year, when the film people come, remember how they treat him?"

Reagan smirked.

"They touch him with makeup, and fix da shirt a certain way, such fuss."

"I remember; it was a bit much." Reagan shook her head.

"He jus' won't worry so much no more. He's one of us."

A teal-necked hummingbird flew in place, drinking the nectar of a tulip, only a few feet from them.

Maura pointed at the bird. "Look at my spirit animal, he remind me to accept change, he be waiting for me."

Reagan shifted her gaze to the dock. Her boat bobbed with the incoming tide. She cleared her throat, "Whenever you're ready, you know we'll all be fine."

Maura shook her head, "I'm close. Jus' so tired."

Reagan put her arm around Maura's back. She'd known her for over ten years, laughed and cried, helped birth Joni, and assisted in her husband's death, with dignity. She would miss her, terribly.

"Okay, when you're ready, I'll help." Reagan held Maura's hand for a while. No one else came or went, except birds, lizards, and cumulus clouds. The quiet wrapped around both of them.

Life comes. Life goes. Reagan remembered Phaeole's wisdom. Thoughts shifted from Maura, to her mother, and back to Maura, who was now breathing softly, unhindered by her strained heart and atrophied lungs. Reagan faced her friend. "Don't think of death as leaving . . . think of it as going, somewhere else, to be with your family who have passed."

Maura found her smile. "You are my family. My children are your children."

Massina walked up to them, “Sun go down, Mama. Time to go back to bure, get off your feet.”

Reagan nodded to Massina and helped Maura stand. She hugged Maura, longer than usual, and whispered, “I love you. Go rest, my friend.”

48

MOTORING back to the resort, Reagan still felt the lightness she had when leaving Phaeole's place, but in addition she felt a deep stab of loss. She hoped Maura would not need her assistance; rather, a deep sleep would move her onward. "I've learned so much from you, my friend. I will keep your smile and heart with me always." She whispered in the wind to Maura.

The trade winds had settled for the day, leaving a glassy reflection of the bow gliding effortlessly through the water. Dusk colors waltzed off the horizon, leaving an auburn tint to the sky. Entering the harbor to the resort, Reagan could make out Roger and her dad at the end of the dock. Earl handed nails to Roger as he made repairs to the tethered slats of wood. He waved to Reagan as she approached.

"How's the surf, R.C.?"

She gave him a thumbs up. Reagan loved hearing these words from him. After so many years apart, he was now living with her and thriving. "Looks like you've been hired."

"Oh yeah, will work for coconuts, and anything else they'll feed me." Earl chuckled.

She tied up the boat and joined them.

"Did you go to the island too?" Roger asked.

"Yup, checked in on Phaeole." She looked back toward the island, and Maura.

"Everything good?" Earl stood.

"I hope so." She noticed how alert and intact her dad seemed. His eyes were clear, his voice recognizable. In fact, he hadn't shown a lapse in memory since he'd arrived in Fiji. Lydia was still working on getting more meds for him, so he had been unmedicated for almost three weeks.

Roger chimed in: "Oh, you missed a call from Lydia. She had some breakthrough. Couldn't get her to slow down her yammerin' about this or that. Wants you to call her when you can."

"Probably figured out my meds." Earl handed a few nails to Roger.

"Do you need them, Dad?"

"I don't remember." He winked at her.

"I wish we knew what the meds were doing. The nurse at the hospital made a point of my dad needing them." Reagan spoke to Roger. "I mean, my mom was always one for overstretching theories."

Roger continued to work on the dock repair. "Not my world, for sure."

Earl rifled through the toolbox of nuts, bolts, screws, and other repair items. A heavy jingle sound resonated within the metal box. "Can't seem to find . . . Ah ha . . . got yah." He held up an old rusted key and a padlock. "It's kinda like this . . . the key won't fit anymore, too rusty and corroded."

Reagan looked to Roger, who shrugged.

"You know, R.C., like a neurotransmitter and a neuron . . . If the key doesn't fit into the lock, then no signal to the brain—the communication system is down." Earl smiled.

"Dad, are you talking about memory loss?" Reagan took a stab at what he meant.

"Yup." Earl answered. He attempted to put the key in the lock, and the orange-colored metal would not fit. "The neurons lose connection—the key won't fit in the lock. Your mom figured out how to keep the connection. I think she said it was remodeling, so the synapse would work."

Reagan's mouth hung open as she stared at her dad in disbelief. "What—"

"She also figured out how to get rid of the crazy inflammation in the brain. I guess that's mostly what I have." Earl tilted his head to the side a few times like he was shaking water out of his ear, "I told her it's just a bunch of saltwater in there. It never really goes away."

Reagan grabbed at pieces of academic information from years ago: neurogenesis, remodeling, receptor sites, and dendrites. And then the hippocampus and cerebral cortex flashed in her brain. "Wow, Dad, this is really amazing."

Roger stood up and put the tools down. "Should I be getting any of this?"

"Yes, and no. What my dad's saying is that my mom may have figured out how to keep the neurons in your brain from dying off even when Alzheimer's progression has damaged them. Maybe . . . I can't be certain I'm getting this right."

Earl added: "You're getting it alright. She also figured out how to save other parts of the brain with some gene adaptation. Something about T . . . something or other. She called it the T gene. It could fight the inflammation better than any med could. That's why the pharmaceutical company wants to shut it down. But I really don't know any of that detail."

Reagan collapsed into the side rail of the dock, in disbelief of what she'd heard from her dad. He wasn't the least bit medical and he just summarized a breakthrough concept for memory loss, a hopeful treatment strategy, and a drug company attempting to stop it from getting to market.

"I need to call Lydia, right away." Reagan headed up the dock. For the first time since Reagan had become a doctor, she thought of her mother in a different light—a brilliant physician with immense compassion rather than a lauded researcher with a monetary agenda.

49

FOR weeks, Lydia had regular communication with epigenetic and aging experts regarding the pills that Earl had been given by Roz. There were several easy-to-identify ingredients, which made sense—anti-inflammatory in nature, all nootropics to improve memory and cognitive decline. Then some bacopa and Huperzine A, all of which had already been touted as memory and focus enhancers. But two ingredients were not identifiable.

"Test it again," Lydia rolled her eyes while holding the phone away from her mouth so she didn't have to adjust her volume. "That's what y'all do there, right." It wasn't a question.

"But, Ma'am, it's not one of our markers. We don't have a match for it." The voice on the other end of the line could have belonged to anyone, but Lydia assumed they were young, too young to understand about looking beyond what you knew.

"Here's the trouble with y'all. Yah don't know what yah don't know." Lydia smirked.

"Excuse me?" The voice on the other end of the phone cleared their voice.

"Jus' break it down the other way, you know from bottom up. Yah jus' expecting it one way, but maybe it's got somethin' else cuz you lookin' at it top to bottom."

"Uh, not following you, Ma'am. This is how we run the test. There's no other way. It says right here."

Lydia hung up the phone and looked upward, "Holy Mother of Mercy, do I gotta do everythin' myself?"

Three short knocks on Lydia's door diverted her attention. She looked through the peephole to see Mike standing with one hand full of papers and a premier coffee in the other.

She opened the door. "Mike! What're you doin' here? Thought you were in Fiji. What hap—"

"Vanilla latte with almond milk, right?" He handed her the cup.

"Oh, you real smooth, honey. Come on in."

"Difficult phone call?" Mike looked around the small apartment.

"How'd you know?"

Mike pointed to the entry, "thin walls."

"Jus' trying to get the recipe to Roz Caldwell's wonder drug."

"You got the samples, right? What else do you need?" Mike walked to the corner chair and sat.

"Should be a piece a cake, right? Run the dang labs and break it all down." Lydia said.

Mike toyed with the plastic rod for the window blinds, twirling it back and forth, creating a Morse-like-code with the blinds. "Reagan's mom was a genetic specialist—something about fixing the problem at its source."

"Yes, she looks at the DNA of her patients and extrapolates nucleic acids . . . oh, huh . . . just maybe." Lydia hesitated. She walked over to the worn-out desk and got a pad of paper and a pen. She jotted quick notes in medical shorthand. "Uh huh, possibly." She wrote fast, not looking up. "Big Mike, you are real good. How did you—" She pulled her Physician's Desk Reference off the top shelf.

Mike got up and paced the room. He noticed every shelf in the room held an odd arrangement of collectibles. He picked up a small statue of a man playing the accordion with his arms, tapping drums with his feet, and holding a harmonica in his mouth. "What's this?"

"That's a gift from a patient." Lydia looked up from her notepad. "He said it reminded him of me, doing so many things at one time."

"Huh," Mike put the toy back in place. "You have quite a collection."

"People say thank you in weird ways, small gifts. Silly, huh?"

Mike picked up a stack of Russian nesting dolls. The hand-painted wooden statues, in descending sizes, had a unique pattern of colors and shapes.

"Careful with those. They be delicate and precious—a chain of mamas, with babies, and their babies in each belly. They live within each other."

Mike thought of Reagan, and her mother, and baby Laura. He put the dolls back in order and placed them back on the shelf.

"What's on your mind, Mike?" Lydia kept her head down while jotting notes and turning pages of the medication reference book.

"Not much." He kept it short.

"That's not like you. What aren't you saying?" Lydia stopped writing and looked at him.

Mike kept his lips sealed and held her gaze.

"I see." Lydia returned to her notes.

The silence lasted for several minutes. Lydia walked to the kitchen and opened and closed drawers, pulled out a frying pan, and threw several pieces of bacon in a pan. When the grease hit the pan, it crackled and the air got dense with the steamy flavors of fatty pork. She returned to the open living room with her arms balancing plates and napkins and strips of fleshy, undercooked bacon.

"Sit," she motioned to Mike.

"Oh no, I'm not hungry." He walked toward the door to leave.

"Mike, why'd you come here today?" She pulled out a chair for him.

"I was passing by . . . and well, just thought I'd say hi." Mike had his hand on the doorknob.

"Huh." She took a bite of bacon. "Not like you. To not say what's on your mind."

Mike let go of the knob. He had nowhere to go. Lydia was a connection to Reagan, but he didn't need her to know. He sat next to her and picked up a piece of bacon. "This is how I like it." He pointed to the uncooked section of meat.

"Uh huh." Lydia leaned back in the chair. "So glad you stopped by to let me know . . . how you like your bacon cooked."

Mike smirked and picked up another piece of bacon and ate it. "When I left Fiji—"

Mike and Lydia were startled when the phone rang. Lydia laid down her plate and napkin and walked over to the old phone, still attached to a base by a coiled rubber chord. "Who's callin'?"

Mike looked away.

"Oh, Lordie be, now . . . slow down . . . slow down." Lydia cupped her hand over the phone and mouthed 'Reagan' to Mike.

The greasy napkin slid off Mike's lap; he walked toward the front door, then glanced back at Lydia. Their eyes met and he stopped for a second, before he turned to leave.

50

"I FIGURED it out." Reagan half-yelled into the phone. "Lydia?" Reagan waited. The distance between them seemed longer than usual. "Hello?"

"I'm here." Lydia answered. "I got it too. The genome . . . twice . . . to be replicated. . . ." Static lasted for several seconds before Lydia's voice broke through again. "That doctor mama of yours, she was really onto somethin'." Lydia's voice receded—the distant static took over.

"Lydia, say that again." Reagan held the phone with both hands.

"That's why she wanted Laura's placenta back at the hospital."

"Must have been why they wanted the DNA test done." Reagan turned to the ocean. Looking upward, past the cumulus clouds, Reagan gripped the phone, "For Dad?"

A gentle sea breeze swept Reagan's hair across her face. She wiped at the tears and moved her hair at the same time. Her dad and Roger sat across the bar, and stared at her. "My mom loved him—she tried to save him, Lydia." Her voice deteriorated. "She needed my DNA, back in Los Angeles when I was there for blood tests for the radiation poisoning, but I refused. Then she tried again, when Laura was born. She always knew where I was . . . she needed our help, our genes . . . to make a functional protein, for Dad. To save him." Reagan dropped her head down and mumbled, "How could I have—"

Lydia's voice calmed her, "Yah didn't know. No one knew."

"That's what Mike said." Reagan responded instantaneously.

"Well, he's right, yah know. He seems to know all kinds of stuff. He was just here and—"

"He was?" Reagan's voice escalated. "Lydia? You still there?"

"Yeah, I'm here."

"What did Mike say?" Reagan asked.

"Nothing really. What's goin' on between you two?"

"Nothing, nothing, just wondering . . . well how . . . how is he?" Reagan stuttered.

"He be jus' fine. What I be missin' down there?" Lydia pressed for an answer.

Jeremy appeared at Reagan's side and handed her a cold lemonade.

"We'll talk more soon, Lydia. Thanks for calling."

"Wait a minute, Reagan. What's goin' on?"

"Jeremy's here and well . . . that's a great discovery of my mom's. Thanks again, Lydia. I'll check in soon."

The line disconnected and Reagan sipped the lemonade. She searched for an escape. "Is it time to feed Laura?"

"What was that call about?" Jeremy rocked Laura in his arms.

"My mom . . . I didn't know . . . I was just so mad at her all the time. I was suspicious . . . you know, all that stuff after Laura was born. Why did she suddenly show up? Now I know . . . if only I'd known then."

Jeremy tilted his head, "What do you mean?"

"All those years, I thought she only cared about her precious work and the recognition. I never imagined—" Reagan stopped midsentence.

"That she was capable of love?" Jeremy handed Laura to Reagan.

"Or caring for us." Reagan whispered.

Jeremy stretched his arms around Reagan and Laura. "I think that's what family does, they keep you on the path home."

Reagan looked past Jeremy. A plume of smoke from the north end of the island spiraled skyward. She recognized the outward sign of silent surrender. She closed her eyes and leaned her head onto Jeremy, "Maura's gone."

"How do you know?"

She pointed across the ocean. "The islanders light a prayer flame when someone dies. They hope it guides their family member to the other side, safely."

Roger and Earl joined them and they all walked toward the edge of the lanai. Squawking flocks of birds headed toward the island, creating a sky full of painted wings. There were a few openings in the low clouds, allowing the blue sky to illuminate a passage.

"Should we go be with the girls?" Jeremy asked.

"Not just yet. They have each other." Reagan said calmly.

"Was she sick?"

"No, just tired." Reagan smiled, "She was done here, time to go be with her husband."

Off in the distance, Reagan saw Romeo and Juliet swimming toward the island. She took the binoculars off the ledge of the lanai and focused on her two friends—half-leaping, half-gliding toward the flock of birds.

51

SEVERAL weeks passed with onshore winds alternating with offshore breezes. Reagan walked down the dock with a small backpack on one shoulder. Mike had called two days earlier. He needed Reagan's signature on bank documents. She was relieved that Roger had offered to join her on the boat ride to Nadi airport. The early onshore winds would make a choppy boat ride and a co-captain would ease her nerves.

"Why wouldn't Mike come to the resort?" Reagan spoke up so Roger could hear her over the outboard engine noise.

"He said the airport was easier for him . . . has a plane to catch later today."

At the entrance to Nadi marina, their boat surged and swayed, as the merging wakes of other big vessels jockeyed for dock access. The landing dock was a chaos of boats fueling, restocking, and gathering passengers. Reagan usually avoided this Fijian traffic, but today she welcomed the distraction.

She hopped off the boat with the bowline in her hands, "It's a bit crowded on the dock, we may have to—"

"No need to tie up. I'm going over to the cargo dock, need more toggle switches for the boat out of service."

Reagan didn't question Roger but doubted he needed more toggle switches to add to his current full inventory, and she hadn't heard of a resort boat out of service.

"Where should I go?" Reagan threw him the bowline.

"Remember, Mike said to meet you inside the restaurant."

"It's a big restaurant." She moved closer to the boat.

"Don't worry, Reagan. Mike will find you."

She stared, blankly, at Roger.

"I'll be back in an hour, so take your time." Roger pulled away from the dock, leaving Reagan standing on the commercial dock with crowds of people around her.

Reagan walked along the short boardwalk to the airport, backpack on her shoulder. She rehearsed what she wanted to say. Her brain raced with urgent messages—*turn around, don't say a thing, don't bring up Jeremy . . .*

"Reagan!" Mike called from the entrance of the crowded restaurant.

Reagan waved at him. Her throat was dry—she'd left her water bottle in the boat. As she got closer, she swallowed hard and couldn't remember what she was or wasn't supposed to say.

Mike looked beyond her, "Are you by yourself?"

"Roger stayed at the marina . . . had to get some supplies." She cleared her throat and softened her grip, "Yes, by myself."

"Follow me, got a table at the window." He nodded toward the windows.

Reagan followed, winding through a maze of people waiting to be seated. He held out a chair for her. "Probably didn't need to get this signature in person, but—" His gaze landed on hers. "I needed to see you, in person."

"I'm glad you came, Mike. I've really—"

A waitress appeared at their table. "Can I get you a drink to start?"

"Two ginger beers, please." Mike answered.

The woman left the table and Mike opened his briefcase. "So, let's first look at the bank draft—"

"Mike, wait. Please . . . can I say something?"

Mike put the stack of papers down on the table.

"I've thought about . . . us . . . or what could have been . . . us. It was so sudden, so unexpected." Reagan leaned toward him.

Mike looked away.

"What I mean is, I hadn't expected to have feelings for you." She lowered her voice.

He looked back at her.

"You being there, every day, meant so much to me. When Jeremy—"

Mike held his index finger to his lips, "It wasn't our time."

"I know, you said that when you left, but it might have been."

"But it wasn't. I came to let you know it's all okay. I have these papers for you to sign to release the bank—"

A waitress dropped off two ginger beers and a basket of chips. "Any food?"

Mike nodded, "This will do."

He sorted through the stack of papers. "Lucky I went to Germany, in person. Someone tried to transfer funds and it wasn't you or your dad. Bank security caught it and traced it back to the pharmaceutical company your mom sold to. The company claimed she hadn't paid in full, said they had authorization of some sort. The bank needs your signature in several places and confirmation of—"

Reagan placed her hand on top of his, "I looked forward to you bringing coffee every morning. It was one of the highlights of my day."

Mike released the stack of papers and put his pen down.

"You rescued me, when I was so low, so out of it. You were there. When Laura needed some love; you were there. And when my heart ached so painfully; you were there." Reagan kept her hand on his.

The waitress came back to their table, "Will that do it?"

They both answered in unison, "No!"

A few customers walked by their table and stared at them, as the waitress walked away.

Reagan waited until they were out of ear-shot. "I am so grateful for you, Mike. I . . . I . . . will always remember you."

Mike's hand stayed under hers for several seconds, before he pulled away and leaned back in the chair. "I've met someone."

"Really?"

"She reminds me of you. Her eyes and smile . . . well, not exactly, but a little similar."

"I'm happy for you."

Reagan lifted her ginger beer, but put down the glass knowing she couldn't swallow without choking.

"I will miss you." He leaned across the table, "Laura too, and your dad, and the girls and—"

"Don't be a stranger. You know where we are. You will always be welcome to stay." Reagan whispered.

Mike answered softly, "In time." He picked up the papers and handed her a pen. "I will make sure this gets into the right hands."

Reagan signed in the places that were flagged with yellow stickies. She didn't need to read any of it. She knew Mike had done the hard part.

At the bottom of the stack of papers, there was a sealed envelope. On the front, in Roz's handwriting, the letters and number: TREM2 were front and center.

"That was in your mom's safe deposit box," Mike said. "The banker said it seemed important to her. It was the only item in the box. Makes me think whatever's in that letter, could be what someone else really wanted . . . you know what your dad said about moving around all the time. Maybe that's why they burnt the place down. Someone wanted *that* destroyed." He pointed to the letter in Reagan's hand.

Reagan stared at it. The T gene—her dad had mentioned it. As much as she wanted to tell Mike about the ground-breaking concept of the protein coding gene TREM2 being the gene to combat brain plaques and inflammation, she didn't open the envelope.

"Aren't you going to open it?" Mike asked.

"Maybe another time." She answered.

52

EIGHT months had passed since seeing Mike and signing the papers. The unstable currents of tropical air settled into spring. Reagan focused on simple things—her island garden, pastel artwork, and daily surf, all while raising a toddler and falling more in love with Jeremy and their small family. The deep scars of what Jeremy had escaped slowly healed. He looked more like himself every day or maybe Reagan had gotten used to them.

Laura was now a year and a half—she was able to walk fast, run several steps at a time, and jump into their arms into the water. She could also swim several feet with her face in the water, eyes wide open. Her golden curls bobbed across her face as she threw handfuls of fish food into the water. "Hehehehe ishy, ishy, ishy. . . ." She broke into giggles as hundreds of schooling fish swarmed towards the feast.

Reagan imitated, "ishy, ishy, ishy."

"Throw it again, again, Laura." Joni towered over her, resembling a small banyan tree preparing to sprout new branches.

"Ehehehe, mor, mor, mor." Laura clanked the back of her knuckles together.

Reagan felt Jeremy's deep stare, while she kept her eyes on Laura at the edge of the dock. She knew Joni would not let her go any farther but nevertheless, she kept guard.

"What's that on your wrist?" Jeremy caressed her hand.

Reagan blushed—she loved it when he kissed the back of her hand. Such a simple, endearing and romantic—

She felt him put something on her finger. She stared at the small abalone ring on the finger next to her pinky.

He looked up at her with a mischievous grin. The slight scar on his face made his smile extend off to one side more than the other. "Marry me."

Joni was the first to answer for Reagan. "Yipeee, a wedding, yipeee . . ." She lifted Laura and spun her around. ". . . And big family now."

Reagan kissed him fully. No words were needed.

Earl and Roger, having heard Joni's words, made their way down the ramp.

Roger slapped Jeremy on the back, harder than Jeremy was ready for, throwing him off balance. "That's my guy. About time, yah know."

Earl approached Reagan, "My dear R.C., already such a beautiful daughter and mother, and now . . . well, I'm just so proud."

The dockside celebration was momentarily halted as the rumble of a large boat's twin engines entered the harbor. An inter-island boat approached them, with larger than usual wakes thrown in the direction of the resort. The dock rolled side to side, causing a small spontaneous dance from everyone.

Reagan strained to see who was being dropped off. "Rog, you expecting guests?"

"No, don't think so, but that darn internet booking has thrown me surprises before. We got rooms. I'll make it work."

The man leapt from the boat to the dock. His glasses fell off his nose, but he miraculously caught them before they dropped through the wooden slats. His gangly legs buckled as he landed, yet kept him upright.

"Windsor?" Reagan squinted. "Is that you? Why—"

Jeremy tipped his sunglasses below his eyes. "Is that the odd student who was here last year? The weird kid who—"

"Hey, not so loud." Reagan put her hand over Jeremy's mouth.

Joni picked up Laura and scrunched her nose at the young man.

"Dr. Caldwell." Windsor extended his hand.

Reagan extended both arms into a hug. "Why are you here?"

"Well, I did what you said, applied to medical school, and for some reason, well . . . I got in." He grinned while pushing his bent glasses back up the bridge of his nose.

"That's great. I'm so proud. But you probably could've called or emailed. Something else bring you here? Are you ready to intern?"

"Not yet. I'm only first year. I just had to come in person, to thank you. My grandfather said, 'well, you go in person'."

"And your mother? How is she?" Reagan asked.

"Mom's gone. She passed shortly after I returned from my visit with you last year. It was the most beautiful thing I've ever seen. So quiet, so peaceful. I held her hand, like you said. I just waited with her."

"I'm sure she knew you were there. She loved you so much." Reagan placed her hand on top of Windsor's wrist. "Is that why you came? To let me know?"

"No, not really, although I did want you to know. The others . . . they sent me."

"Who sent you?" Reagan asked.

"My classmates . . . well, the ones who checked the box."

"What box? I'm not following, Windsor." Reagan looked over at Jeremy.

Everyone was quiet. All gazes were on Windsor.

"You know, the one that says you'd be willing to work for a nonprofit hospital. And, of course, I checked it so here I am. I really wanted to thank you, again—for your generosity. It was so unexpected." He spoke with confidence, so different from his last visit with her.

Reagan looked to Roger, then Jeremy—both standing expressionless.

"They wouldn't tell me at first, but I'm getting good at learning how to ask the right questions." Windsor spoke slowly. "You taught me to wait and listen."

Reagan thought he looked taller and more filled out than their last meeting. He was still knocked-kneed and his arms were too long for his trunk, but there was a new confidence.

Reagan raised her eyebrows. "I'm not sure what you're talking about."

"It started with the bank calling me, recommending I set up a savings account or money market account, to accrue interest." Windsor looked at each person in front of him, then went on, "Then I found out a bunch of students had been helped, not just me."

"Still not sure what you mean." Reagan's voice lowered.

Windsor broke into a short laugh. "Yeah, sure you don't."

There was a palpable silence. Even Laura kept her thumb in her mouth.

"What you did, you know, what you paid for." Windsor extended his arms outward, with his palms to the sky. "My whole medical school is paid for, and many of my classmates', the ones who checked the box."

Reagan looked up to the clouds. A spiraling jet stream joined the cumulus puffs, while a flock of pelicans flew single file beneath them. "Well, Windsor, I look forward to having you as an intern. Deal?"

"You got it, Doc."

Several days after Windsor had left, Reagan and Jeremy laid side by side in a swinging hammock while Joni and Laura played on the shoreline a few yards away. They watched their daughter splash water toward a small school of yellow tang. Joni was at her side the entire time.

"I've been thinking," Reagan pushed off the palm tree, sending the hammock back in motion. "It's really strange . . . I've received over twenty thank-you emails. There are several million dollars in donations. There wasn't that much money in my mom's account."

Jeremy looked away, "Huh."

"That's all you got, huh?" Reagan lifted his chin and turned his face toward her. "What do you know?"

"I've been doing some light reading, you know . . . the kind you always tell your patients to do, stuff that's easy on the brain." Jeremy tapped his head.

"And?"

"Well, I reread that book your mom gave you in the hospital . . . the one about the tree."

"You've been reading *The Giving Tree*?" Reagan smirked.

"Yes, several times now . . . well, actually, it's the only book I have."

"Good job keeping it light." She met his eyes. The swirling shades of her favorite colors drew her in. She searched deeper, past the colors and the dark pupil, past the whites of his eyes. There was new depth.

"You know that damn tree was happy the more he gave away."

"Really?" Reagan propped on one elbow.

"Well, it took that boy in the story a long time to figure it out, and I don't want to be that guy. I want to be the tree."

"So, that's what you're going for, the tree." Reagan chuckled.

Jeremy kissed her gently at first, then with more passion. He paused a moment, just enough to speak. "I'm goin' for happy."

Like a slow setting sun over the horizon, Reagan let her eyes drift shut. She leaned into Jeremy and embraced his words, the moment, and her world. A small flock of pelicans glided in line, over them. As she opened her eyes, she couldn't be certain, but the last one, trailing behind the others, may have glanced down at her.

53

THE Dean of Admissions at Northwestern Medical School scratched his head as he read and reread the confidential letter.

To Whom it May Concern,

This endowment must be confidential. It may only be revealed after a medical student's freshman year has been achieved, for any student who chooses to work for a nonprofit medical institution. All tuition will be covered at that time, retro one year and paid forward in full until graduation.

The CEO of All Animals Matter, a nonprofit organization in Albuquerque, New Mexico, read the letter out loud to a colleague.

To Whom it May Concern,

Please accept this anonymous donation to be used for any Doctor of Veterinarian medicine who will commit to five years of employment with your organization, to pay off all their student loans in addition to their salary for five years.

The director of Partners in Healing, picked up the phone and called his colleague in Ecuador: "Hey, Tom, what do you know about this donation—"

Tom interrupted, "We got one too. Six figures! What are the chances?"

The founder of Remember When opened the sealed letter with no return address and counted the zeros on the check, repeatedly.

> *Please use this donation to better assist your research in the pursuit of treatment solutions for memory loss, dementia, and Alzheimer's disease. Please find attached patent pending and exclusivity information to be used at your will.*

Sixteen other letters and checks to various nonprofit organizations around the world were received with similar shocked responses.

As usual, Sydney Annex was overwhelmed with patients needing care. It was the summer solstice in Australia, with the sun moving slower than usual to anyone waiting patiently, and a holiday week to muck up the usual flow.

"Make sure she gets to the lab—full blood panel. Ask Poppy to sit with her a bit and just chat. I'll check back in as soon as I can." Dr. Yiung was concerned about the pale, young girl, with bruised arms and legs. She wouldn't say if she'd fallen. Poppy would find out.

He felt unusually tired; his caseload—impossible, so many patients in one day. Unexpected medical issues always spiked the week of Christmas. Dr. Yiung caught a glance from an intern holding her hand up. Sighing, he headed her direction.

"Doctor, please go out to the parking lot . . . it's crazy—"

"What is it, Anna? I'll grab my EMS bag."

"No Doctor, it's not that kind of an emergency. Please just go to the parking lot. They're waiting for you."

"The parking lot? Anna, really, I've got too many—"

Dr. Yiung fought against his own lethargy; he shrugged and proceeded to the parking lot. *What now?*

A large crowd had gathered around the immense containers being offloaded in the main parking lot. Traffic was backed up as far as he could see. The doctor counted at least 15 towering containers, as a large crane maneuvered the cargo, all labeled *Fragile,* with arrows and instructions written on each side.

"Hey Doc," one of his patient's called out, "are those coffins for us or what?"

"I hope not, Russ. Maybe they're full of your favorite Aussie beer." Dr. Yiung didn't find his own joke amusing.

"G'day, mate. You in charge? Need a signoff." The burly driver handed a clipboard to Dr. Yiung.

"What is all this? I mean . . . I didn't order anything . . . certainly not anything this big or this many. What's in all these crates?"

"Oh, come on, Doc. How can you *not know* you ordered three MRI's, four X-ray machines, a CT scan, six ultrasound machines, and something—I don't know—special instructions . . . nuclear medicine? Here, mate, you figure it out." The trucker jammed more loading documents onto the clipboard.

Dr. Yiung stood motionless, staring quizzically at the crates, then to the wrinkled papers. He noticed the stamp on the invoice, across the docket number: PAID RC Foundation.

A smile crept ever so slowly across the doctor's pursed lips, wiping away the exhaustion of his day. "Of course."

"Doc, can you just sign off, right here. Gotta get on with m'day." The driver wiped the sweat off his forehead with a dirty handkerchief.

"Sorry, I didn't quite understand . . . I just didn't know who would do such a thing." Dr. Yiung laughed while looking skyward. "Thank you, Reagan."

"M'name's Ian." The trucker grabbed the clipboard and walked away.

Dr. Yiung laughed deeper than he had in a long time. "I was talking about my friend, Reagan Caldwell."

Soli Bula

Made in the USA
Middletown, DE
26 March 2022

63133659R00146